THE BURIED CROWN

ALLY SHERRICK

Chicken House

2 PALMER STREET, FROME, SOMERSET BA11 1DS

Text © Ally Sherrick 2018
First published in Great Britain in 2018
Chicken House
2 Palmer Street
Frome, Somerset BA11 1DS
United Kingdom
www.chickenhousebooks.com

Cover design and interior design by Steve Wells
Illustrations © Alexis Snell
Typeset by Dorchester Typesetting Group Ltd
Printed and bound in Great Britain by CPI Group (UK) Ltd, Croydon, CR0 4YY

The paper used in this Chicken House book is made
from wood grown in sustainable forests.

1 3 5 7 9 10 8 6 4 2

British Library Cataloguing in Publication data available.

ISBN 978-1-910655-32-0
eISBN 978-1-911077-61-9

For my mum, who loved books.
And my dad, the original George.
With all my love.

Also by Ally Sherrick

Black Powder

CHAPTER 1

Berlin, Germany – Early July 1940

SS-Hauptsturmführer Kurt Adler sat in the marble-tiled hallway waiting to be called. An hour had passed since he'd first arrived and still the pair of great ebony doors in front of him stayed firmly shut.

He stared up at the steely-blue gaze of the man in the portrait hanging above them.

He hadn't been told exactly why the *Führer* wanted to see him – though it would be about the mission, of course. Top secret; the orders for it had come from the man himself. A flush of pride swept through him. It was a supreme honour to have been chosen to lead it and he would make a success of it – or die in the attempt.

He glanced at the fair-haired young private sitting next to him. He was dressed in the uniform of the regular army, not SS. A pale-cheeked bookish type who looked like he'd be more at home in a library than on the battlefield; probably waiting to deliver a message when the secretary came back.

The clock on the wall behind the desk chimed the hour. One . . . two . . . three. Adler's stomach tightened. It couldn't be long now, surely? He shot another look at the private. He had taken his cap off and was picking with nervous fingers at the silver-winged eagle badge sewn on the front of it. Adler clicked his tongue against his teeth. If he was the man's commanding officer, he'd give him a piece of his mind.

A barked order behind the doors, followed by the sound of hurrying footsteps, jolted him out of his thoughts. A few moments later, the right-hand door swung open and a small rat-faced man wearing the brown jacket and swastika armband of the Nazi party stepped out into the hall.

Adler stiffened and sat to attention. The young soldier beside him did the same.

The rat-faced man mopped a handkerchief across his sweaty forehead, then straightened his back and fixed Adler with a pair of quick, black eyes. 'Hauptsturmführer Adler?'

Adler jumped to his feet and gave a quick salute. 'Yes, sir.' He made to step forwards, but the rat-faced man's attention had turned to the other man.

'And you are Schütze Hans Ritter?'

The private blinked and stood up, what little colour there was draining from his face. 'Yes, I—'

Adler gave him a sharp jab in the ribs. 'Your cap, man!'

Ritter fumbled the cap back on and arrowed his hand to the side of his head.

The rat-faced man looked them both up and down then motioned to them with a flick of his fingers. 'This way, and look sharp. His Excellency can only spare a few minutes. He is due at a medal-giving ceremony in half an hour.'

Adler frowned. What could the *Führer* possibly want with someone like Ritter? He gave a small cough. 'Surely there has been some mistake. This man here, he is not with me, he's—'

The rat-faced man narrowed his eyes. 'Are you questioning the *Führer*?'

Adler felt his cheeks grow warm. 'No, sir.'

'Good, because if you are, it will be the last thing you do.' He threw Adler a warning look and gestured for them to enter.

Ritter made to go first, but Adler pushed him aside. 'You should remember your place, Schütze Ritter. I am the superior officer here.'

As Adler stepped through the door, he blinked and stared about him. The room was in semi-darkness, a set of black blinds drawn low across the row of long oblong windows to his left. A line of red flags hung in the spaces between, the familiar white circle and swastika emblem on each of them glowing dimly in the half-light. To the right of the two soldiers stood a great marble fireplace, a pair of carved gilt chairs and a table set in front of it. But it was the green glow at the far end of the room which drew Adler's attention the most.

It came from a lamp set on a black polished desk. As he peered past it, trying to make out what lay beyond, a dark shape shifted in the shadows.

'Approach.'

Adler stepped smartly forwards, his boots clicking against the marble floor tiles. The younger man held back for a moment, then followed suit.

'Halt!' The word ripped through the air like a pistol crack.

The two soldiers jerked to a stop. Adler snapped his heels together, threw back his shoulders and forked his arm in the Nazi salute.

'*Heil, Mein Führer*! SS-Hauptsturmführer Kurt Adler, and er . . . Schütze Hans Ritter, reporting for duty!'

There was a creak of leather and a pale palm shot into view. It hung there for a moment then slid back into the shadows.

Adler dropped his arm to his side and waited. Silence, except for the low ticking of a clock and Ritter's hurried breathing. He frowned. Did the *Führer* expect him to say something? He cleared his throat. 'It is an honour to meet you, *Mein Führer*. I—'

'Silence!'

A man's face appeared suddenly out of the gloom. He had the same oiled hair, neatly clipped black moustache and hard-set jaw as the portrait. But the eyes . . . A cold shiver slid across the back of Adler's neck. The eyes were different. Fiercer; more penetrating. Eyes that could light a fire in you. Or freeze your blood to ice.

Adler swallowed and forced himself to meet their gaze. 'You know why you are here?'

Adler gave a clipped nod. 'Yes, *Mein Führer*.'

'Good.' The *Führer* swept a hand across his forehead and gave a sharp cough. 'The English and their so-called allies thought they could stop us from taking France. But they were *wrong*.' He hammered the desk with his fist as he spoke the last word.

Ritter jumped, but Adler gritted his teeth and stood his ground.

The *Führer* pulled back his chair and got to his feet. 'Now we will take the war to them.' He stalked round the desk and came to stand in front of them, shoulders back, arms thrust behind him. He fixed them with an ice-cold stare. 'This mission will deal them a fatal blow. A blow from which they will never recover. Then they will be forced to recognize the truth: that our glorious Third Reich reigns supreme.'

Adler drew himself to attention again. 'Yes, *Mein Führer*! But . . .' He licked his lips. 'But if I may be so bold, what is this man doing here?' He shot Ritter a look of contempt.

The *Führer* frowned. 'You and your men have been hand-picked for your skills operating undercover in the field. But Schütze Ritter has been selected for quite another reason.' He threw the private a grim smile.

The younger man swallowed and shifted nervously under the *Führer*'s steely gaze.

The *Führer*'s eyes swivelled back to Adler. 'As you may know, since I became Chancellor of our beloved Fatherland, I have made it my business to collect treasures. Treasures to glorify the Reich.'

Adler gave a quick nod. He had heard about the *Führer*'s love of precious artefacts – how he had assigned a special force of men to track them down from the monasteries, museums and castles of the occupied territories and deliver them to a secret bunker to which only he and his most trusted ministers had the key.

The *Führer*'s harsh tones snapped him back to the room. 'My collection is almost complete. But there is one treasure not yet in it. One I desire above all others. And I am told that Ritter here knows all about it. Isn't that so, Ritter?' He turned and locked his eyes back on the younger man's face.

Ritter blinked and took a step backwards. 'You mean . . . the dragon-headed crown? But . . . but how do you—'

The *Führer*'s expression darkened. 'Remember who I am, soldier!' He jabbed a finger at the shadowy outline of a giant eagle hanging on the wall behind him. 'Like the emblem of our great nation, I have eyes and ears everywhere.'

Adler gave Ritter a haughty stare. 'I apologize, *Mein Führer*. Schütze Ritter should know better than to interrupt. But forgive me, I don't quite see what this crown has to do with our mission?'

The *Führer*'s eyes shrank to two cold blue chips. He took a step forwards and jerked up a hand as if to strike him. Adler flinched. The *Führer* snorted. Lowering it again, he flicked his gaze back to Ritter.

'You have heard of the legend attached to it, Schütze Ritter?'

Ritter's face paled. 'Yes, *Mein Führer*. That . . . that whoever has the crown will rule the kingdom.'

The *Führer*'s eyes glittered with a fiery blue light. 'Precisely!'

Adler raised his eyebrows. Surely the *Führer* didn't believe in such things?

The *Führer*'s jaw tightened. 'Is something troubling you, Hauptsturmführer?'

'Well . . . I . . . er . . .' Adler cleared his throat. 'If I may be so bold, *Mein Führer*. Such legends . . . aren't they just stories?'

Two red spots of anger appeared on the *Führer*'s pale fleshy cheeks. 'Not this one.'

Adler curled up his fingers, bracing himself for the tongue-lashing that would surely follow.

But it didn't come.

Instead, the *Führer*'s face had taken on a mysterious, faraway look. He drew in a breath and began to pace up and down in front of them.

'The crown belongs to a great line of ancient kings. The original kings of England. Once it is mine' – he stopped and turned to face them, eyes sparking with fresh blue fire – 'England will become mine too, and the Third Reich will control the greatest empire in the world. That is our destiny.' He let his last words hang in the air. Then, taking a quick breath, he focused his gaze back on Adler. 'Do you understand now why I must have the crown, Hauptsturmführer?'

Adler straightened his back and clicked his heels together. 'Yes, *Mein Führer*. Of course, *Mein Führer*.'

The *Führer* tilted his head a fraction as if satisfied by Adler's answer, then frowned and narrowed his eyes. 'But it must be our secret. Your mission's original objective still stands. The crown is what the English might call "the icing on the cake".'

'Yes, *Mein Führer*.' Adler nudged his comrade. The two soldiers drew themselves to their full height and gave another salute.

'Now, go and prepare. You have two months. And remember, the future of the German Reich depends on your success.' The *Führer*'s lips pressed into a thin white line.

A bead of sweat trickled down the side of Adler's left cheek. He clenched his jaw and jerked back his head. 'We won't fail you, *Mein Führer*. Of that you can be assured.'

'Good. Because if you do, I need not remind you of the consequences . . .' The *Führer* shot them both one last skewering look, then swung round and strode back to his desk.

The two men saluted. Spinning on their heels, they marched back past the fireplace towards the doors.

As they reached them, Adler glanced quickly over his

shoulder. But the *Führer* had melted into the shadows and the only thing visible now was the eagle: black eyes glittering; wings and claws outstretched.

Watching. Waiting. Preparing to strike.

CHAPTER 2

Suffolk, England – Friday 6 September 1940

George was picking stones out of the trenches in the potato field when he heard the plane. He jumped up and scanned the sky, shielding his eyes against the sun's glare.

He couldn't see it first off, but then he spotted it, climbing up from the horizon into the clear blue space overhead. A Spitfire. He'd know the shape of those wings anywhere. And the sound of the engine too. The low hum which built to a blood-tingling roar as it approached.

It'd be from the local airbase: the one Charlie was stationed at. 'Course Charlie was still in training at the moment; but the minute he was finished he'd be up there fighting alongside the best of 'em. In a Spitfire too with any luck, though he didn't know for definite because Charlie hadn't been allowed to say.

George was worried for him, but he couldn't help being proud too. His own brother, a sergeant in the RAF. What would Mum and Dad have made of that? As their faces swam into view, he felt the familiar ache in his chest. He blinked and fixed his eyes back on the plane. For a moment, as it rose higher still, he was up there with it, swooping and soaring like a hawk. But then, as the Spitfire dipped its nose and levelled out, another noise cut through the air – a high-pitched saw, like the sound of an angry wasp.

George swung round. A second plane was approaching. Lower down than the first and flying fast. Not a Spitfire. Not making that noise. A Hurricane, maybe? He scrunched his eyes. From this distance, it was hard to say . . .

He turned back to look at the Spitfire. It was climbing again now, engine a distant growl, wings shining silver in the sunlight. Then, as the other plane flew beneath it, the Spitfire tipped on its side and arced down. For a moment, George thought it was play-fighting and would pull up short. But it kept on coming, the noise from its engine tearing through him, sending hot and cold shivers up and down his spine.

And then it opened fire.

Rat-tat-tat-a-tat! Rat-tat-tat-a-tat!

As the target pulled away sharply, George spotted the black swastika painted on its tail. It was a Messerschmitt

109. He could see that now. A dogfight! And here he was – George Penny – with a grandstand view.

The Spitfire tore after the enemy fighter and fired again, leaving a trail of white smoke behind it. The Messerschmitt swerved to avoid it. George held his breath, waiting for it to turn back and fight. But it didn't. Instead, it took off back in the direction it had come. As he watched it disappear from view, there was a roar above him. The Spitfire did a victory loop and tipped its wings. George waved at it and punched the air. Old Hitler might have scored one against them at Dunkirk, but if he had thought that was the end of things, he hadn't bargained for the RAF. They'd been stopping the Jerries up in the skies now for nearly two months!

A door banged in the distance. George's heart lurched. Bill Jarvis. It must be. He shot a look over his shoulder. There was no sign of him yet. He glanced down at the half-full bucket of stones. Better get back to work. Last time Jarvis had caught him slacking, he'd given him such a beating he hadn't been able to sit down for a week.

He gritted his teeth. If only Charlie knew what it was really like here . . . but there'd been no way of telling him. He couldn't send him a letter, because Jarvis had stolen the money Charlie had given him the day he'd arrived. And then Charlie had written and said all leave had been cancelled. Anyway, he didn't want to make a fuss. Not after Charlie had gone to so much trouble to find him somewhere to stay in the first place.

He looked back up, hoping to catch one final glimpse of

the Spitfire before it headed back to base. It was still up there, flying high above him. But now two more black shapes had appeared in the sky to its right. Fighters. Enemy ones – and bearing down fast.

'Watch out!' He jumped up and down, waving and pointing frantically, but it was no use. The pilot was never going to see him from up there.

And then the two Messerschmitts were upon him, all guns blazing.

There was a flash of silver as the pilot rolled the Spitfire and veered into a steep dive before pulling up hard and climbing steeply away.

George tensed. *Come on! Come on! You can do it!*

But suddenly the engine sputtered and the plane began to spiral down. As it struggled to regain height, the two Messerschmitts closed in and fired again. And this time the bullets found their target. A trail of thick grey smoke poured from the Spitfire's rear end.

'No!' George's stomach clenched as the plane zigzagged crazily across the sky. He willed it to lift up again but it kept on falling, plummeting towards the coast like a spent rocket. He couldn't bear to watch . . . He scrunched his eyes tight shut. A few seconds later there was a thudding bang. He groaned and hugged his arms to his chest.

'Oi, you! City Boy!' A rough hand gripped his shoulder and swung him round. 'I'm not given' yer board and lodgen' so's yer can stand there dreamen'.'

George blinked. The stocky figure of Bill Jarvis stood before him, legs straddling the potato trench, hands fisted on his hips.

'There was a Spitfire . . . It—' George pointed up at the sky. But all that was left was a criss-cross of white vapour trails and a plume of black smoke on the distant horizon.

'The sooner yer stop gawpen' at some young fool tryen' to prove himself a hero, and get back to yer work, the better.' Jarvis stepped forwards, right hand slipping to his belt buckle, a ferrety glint in his eyes.

A spurt of anger shot through George. For a heart-thumping moment he pictured himself picking up the bucket, swinging it at Bill Jarvis's head and making a run for it. But as Jarvis took another step towards him, his courage leaked away. Cheeks burning, he lowered into a squat and grubbed up another stone from the gritty brown soil.

'That's more like it.' Bill Jarvis's face cocked into its familiar sneer. 'Now, I'm off into town to meet a contact of mine and do a bit of traden'. When I come back I want this whole trench picked clean. If not, yer'll be goen' to bed hungry again.' Flexing his knuckles, he shot George a warning look, then turned and stomped back across the field and through the rusty farmyard gate.

George kept his head down. When he was sure Jarvis had gone, he got to his feet again and peered back up at the sky. There was no sign of the two Messerschmitts, but the plume of smoke was still there, fading now into the blue. Had the pilot managed to bail out before the plane hit the ground? He hoped so. But what if the same thing happened to Charlie? He shivered and did his best to squash the thought back down.

A series of frantic barks rang out from across the yard.

'Shut yer noise, fleaball!' There was a sudden yelp followed by the rattle of metal and the bang of a door. 'That'll teach yer, yer mangy cur.'

The knot in George's stomach grew tighter. It was bad enough when Jarvis took the belt to him; but it hurt even more when he gave poor Spud a hiding. The dog was the only good thing about being here. That, and being close to Charlie. Spud had been near to starving when George had first arrived; hadn't even had a name until he gave him one, though he'd kept it a secret from Jarvis.

He slid over to the gate, staying low to keep out of sight. A cart laden with a bunch of potato sacks stood in the sun-scorched yard. Bill Jarvis was up front, shunting his moth-eaten pony between the wooden shafts. There was no sign of Spud. What'd he done with him? George pulled back to avoid being spotted. He was desperate to check on him, but he couldn't risk it. Not while that great bully was still around. A bead of sweat trickled down the side of his face. He wiped it away with his shirtsleeve and waited.

At last, after what seemed like an age, Jarvis finished hitching up the pony and climbed on board. At a flick of his whip, the animal jerked into motion. The cart jolted forwards, scattering a bunch of scrawny chickens before turning out through the gate and on to the stony track that led towards town.

George waited until it had disappeared from view. Then, yanking open the gate, he dashed into the yard. He snatched a look at the cottage, sagging under the weight of its mouldy thatched roof. Spud wouldn't be in there – Jarvis never let him indoors; even at night. He cocked his head and listened again. The cart was a distant rumble now, mixed in with the faint cry of gulls echoing up from the river. Above it a new sound pricked his ears. A stomach-twisting whine of pain. It was coming from the ramshackle barn opposite.

Tearing across to it, he heaved the door open and stepped inside. He blinked against the dark, nose wrinkling at the sour-sharp stink of soiled straw.

'Spud? Where are you, boy?' There was a rasp of metal from the darkest corner and the whimpering started up again. George crept towards it, heart thumping, afraid of what he might find. A black furry shape shifted against the wall and the whimper became a low growl.

'It's only me, boy. Don't be frightened. I ain't going to hurt you.' George knelt down and held out his hand. As a biscuit-brown snout poked out from the shadows, there was another cold clink of metal.

George's stomach lurched at the sight of the chain.

'Oh, Spud! How could he do that to you?' Tugging the end of it free from the hook Jarvis had fixed it to, he gently worked it loose from the dog's matted fur and slipped it over his head. 'Wait there, boy. I'll get you something to drink.' He picked up an old milk-churn lid and ran out into the yard. Filling it with water from the pump, he hurried back into the barn.

'Here you go.' George knelt in the straw and watched as the dog dipped his head and drank long and hard.

He was fetching more water when he heard the crunch of bicycle tyres on the gravel outside. He let the pump-handle fall and watched as the portly figure of the postman came wobbling down the trackway towards the farm.

As the bike ground to a halt, a flash of excitement tore through him. What if it was a letter from Charlie?

'Mornen'. The postman clambered off the bike and propped it against the wall. He had the same weird way of talking they all had round here. Puffing out his cheeks, he took off his hat and walked through the gate towards him. 'See that dogfight, did you?'

George shivered as the last moments of the Spitfire's flight played again like a newsreel inside his head.

'Looks like old Jerry got the better of us in that one. Still, at least our lad'll live to fight another day.' The postman came to a stop in front of him. He pulled a damp-looking handkerchief out of his pocket and mopped at the sheen of sweat glistening on his forehead.

George's stomach fluttered. 'You mean he bailed out?'

The postman nodded. 'I saw the parachute comen' down when I was on my way up here. Let's just hope he didn't have a rocky landen'. The sooner he's back up there keepen' those Jerries at bay, the better.' He gave a small cough. 'Mister Jarvis about, is he?'

George tensed. 'No. He's gone into town.'

The postman shot him a sympathetic look. 'I feel sorry for you, lad. Crooked Bill's a hard taskmaster and no mistaken' it.' He frowned. 'How come you've ended up with him anyway?'

George felt his cheeks flush. He didn't want him knowing the whole story. It was embarrassing. And besides, it was none of his business anyway. He licked his lips and toed at a weed growing from beneath the wall next to him. 'My brother's training to be a pilot at the airbase. He thought I'd be safer out here than back in London.'

'Not here you won't.' The postman's frown deepened. 'Haven't you been listenen' to the news? Old Herr Hitler's plannen' to invade any day now. All this' – he waved his handkerchief at the sky – 'is part of his cunnen' plan. Getten' the Luftwaffe's planes to try and soften us up first before he makes his big push by sea. Which means if he and his Nasties come this way, we'll be right in his path.'

George's eyes widened.

The postman looked over his shoulder. As he bent in closer, George got a whiff of salty-smelling sweat. 'Rumour has it, some of them Home Guard volunteers have been holed up in the woods hereabouts on special trainen' just in case. Not that them and a bit of barbed wire on the beach'll stop the Jerries if they do decide to come.' He stuffed his handkerchief into his trouser pocket and cleared his throat again. 'Anyway, don't mind me.' Opening the leather satchel which hung from his shoulder, he rummaged inside and fished out a grey envelope. ''Ere y'are.'

George put the milk-churn lid down on the ground and dried his hands hurriedly on his trousers. As he took the letter from the postman, his heart lifted then sank again. It was Charlie's handwriting all right, but it was addressed to Bill Jarvis.

'I'll be off then.' The postman climbed back up on his bike. 'And if I were you, sonny, I'd try and stay on Crooked Bill's good side. He's got a nasty temper on him, that one.' With a wave of his hand, he swayed off down the track in the direction of town.

George pulled a face. Good side? Bill Jarvis didn't have a good side. Leastways there'd been no sign of it in the five weeks since he'd got here. And why was Charlie writing to Jarvis and not him? He ran his fingers over the familiar inky scrawl and frowned. There was only one way to find out.

Stuffing the envelope into his pocket, he scooped up the milk-churn lid and headed back inside the barn.

CHAPTER
3

As George approached, Spud shot up from the pile of dirty straw he was lying on and backed trembling into the corner.

'It's all right, boy. It's only me. Here you go.' George set the lid on the ground and sank down beside him. Giving his hands another quick wipe, he pulled the envelope out of his pocket and turned it over. The flap hadn't been sealed properly on one side. He wavered for a moment, then, poking a finger into the gap, slowly, surely he worked it free. Hands shaking, he slid out the piece of flimsy white paper inside. As he unfolded it, a ten-bob note fluttered out and landed in his lap. He gasped. What was Charlie doing sending Bill Jarvis a whole wodge of money like this? He picked it up and stared at it, then turned his gaze back to the letter. It was dated Monday 2 September. Four days ago.

He took a breath and began to read:

Dear Mr Jarvis,

I'll be finished with my training at the end of this week. I was hoping to get a pass to come and see George, but it looks like they'll be sending me off up to fight the Jerries just as soon as I'm done.

This may be the last time I can write for a while — I'm expecting to be kept pretty busy up there — so I thought I should send you some more money for his keep. Hopefully it'll be enough to tide him over for the time being. And I've got a bit more put by for him too, if the worst happens...

Well, it's lights out now so I'll sign off, but if you could pass a message on to George for me I'd be grateful. Tell him I love him. And tell him to be sure and keep the promise he made. He'll know what I mean.

And thank you again for agreeing to take him in. It means a lot, being so close to each other, even if I haven't managed to get across and pay him a visit yet.

Yours sincerely
Charlie Penny

George dropped the letter and slumped back against a bale of prickly straw. It felt like someone had punched a hole in his stomach and filled it full of stones. '*If the worst happens.*' He knew what that meant. It meant Charlie being shot down over the sea and drowning; or crash-landing and his plane exploding in a ball of flames. Or else his parachute not opening properly and . . . The old familiar tightness gripped his chest. He did what Charlie had showed him, taking deep breaths, holding them for a count of five and blowing them out again slowly until it began to fade.

He couldn't let himself think like that. Charlie was relying on him. That's what the promise was about, wasn't it? Why Charlie had asked Bill Jarvis to remind him.

He slipped his hand in his trouser pocket and pulled out the ring. As he held it up, a sliver of light from a knothole caught the letters engraved on it, making them pulse with a sudden gold fire:

Together Always

It was what Mum and Dad had promised each other on their wedding day: Charlie had told him that when he'd given the ring to him, the day he'd left for his basic training – nearly a year ago now. George closed his eyes and let the scene come flooding back.

They were on the platform at Liverpool Street station, waiting for Charlie's train to leave. It was crowded out with all sorts: city gents in suits and bowler hats striding off to work; soldiers kissing their wives and sweethearts goodbye; crocodiles of evacuee kids following their teachers, each with a gas-mask box strapped across their chest, a luggage label tied to their coat and a small suitcase or pillow-case with their belongings in it, clutched in their hand – all of them being sent off to live with strangers in the country.

By rights George should have been one of them, but he'd refused to go, saying he'd only leave London if he could be close to Charlie. And in the end Charlie had caved in and arranged for him to stay with their neighbour, old Mrs Jenkins, until he could find a place for him near the airbase – though it'd taken a lot longer than either of them had thought.

As the crowds milled around them, Charlie looked down at George and frowned.

'It don't feel right leaving you, Georgie, but you understand, don't you? I've got to do my bit to try and stop old Adolf, or life won't be worth living.'

George bit down on his lip and nodded. He was trying his best to be brave but it was hard . . .

'Good lad. I'll write once a week, and come back and see you every leave too. And don't go giving Mrs Jenkins any grief, will you? It's good of her to take you in.' He glanced back to where their elderly neighbour stood at the entrance to the platform and raised a hand.

A whistle shrilled. Doors slammed. People began to shout their farewells.

Charlie ruffled George's hair. 'Nearly time, Georgie. Here, look. I've got something for you.' He fished a small leather-covered box out of his coat pocket and lifted the lid to reveal a pair of gold rings nestled against each other on the black velvet cloth inside.

George frowned.

'Mum and Dad's wedding rings. The coppers gave them to me after the accident. I didn't tell you before cos, well, I thought it would upset you.' Charlie blinked and puffed out a breath. 'But I reckon you're old enough now.' He picked up the smaller of the two rings and showed George the inscription. Then, pressing it into his hand, he fixed him with a steady gaze. 'Keep it safe, George, and I'll come back to you, whatever happens.' He took the second ring out of the box, slid it on to the middle finger of his right hand and tipped it towards George. 'D'you swear?'

George curled his fingers round his ring and touched it to Charlie's. 'I swear!'

Charlie nodded. He drew in a breath and pulled George to him, holding him tight; so tight one of his buttons spiked George's cheek. But it didn't matter. Nothing mattered except Charlie staying safe.

The whistle sounded again. Charlie pushed him gently away. 'I'd best get going. Don't forget now, Georgie.' He held up his finger so the ring caught the light. Flashing George a quick smile, he picked up his bag and jumped on board the train. As he turned round to wave, there was a sharp hiss of steam and a juddering clank. The train lurched forwards and the crowd surged towards it, blocking him from view. By the time George had managed to elbow his way up to the front, it was too late. The train had already left the platform and was snaking away out of sight down the track . . .

Something wet and whiskery nuzzled the back of George's hand. He blinked and lifted his head. A pair of brown eyes shone back at him from the gloom.

'Sorry, boy.' He ran his fingers through Spud's fur and gazed at the ring again. He'd make sure and keep it safe, just like he'd promised; then Charlie would be safe too. He swallowed hard. If only he could see him. Wish him luck before his first mission.

A sudden thought flashed into his head. He could go now. What was stopping him? The airbase was only about three miles from here – Charlie had told him that. He'd follow the road into town and ask for directions from there. And he'd take his things too. Because Charlie wouldn't want him to come back here. Not when he told him how awful Bill Jarvis was.

His stomach fizzed with excitement. He tucked the letter and money back in the envelope and stuffed it in his pocket with the ring.

'Stay there, boy. I'll be back in a minute.' Patting Spud on the head, George jumped up and ran out into the yard. He was heading round to the cottage when a winged shadow fell across the ground in front of him. He stopped in his tracks and glanced up, squinting against the sun. It looked like one of them crows Bill Jarvis was always taking potshots at, except bigger. Much bigger. Lucky for the bird Jarvis wasn't around or he'd probably blast it out of the sky and hang it from a fence post like all the others. He shivered at the memory of the lines of black feathered carcasses rotting in the sun.

When he reached the cottage, he pushed open the door and stepped into the dark, grimy kitchen. His stomach rumbled at the smell of fried onions from last night's dinner. He'd had nothing to eat since then, apart from a bit of stale bread and dripping at breakfast. But there was no time to worry about food now.

He hurried into the passage and up the stairs to the tiny cupboard of a room he'd been sleeping in since he'd first got here, what seemed like a lifetime ago. Yanking his knapsack out from under the bed, he stuffed his spare underwear, pyjamas and identity card inside it.

He was about to go when he spotted the dog-eared cover of the cigarette card album poking out from beneath his pillow. He couldn't leave that behind: Charlie had sent it to him last month for his thirteenth birthday, together with a whole bunch of cards – 'Planes of the Royal Air Force' – to stick inside it. It was the only present he'd got; that and a clip round the ear from Bill Jarvis for being late collecting the eggs.

George scooped up the album and leafed through the pages of brightly coloured cards. There were pictures of a Hawker Hurricane, a Blackburn 'Skua' dive-bomber and a Wellington. Not forgetting his favourite. He stared down at the card showing the Mark I Supermarine Spitfire, then lifted up the album and buried his nose in the pages. The cards gave off the same sweet smell as the tobacco Charlie used to roll his own. A lump rose in George's throat. He missed his brother so much. But at least he'd see him now. If they let him on to the airbase . . .

Sliding the album inside his knapsack, he headed downstairs and back out round to the barn. 'Come on, boy. Let's get out of here.' He tied a loop in a piece of old rope, slipped it gently over Spud's head and led him out into the yard.

He paused for a moment to glance about him. He wouldn't miss this place one little bit. He'd had his fill of cleaning out stinky pigsties, shovelling manure and getting pecked to bits by bad-tempered hens. And he never wanted to see another potato as long as he lived. Wherever he went next, one thing was certain; it wasn't going to be a smelly old farm. Giving a quick tug on Spud's makeshift lead, he strode out through the gate and set off in the direction of town.

It was as the crossroads came into view that he saw the pony and cart. They were in the shade of a clump of trees a little before where the track divided. George's heart did a quick somersault. There was no way Jarvis could've got into town and back. Not in that time. But where was he? He glanced about him. There was no sign. He puffed out a breath and tugged on Spud's lead again. The sooner they got past the cart and on to the main road the better.

As they slid alongside it, the pony jerked its head round and bared its chipped yellow teeth.

George froze, then slowly held out a hand. 'It's all right, horsey. It's only us.'

The animal stared at them uncertainly for a moment, then gave a loud snort and went back to munching on a clump of dusty-looking grass at the side of the track.

George and Spud hurried on. They had reached the junction and were about to dash across it when Spud jolted to a sudden stop.

'What is it, boy?' George followed his gaze down the left-hand fork. And then he saw them too: Jarvis and another man, standing some distance off in the shadows beneath a bank of trees, hunched over what looked like a sack of potatoes. Jarvis had his back to them. The other man, who was a head or two taller, stood side-on, his fair hair and pale, hollow-cheeked face lit by a shaft of sunlight shining through the branches above their heads.

George's stomach clenched. They had to get out of sight and quick. Clamping a hand over Spud's quivering snout, he yanked him behind a nearby bush and peered back through the leaves.

Jarvis had picked up the sack and was holding out his right hand. The younger man cast about him, as if checking the coast was clear. Reaching inside the heavy-looking black overcoat he was wearing, he dropped a handful of coins into Jarvis's outstretched palm. Jarvis shoved the sack at him with a grunt and began to count the money.

Instead of waiting for him to finish, his companion hoisted the sack over his shoulder and set off at a brisk march away round the bend.

George frowned. Who was he and what was he dressed like that for when it was such a scorcher? Unless . . . maybe he was one of those Home Guard types the postman had mentioned, camped out on some kind of secret training exercise. He shook his head. Whoever he was, he'd got to be desperate, buying a bunch of rotten potatoes off Bill Jarvis.

He glanced back at Jarvis. He was busy pocketing the coins. Any minute now he'd turn round and come marching towards them. His stomach gripped again. Time to get out of here, while they still had the chance.

He tugged on the rope. But Spud stood there shivering, eyes wide with fear.

George pulled on the rope again. Still Spud refused to budge.

'Come on, boy, or it'll be too late.'

As he spoke the words, a shadow fell across them, blotting out the light.

'Too late fer what?'

CHAPTER
4

Keeping a tight grip on Spud's lead, George steeled himself and turned round.

Jarvis stood in front of him, his whiskery face tight with rage. 'And just where d'yer think yer off to, City Boy?'

'I-I thought I'd take him for a walk.' George nodded at Spud.

Jarvis's eyes flicked to the dog then to George's knapsack. 'What kind of a fool d'yer take me fer? Get in the cart.'

George stood his ground, fists clenched.

'Disobey me, would yer? Well, let's see if I can't change yer mind.' Quick as a flash, Jarvis wrenched the rope from George's grasp. Yanking Spud to him, he snatched up a broken bit of tree branch and rammed it against the side of the dog's skull. Spud gave a terrified whimper.

George's heart jolted. 'Don't hurt him. Please!'

'Well, do as I say then.' Jarvis drew back the branch. Spud struggled against him, but it was no use. Jarvis had him reined in good and proper.

George held up his hands. 'All right, all right.' He turned and stumbled back up the track. As he reached the cart, the pony lifted its head and gave a quick whicker of recognition. He gritted his teeth and hauled himself up on to the hard wooden seat.

Jarvis strode past him to the rear of the cart, dragging the cringing dog at his heels.

George's heart did another flip. 'It'll be OK, boy. I promise.'

'Stop yer blitheren'!' Jarvis flung down the tailgate. Grabbing Spud round the middle, he lifted him up and threw him inside. The dog gave a sharp yelp as he hit the wooden boards, then fell silent.

Jarvis slid the end of the rope through a hook and tied it tight. Slamming the tailgate shut again, he stalked round to the front of the cart and swung himself up next to George. 'Now.' He snatched up the whip and thrust the butt of the worn leather handle against his chest. 'Where's my letter?'

George felt the blood drain from his face. How did he know? If he found out he'd opened it . . . He swallowed hard and forced himself to look his tormentor square in the eyes. 'Wh-what letter?'

Jarvis dug the whip handle deeper. 'Don't mess with me, City Boy. That old fool of a postman passed me a while back. He said he'd given it yer. Now hand it over, or else.'

He tugged the whip handle free and stroked a grimy finger along the snake of black leather that dangled from it.

A sour flush of liquid spiked the back of George's throat. Clenching his jaw, he reached in his pocket and pulled out the crumpled grey envelope.

Jarvis seized it and flipped it over. His eyes flashed with fresh anger. 'Why, yer little—' He pushed open the flap and plucked the letter free. His expression changed at the sight of the ten-bob note. Pocketing it with a greedy smirk, he turned back to the letter, bunched up his forehead and began to read. When he'd finished, he screwed it into a ball, tossed it to the ground and fixed George with a knife-sharp stare.

'So yer precious brother's finally taken to the skies, has he? Well, let's hope Lady Luck's smilen' on him, because the way I heard it, those Jerry planes are shooten' the new boys down ten-a-penny.'

George's throat tightened. 'Charlie'll be all right. I know he will.'

Jarvis gave a hard-sounding laugh. 'Yer do, do yer? Sounds like old Charlie-boy might not be quite so sure.' He pulled the ten-bob note from his pocket and waved it in George's face. 'And what about this? Thought yer'd rob me and hightail it out of here, did yer?'

A spurt of anger shot up inside George. 'Give it back. It ain't yours!' He scrambled to his feet and made a swipe for the money. The cart rocked from side to side, sending Spud into a frenzy of barking. The pony whinnied and pitched forwards.

Jarvis yanked George down and dragged on the reins. 'Whoa! Steady boy!' He glared at him, then, swivelling round in his seat, he drew the whip back and cracked it down an inch from Spud's nose. The dog gave another yelp and jammed himself trembling against the tailgate. 'Let that be a lesson to yer.'

George's eyes filled with tears. 'Spud. No!' He reached out to him, but Jarvis clamped a muscled arm across his chest.

'Spud? What kind of a stupid name is that?' He puckered his lips and shot a glistening gobbet of spit into the back of the cart.

George struggled against him.

'Leave him!' Jarvis jerked George round to face the front. 'And if yer try runnen' away again' – he narrowed his eyes and tipped his head at the back of the cart – 'I promise yer this, old Spud's life won't be worth liven'.'

George shivered. He threw a quick glance over his shoulder, but Spud had buried himself beneath a pile of old sacks and only the dusty white tip of his tail was visible. He slumped his shoulders and fixed his eyes on his boots. The cart lurched forwards. A few moments later he felt it swing round, and when he looked up again, they were rattling up the track in the direction of the farm.

When they arrived, Jarvis bundled Spud out of the cart and dragged him back into the barn. Then he marched George to the potting shed and set him to work on a crate-load of mouldy potatoes with an order not to come indoors until he'd 'tidied' the lot of them.

As he dug the green shoots from the potatoes' leathery skins, George did his level best not to think about what Jarvis had said about Charlie. What did *he* know anyway? Besides, he had the ring, didn't he? His thoughts turned back to Spud again. There was no way of going to check on him, not with that rotten bully on the prowl. But one thing was for sure, the minute he got the chance he'd rescue him and they'd be out of here faster than you could say 'Spitfire'. He heaved a sigh and shovelled another load of potatoes on to the workbench.

The sun was going down when he finally finished. Slinging his knapsack over his shoulder, he opened the door and peered out into the yard. There was no sign of Jarvis. Maybe this was his chance? He darted across to the barn. But when he reached it, his heart sank. The mean so-and-so had gone and fixed a rusty great padlock to the door. He went to call Spud's name, then thought better of it. If Jarvis heard him, it would only make things worse for both of them. Best wait till later.

He clutched his stomach. It was griping something awful. He'd have to go and face him if he wanted any supper. As he rounded the barn, he shivered. An oil lamp was shining at the kitchen window. Jarvis hadn't bothered putting up blackout curtains. Said the ARP wardens were too lazy to come and check this far out of town. George steeled himself and pushed open the door.

But he was in luck. When he got inside, Jarvis was lying face down on the kitchen table fast asleep, his right hand curled round an empty bottle of his favourite home-made 'tater' vodka. George's mouth watered at the sight of the half-eaten plate of sausage 'n' mash in front of the man. Snatching up what was left of a sausage, he hurried back outside.

As he drew closer to the barn he heard the rattle of a chain. He squatted down. 'Here we are, boy.' He pushed a bit of the leftover sausage through a gap in the planks. There was a snuffling sound followed by a low whimper. George's chest tightened. 'I know, Spud. I'm sorry. He's gone and put a padlock on. But I'm going to get you out of there soon, I promise.'

His stomach rumbled again. He looked down at the other bit of sausage and hesitated, then shoved it through the gap quickly before he had a chance to change his mind. 'Try and get some kip, boy. I'll come back in the morning.' Trailing a hand across the gap, he got to his feet and set off back to the cottage.

Bill Jarvis was where he'd left him, slumped across the table and snoring loud enough to raise the dead. Tiptoeing over to the cupboard, George helped himself to a slice of dry bread. He crammed it into his mouth and crept up the stairs to his room. Changing into his pyjamas, he slid Charlie's album out of his knapsack and leafed through it for a bit in the shadows, before tucking it under his pillow and climbing into bed.

In spite of the scratchy blanket and the lumpiness of the mattress, it didn't take long for him to drift into sleep. And with sleep came the dream. The one he'd been dreaming on and off ever since he got here . . .

Him and Charlie were building the Anderson shelter in Mrs Jenkins's back yard to keep her and George safe from old Hitler and his bombs. They'd already dug out the pit and were busy fixing the corrugated metal walls and roof in place. When Charlie had finished tightening the last bolt, he climbed down inside to inspect their work. But as he turned round to give George the thumbs up, something strange happened: something that hadn't happened before.

A tide of grey mist slid up over the top of the shelter. As it snaked across the roof and walls, they melted away, leaving Charlie standing on his own in the middle of the pit, a blank look on his face. And then the ground beneath him shuddered and the sides of the pit began to collapse.

George tried to shout a warning, but his mouth was blocked and no sound came. He made to jump forwards, but his feet were stuck too. He twisted and turned, trying to break free, but it was no use. When he looked up again, Charlie had gone – and in his place there was nothing. Nothing but a black gaping hole and a mound of thick, dark earth.

And then he heard the voice. Faint and faraway. *Charlie!* Dashing to the edge of the hole, he flung himself down and peered in.

At first all he saw was a swirling pool of mist. Then a faint golden glow rippled up beneath it and a dark shape snaked into view. He watched open-mouthed as the shape curled itself around the light, squeezing its shadowy coils about it until no more than a pinprick was visible. The ground rocked again and the mound began to tremble, sliding forwards and shooting a torrent of black earth into the hole.

Charlie! No!

George jolted awake, gasping for breath. He peered about him. A finger of moonlight shone through a hole in the tattered curtains. He blinked and blew out his cheeks. A bad dream, that was all. He snatched up his trousers from the end of the bed and reached inside the pocket for the ring. He puffed out another breath. Still safe.

He pulled it out and ran a fingertip across the inscription. Then, slipping it on to his right thumb, he lay down again and sank back into sleep.

CHAPTER 5

Saturday 7 September

The rusty crowing of Bill Jarvis's vicious one-eyed cockerel woke George with a start. He scrunched his eyes against the light and groaned. What jobs had Jarvis got lined up for him today? More stone-picking? Or maybe he'd be back on dung duty again, cleaning out the pigs or shovelling up the pony's doings? Then he remembered the dream. He shivered. It wasn't real; he knew that. But it had spooked him good and proper. The sooner he and Spud got away from here and he got to see Charlie again, the better. If only he could find the key to the padlock . . .

A thud of boots sounded on the stairs below. He rolled over, pulling the moth-eaten blanket over his head, and held his breath.

A few seconds later, the door banged open. 'Get dressed, City Boy! We're goen' into town.' A hand whipped the blanket back and yanked him up.

George twisted free and hugged his arms across his chest. 'Why?'

'To buy a Meccano set. Why d'yer think?' Jarvis's blood-shot eyes darted to George's pillow. 'What've yer got stashed under there?' He bent over and snatched the album free.

'Give it back!' George made a grab for it, then drew back his hand. The ring was still on his thumb. He couldn't risk Jarvis taking that too. He slid it off and stuffed it in the waistband of his pyjamas.

Jarvis flicked through the pages of the album and gave a grunt. 'Fat lot of good all these fancy planes are goen' to be when the Jerries get to work on London.'

George's chest tightened. 'What d'you mean?'

'Rumour is Mister Hitler's proper riled up about our brave boys goen' off and bomben' Berlin the other day, so he's plannen' a little attack of his own.' Jarvis gave a sarcastic laugh.

'I don't believe you.'

Jarvis's eyes narrowed to two mean slits. 'Call me a liar, would yer? We'll see about that.' He flipped the album shut. Gripping the paper cover with both hands, he ripped it in half and let it fall to the floor.

'No!' George jumped off the bed and gathered up the pieces. He stared down at the torn cards and let out a strangled sob. 'Just you wait till Charlie finds out . . .'

Jarvis turned down his mouth in a look of mock sorrow and shook his head. 'But yer big brother's not here to tell, is he?' He grabbed George's clothes and threw them at him. 'Now hurry up and put these on.' He stomped over to the door. When he reached it, he whipped round and shot George a sneering look. 'And grow yerself some muscles while you're about it. Those taters aren't goen' to bag themselves.' He turned and clumped off down the stairs.

George's eyes filled with angry tears. He blinked them away and pressed the torn halves of the album together to make a ragged join. He could probably glue them, but it wouldn't be the same. He pushed them back under his pillow and changed into his clothes. Then, slipping the ring into his trouser pocket, he trudged downstairs. As he stepped round into the sun-bright yard, he glanced over at the barn door. His heart squeezed at the thought of Spud chained up in the dark all alone.

I'll rescue you soon, boy, I promise.

It was busy when they arrived in town. There were queues of shoppers outside the butcher's and grocer's, and a bunch of Boy Scouts and Girl Guides were traipsing around waving placards and shaking buckets of change in aid of the Spitfire Fund. As the cart rattled past a pair of gossiping women, they looked round and shot sharp looks at Bill Jarvis before turning their backs on him. A bit further on an old man shook his fist and made what sounded like a rude remark. But none of it seemed to bother Jarvis.

Steering the pony down a side street, he turfed George out with a first sack of potatoes and told him to get selling. But it was hard work going from door to door. Plenty of people were wise to Jarvis's tricks – stacking a few good taters on top of a bunch of the mouldy ones he'd forced George to 'tidy' – and sent George away with a flea in his ear. The only ones who bought off him were old folk who hadn't been able to grow any of their own. He hated being made to trick them, but if he refused to carry on, he knew he'd be in for a beating.

The sun was almost overhead when Jarvis glanced down at the battered pocket watch hanging from a fob on his grubby waistcoat. He swirled his fingers through the mound of coins in the collecting bag and gave a brown-toothed grin.

'Time fer a bit of refreshment.'

He signalled to George to climb up beside him, then with a tug of the reins steered the pony up the hill in the direction of the market square. With the shops shut for lunch, the place was a lot quieter than it'd been earlier. George wiped the sweat from his forehead. The sooner they got out of this heat the better.

As they trundled into the square, he spotted a small group of boys hunched over a game of marbles at the back of the old Shire Hall. One of the boys lifted his head as they passed and gave his neighbour a quick poke in the ribs. The second boy rose slowly to his feet and fixed George with a cold-eyed stare.

George's heart sank at the sight of his mean ratty face

and close-cropped black hair: Raymond Scroggins, the local police inspector's son – another reason why he hated this place. Scroggins had cornered George the day he'd first arrived, while he was waiting for Bill Jarvis to come and pick him up from the railway station. Asked him a whole bunch of questions. What was his name? Where was he from? What was he doing here? As soon as George mentioned Charlie and told Scroggins he was in the RAF, the other boy had seemed to bristle, and without understanding why, George knew that from here on in, he would be his enemy through and through.

Fortunately he'd only been back into town once since then, so he'd managed to keep out of his way. But it was clear from the look on Scroggins's face now that he hadn't forgotten him.

As the cart jolted by, Scroggins pointed at George, then turned and whispered something to the other boys. They fell about laughing, holding their bellies like he'd just told them the funniest joke ever. George curled his fingers into fists. What was his problem?

Keep your cool, Georgie, keep your cool. They're not worth your trouble. A bunch of cowards, the lot of 'em. It was Charlie's voice, clear and calm.

He sucked in a breath. Charlie was right. Best just ignore them. Gripping the cart seat with both hands, he set his eyes on the road ahead.

A few seconds later a stone whistled past him, clipping the side of his face. He clutched a hand to his cheek and cried out in pain.

'Whoa!' Bill Jarvis yanked on the reins and the pony clattered to a halt. 'What's wrong with yer?' He swivelled in his seat.

'Nothin'. I . . . er . . .' George shot a look over his shoulder, but Scroggins and the other boys were nowhere to be seen.

Jarvis gave a low growl. 'Stop wasten' my val'able drinken' time.' He flicked the reins and the pony jerked forwards. When they reached the top of the square, he yanked the wooden brake on and jumped down from the cart.

'Wait here and guard what's left.' He jabbed a thumb at the remaining sacks of potatoes. 'Yer can flog the rest of 'em when I'm finished.'

'Wh-where are you going?'

'To the pub.' Jarvis jerked his head at a crooked old building behind him.

'But what about me?'

'There's a pump over there. Yer can fetch yerself and the nag a drink from that.' He looked at his pocket watch again. 'It's half past twelve now. I'll be out at two. And don't go getten' any ideas about runnen' off again – or else.' Hitching up his woollen farm breeches, he turned, pushed open the pub door and disappeared inside.

As the door banged shut, George glanced down the street. He could make a dash for it now; head back to the farm and work out a way of getting Spud free. But what if Jarvis came out to check on him? He'd soon catch him up. Unless he took the cart . . . He grabbed hold of the brake with both hands and pulled on it, but try as he might, he couldn't make it budge.

He slumped his shoulders. It was no use. He'd just have to sit it out and wait. He glanced over at the pump and gave a dry swallow; might as well do as Jarvis said and get himself and the pony some water. He climbed down from the cart and trudged over to it.

There was a wooden bucket next to the pump. He filled it and was setting it in front of the pony when the sound of shouting echoed across the square. He spun round, frowning. The noise was coming from further down. Back behind the Shire Hall. Scroggins and his gang from the sound of it. And now a girl's voice too. High-pitched and quavering. Like she was trying her best not to burst into tears.

George licked his lips. He didn't want any trouble. Best ignore it. Someone else would come along soon and sort them out. But as he turned back to the pump to fetch himself a drink, the shouting grew louder. Suddenly an ear-piercing scream ricocheted round the square. He clenched his jaw. It was no use. He couldn't just stand here and pretend it wasn't happening.

Throwing a quick look back at the pub, he sucked in a breath and set off down the hill.

CHAPTER 6

Scroggins and his gang were standing in a semi-circle at the foot of the Shire Hall steps around the figure of a pale-faced girl with bobbed brown hair and a blue and white checked dress. From the look of her, George guessed she was probably about his age. As he approached, the boys moved in closer and the girl backed up on to the first step, drawing the small wicker basket she was carrying to her chest.

Raymond Scroggins took another step forwards and jabbed a finger at her. 'Go back home and tell Mister Hitler we're going to give him what for, Nazi-girl!'

'I-I am not a Nazi. Please!' She stumbled up the remaining steps, her brown eyes wide with fear.

'Yes you are. Same as that dirt-grubbing granddad of

yours. Come on. Give us a Heil Hitler.' Scroggins flipped his hand into a mock Nazi salute. His friends copied him.

'Hey! What if she's smuggling a secret message in her basket?' A scrawny, carrot-haired boy leapt up the steps after her. As he made a grab for the basket, the girl cried out and swung it away from him. A bunch of eggs flew out, smashing against the pavement in small yellow explosions.

Scroggins and the others burst into gales of raucous laughter.

George balled his fingers into fists. He'd seen enough. 'Oi! Leave her alone!' He flew at the boys, knocking them aside like skittles, then dashed up the steps and wheeled round in front of the girl, knuckles raised.

'If it isn't old Georgie-Porgie.' Raymond Scroggins's eyes shrank to two pale green slits. 'Think you're some kind of a hero, do you? Well, we know different, don't we, lads? How does that rhyme go?' He scratched his head and gave a mock frown, then opened his thin-lipped mouth and half sang, half yelled:

'Georgie-Porgie pudden 'n' pie . . .' He raised up his arms and glanced around him.

The other boys smirked at George, then joined in at the top of their voices.

'Kissed the girls and made 'em cry!'

Raymond Scroggins paused. He shot the girl a sly look and signalled to the others to start up again.

'When the boys came out to play,
Georgie-Porgie ran away.'

He bared a set of ratty yellow teeth and took a step up.

'Go on then, Georgie. Give her a kiss!'

George's cheeks flushed. Heart thumping, he jerked his fists higher. 'Get back or . . . or I'll—'

'You'll what? Get that big brother of yours to try and dive-bomb me?' Scroggins stuck out his arms and mimed being a pilot spinning out of control. The other boys exploded into more fits of laughter.

A ball of hot fury ripped through George's chest. 'Don't you talk about Charlie like that!'

Scroggins gave a loud snort. 'Oh dear, Georgie-Porgie. Can't you take a joke?' He took another step up.

CRUNCH! George's right fist made contact with his nose.

'Arrghh!' Scroggins's hands flew up to his face. He lurched backwards down the steps and toppled to the ground.

The rest of the boys drew back, exchanging fearful looks. One by one, they melted away until only Scroggins was left, cowering among the mess of broken egg yolks and shells.

George glared at him. If he thought he was done with him, he had another think coming. He jumped down the steps, drew back his fist and took aim again.

'No! Don't!' Cool fingers clutched his arm and forced it down to his side.

He spun round.

The girl shook her head and fixed him with a wide-eyed look. 'If you do, you will be as bad as them.' She spoke with an accent: not country like the people round there; not London either.

He frowned. 'But they were going to hurt you.'

'It does not matter. Look. A policeman. We had better go before he sees us.' She pointed to a figure in a dark blue uniform and helmet, cycling up the hill towards them.

George snatched one last look at the hunched, shivering figure of Scroggins, then hurried after her.

'This way.' She darted across the road to a large red-brick house. Running up the steps, she pushed open the door and slid inside.

George faltered. He looked over his shoulder. The copper was getting closer. Any minute now Scroggins would be up on his feet, pointing the finger. But if Jarvis came out of the pub and found him missing, he'd have his guts for garters. He ought to go back . . .

'Come on!' The girl had reappeared at the door. She motioned for him to follow. Reluctantly he climbed up the steps and crossed the threshold into the shadowy space beyond.

A long hallway stretched ahead of him, with doors leading off on both sides and a staircase at the far end. George wrinkled his nose. The air smelt of dust and mothballs. It reminded him of the old wardrobe in Mum and Dad's bedroom back at home. The one he used to hole up in when him and Charlie played hide 'n' seek. He pinched his nostrils to stop from sneezing.

The girl's breath came in short sharp pants behind him. 'That was close.'

He turned. She stood in the shadows, with her back against the door, chest heaving, a hand raised to her throat.

He scowled. 'Bully boys. They didn't hurt you, did they?'

The girl's eyelids flickered. She gave a small shudder and shook her head. 'Thank you for helping me.' She slid her hand down and held it out to him, doing her best to keep it from shaking. 'I am Katharina. Katharina Regenbogen. But you can call me Kitty, if you like.'

George stuck out his own hand, then snatched it back, frowning. '*Raygonbogon?* What kind of a name is that?'

The girl flushed. She drew her hand quickly up to her cheek and hooked a bit of hair over her right ear instead. 'It means rainbow in my language.'

His frown deepened. 'Your language? What's that then?'

The girl hesitated then pulled back her shoulders and looked him full in the face. 'German.'

George's eyes widened. So Scroggins was right. She *was* one of them! He shot her a bitter look and made to push past her.

But the girl blocked his way. 'You cannot go out there yet. If that . . . that boy has told the policeman what you did and he catches you, you will get into trouble. His father is a policeman too.'

George's jaw tightened. She was right. He took a step back and looked her up and down. 'What are you then? Some kind of girl spy?'

She made a sharp clicking noise with her tongue. 'I thought you were different from those other boys.'

George felt a hot rush of shame. 'I'm sorry. I—'

She shook her head and sighed. 'It does not matter.' She reached for the door handle and pulled the door open. A waft of hot, syrupy air slid inside. 'Perhaps it is better if you go after all.'

'No, really.' He pushed the door shut again. 'I shouldn't have said it. It's just . . . well, the Germans, they're our enemies, ain't they?'

She gazed down at the red floor tiles and gave a juddering sigh then looked up again, eyes glistening. 'I am German, but I am Jewish too. Which means Hitler is my enemy also. Do you understand?'

George blinked. 'I . . . I think so, yes. There was a Jewish boy in my class back at home. His name was Daniel Goldberg. He was born here, but his uncle and aunt lived in Germany. He told me once about how hard things got for them and all the other Jews after Hitler took control.'

Kitty heaved another sigh. 'It is more than that.'

'What d'you mean?'

'Hitler hates us. He wants to . . . to kill us.'

George's frown deepened. 'Kill you? Why?'

She bit her lip and glanced down at the floor again. 'He blames the Jews for the state Germany was in before the start of the war. He accuses us of being traitors. Of stealing and cheating and telling lies. But all the things he says about us' – she shot her head up again, eyes gleaming – 'they are not true. *He* is the one who is evil. Him and his . . . his Nazis.' She wiped her mouth with the back of her hand.

'So . . . so what are you doing here?'

Kitty paused then took a deep breath. 'I was lucky. *Opa* – my grandfather – he lives here. He came for his work years ago and stayed. My parents . . .' Her fingers fluttered to a thin gold chain round her neck and tugged on a small six-pointed star that hung from it. She pressed her lips together, swallowed and went on. 'They managed to get me on one of the special transports that came to England before the war began.'

'Didn't they come too?'

'No. The transports were only for children.' Her voice trailed away. She clutched at the star pendant again.

'What happened to them?'

'They . . . they are still there.' She kept her head down, her voice no more than a whisper now. 'In Germany.'

George's chest cramped. He knew what it was like, being separated from the people you loved. Not knowing about them. Wondering when you'd see them again . . .

Footsteps sounded above them. 'Kitty. *Bist Du das?*'

George shot a look up at the ceiling and back at Kitty.

'My grandfather. We live in the apartment upstairs.' She slid past him and darted to the foot of the staircase. '*Ja, Opa. Eine Minute.*' She turned back to face George. 'I was going to invite you up for something to eat and drink. But perhaps you would not like to, how do you say it, take tea with the enemy?'

He felt his cheeks redden. 'Er . . . well . . . thanks, but I'd better not.'

She tilted her head and fixed him with a steady-eyed gaze. 'What is the matter? Do you think we might try and poison you or something?'

'No. It . . . it ain't that.' He threw a glance over his shoulder. 'Oh, all right then. But I can't stay long. I'm meant to be guarding the potatoes.'

She raised a dark eyebrow. 'I did not realize they could be so dangerous.'

'They're not, they're . . . Oh. Ha ha! Very funny!' He rolled his eyes.

Her lips twitched. 'You will come then?'

He nodded.

'Good.' She turned and called up the stairs again. '*Opa*? We have a visitor.' Flashing George a quick smile, she gripped hold of the banister and started to climb.

He held back for a moment. He had a bad feeling about this. If someone pinched them potatoes while he was gone, Bill Jarvis would kill him. And Spud too. But it was too late now. Kitty's granddad was expecting him.

Giving his hair a quick smooth, George took a deep breath and plodded up the stairs after her.

CHAPTER
7

As George reached the top of the stairs, an old man with a shock of white hair stepped out on to the landing from a door on the left. He was dressed in a pair of worn brown corduroy trousers, a baggy-sleeved shirt and a dark-green waistcoat. In spite of his hunched shoulders and stooped back, he was tall. Easily a whole head taller than Bill Jarvis.

He peered at George, blue eyes glinting above the pair of half-moon glasses perched on his nose. 'And who is this, *Liebling*?' He turned and cocked a tufty white eyebrow at the girl.

'Oh! Sorry, *Opa*.' She threw George an embarrassed glance. 'I never asked.'

George pulled back his shoulders and stepped forwards.

'I'm George. George Penny.'

'Penny?' The furrows on the old man's forehead deepened for a moment, then cleared. His eyes danced with a sudden twinkle. Digging his hand in his trouser pocket, he pulled out a large copper-coloured coin, flipped it in the air and caught it in his lined palm. 'Like this?'

George lifted his shoulders into a shrug. 'I s'pose.'

'Good! *Sehr gut!*' The old man's face lit up with a warm smile. 'And I am Ernst Regenbogen, Kitty's grandfather. Welcome to our home, George Penny. Go in, please.' He clapped a hand on his back and gestured to the door behind him.

George threw a quick look down the stairs and swallowed. 'Er, I was thinking. Maybe it'd be better if I came back another time.'

'It is all right. Kitty has finished her lessons for the day.'

'Lessons?' George frowned.

'I do not go to the school. *Opa* teaches me at home. It is . . .' Kitty's face clouded for a moment. 'Easier.'

'What my granddaughter means is that we have all the books we need here. Though if she spent a little less time reading fairy tales, we would get a lot more done.' Ernst Regenbogen winked at Kitty and steered George towards the open door. 'Now, from the look of those red cheeks of yours, you could do with a glass of water.'

George ran his tongue over his lips. He'd forgotten in all the kerfuffle with Scroggins and his gang how thirsty he was. Hungry too. He nodded.

'Good. Kitty, *Liebling*, come and help me, will you? My

arthritis is paining me a little more than usual today.' Rubbing his right hip, the old man turned and limped towards a door on the right, halfway down the hall.

'Yes, *Opa*. Go in and sit down, George Penny. We will not be long.' Kitty shot him another smile and followed after her grandfather.

The fluttering started up in George's stomach again. Jarvis had said he'd be out at two. But what if he left the pub sooner? What time was it now? He stepped inside and scanned around, looking for a clock.

The room was three times the size of their front parlour back at home, with a ceiling twice as high. The afternoon sunshine streamed in through a row of tall windows, spilling across the paper-covered surface of a large wooden desk and on to a faded green sofa and a pair of sagging armchairs arranged on a large rug in the centre of the room.

There was a telephone on a small table by the door, but no sign of a clock. There were plenty of books, though, and not just in the bookcases which ran floor to ceiling on every wall. There were towers of them sprouting up from the floorboards, and piles stacked against the back of the sofa and skirting boards like flights of ramshackle steps.

George had never seen so many in one place before; not even in the headmaster's office that time he'd got the cane for accidentally kicking a ball through the classroom window. But it wasn't just the books; there were mysterious looking knick-knacks too; a whole bunch of them scattered across the shelves and window sills. Lumps of rusty metal, broken bits of pot and, on a table next to the sofa, a dented tobacco tin containing a handful of black discs that looked as if they might once have been coins.

Stepping over to it, George picked up one of the discs and ran his finger over the faint outline of a man's head. The wail of a kettle wound its way in through the door. He dropped the coin back in the tin and flopped down in one of the chairs.

Moments later, the old man limped into the room. He was carrying a tray stacked with tea things and a glass of water. Kitty followed behind, clutching a plate of dark-brown biscuits. She slid past him and cleared a space among the papers on the desk.

'So . . .' The old man set the tray down and turned back to George. 'My granddaughter tells me that you are a hero, like your namesake?'

'Namesake?'

'Saint George, the dragon-slayer.' The old man winked again.

A fresh wave of heat surged into George's cheeks. He threw Kitty a sharp glance, but she kept her head bent, busying herself with the cups and saucers.

He gave a shrug. 'Not really. But that Raymond Scroggins should pick on someone his own size.'

The old man drew in a breath and nodded. 'Quite so. There are bullies everywhere. It is important that we stand up to them, now more than ever. Because if we let them win . . .' A sad, faraway expression stole into his eyes. He gave a deep sigh and focused them back on George. 'Here, my young friend. Your water.' He handed the glass to

George. 'And a cup of tea too. You sound like you have earned it.' He lifted the teapot and poured a stream of steaming brown liquid into each of the cups.

George tilted the glass to his lips. The water was warm and metallic-tasting, but at least it was wet. Gulping it down, he exchanged the empty glass for the cup and saucer the old man offered him.

Kitty thrust the plate at him. 'Have a biscuit.'

He eyed them suspiciously.

She stifled a giggle. 'I was not being serious about the poison.'

'I know that!' He pressed his lips together and scowled back at her.

The old man frowned. 'Come now, *Liebling*. Do not tease our guest. Take one, George. I think you will like them. It is an old recipe my wife used to make.' His face clouded for a moment before brightening again. 'Her lebkuchen biscuits were the talk of our little corner of Bavaria.'

George grabbed a biscuit and bit into it. It was softer than it looked. A warming mix of honey and spices exploded on his tongue. He closed his eyes and imagined himself back in the kitchen at home, sinking his teeth into Mum's special ginger cake – the one she used to make for birthdays and the like.

'Tasty, yes?'

George nodded. He took another mouthful and washed it down with a slurp of tea. 'Where's your wife now, mister?'

Ernst Regenbogen blinked and gave a small cough. 'She died many years ago. Before Kitty was born.' He sank down on the sofa. Kitty slid alongside him and squeezed his hand.

'Oh. Sorry.' George fumbled with the spoon on his saucer. It felt like he should say something else. 'My mum and dad. They're . . . they're both dead too.'

As he said the words, his chest spiked. He sucked in a breath and looked away. When he looked back again, Kitty and the old man were staring at him questioningly. He swallowed hard and forced himself to go on.

'There was an accident at the gasworks. Three years ago.'

They didn't say anything, but he could tell they were listening. Really listening. And suddenly it was like someone had turned on the taps inside him and it all came pouring out. How, a few days before George's tenth birthday, Dad had gone off to work at the gasworks as usual, but he'd forgotten to take his flask of tea. So Mum had chased after him with it. But just as she'd caught up with him there'd been a massive explosion. And then how Charlie and him had waited and waited until finally the police arrived with the news.

What he didn't tell them was how, shortly after, he'd had the first of what Charlie called his 'turns': a suffocating tightness in his throat and chest and a strange shivery feeling that came over him, chilling him to the bone.

That was private – just for him and Charlie to know. Instead, he told them about how Charlie had joined up to 'do his bit', then arranged to move him here, though he didn't tell them either what a bully Bill Jarvis was, or about his plans to run away. They'd probably try and persuade him not to, and he didn't want an argument.

When he'd finished speaking, the old man set down his cup and saucer. He leant across and laid a warm hand on George's shoulder. 'How dreadful. You must miss your parents very much.'

George's chest cramped again. He did, but he'd never showed it. Except to Charlie. He was the only one who understood . . . A sudden rush of panic gripped him. What if Bill Jarvis was right? What if he lost Charlie too? He took another breath and slid his hand in his pocket, feeling again for the reassuring curve of the ring.

The old man sighed. 'You have our heartfelt sympathy. We know a little about how you must feel. Isn't that so, *Liebling*?' He gave Kitty a tender look.

She nodded and bowed her head, fiddling with the pendant on her necklace again.

'Thanks, mister.'

'Call me Ernst, please.'

'All right, mister, I mean Ernst.' George cleared his throat and glanced over at the nearest bookshelf. 'What kind of work do you do?'

Kitty jerked up her head. 'He is a famous archaeologist.'

Ernst Regenbogen smiled. 'Not so famous. But an archaeologist, yes.'

'What's an arc— an arc— . . . one of them?'

'An arc-ee-ol-ogist.' Kitty sounded the letters out like he

was a baby. 'They dig old things up, don't they, *Opa*?'

George curled his fingers. If she thought he was going to take English lessons from the likes of her . . .

The old man got to his feet and patted George on the back. 'Do not mind my granddaughter. She is like her father when he was a boy. Fond of showing off from time to time. He is the one who taught her to speak such good English.'

Kitty's cheeks flushed pink. 'I was not showing off, I was explaining.' She thrust her arms across her chest and gathered her lips into a pout.

'She is as stubborn as him too, at times.' The old man winked at George. 'But come, let me show you.' He led him over to one of the bookcases and pulled an object down from one of the shelves above George's head.

George peered at the fist-sized oval stone. 'What is it?'

'A prehistoric axe head.' The old man traced a wrinkled finger round the hole in its centre. 'I found it on my first dig when I was a student back in Germany. It is cracked just here. You see? So the dig leader said I could keep it. The other bits and pieces are small, unwanted things I dug out of spoil heaps.' He held the stone out to George.

George stroked a fingertip along the thin black diagonal line that ran across its polished surface.

Kitty pushed in alongside them and seized a framed photograph from the shelf below.

'*Opa* worked on one of the most famous digs ever, right here, just before the war. Look! That is him, there.' She pointed at a tall figure in a floppy hat standing with a group of men in front of a grass-covered mound. 'Guess what they found beneath it.' She tapped the mound with her finger, eyes sparkling.

George shrugged. 'I dunno. What?'

'A ship.'

'A *ship*? Are you pulling my leg?'

Kitty shot him a puzzled look. 'Why would I want to do such a thing?'

The old man chuckled again. 'No, *Liebling*. He means, *are you joking?* But Kitty is right. We did indeed find a ship. Or rather, the ghost of one.'

'Ghost? What d'you mean?'

'The outline of a great longship, over ninety feet in length and with space enough for forty oarsmen.'

George's eyes widened. Who was joking now?

'Hard to imagine, I know. But it is true. The nails were still there, caked in rust. And the imprint of the wooden planks used to build it. But the timbers had long since rotted; eaten away by the sandy soil.' Ernst Regenbogen rubbed a hand over his leg and gestured to the sofa. 'Do you mind if we sit down again?'

'That was not the only thing they dug up, was it, *Opa*?' Kitty darted past them to the desk and snatched up a slim rectangular cardboard box. As they sat on the sofa, she squeezed in between them and opened the lid to reveal a pile of photographs. She leafed through them, pulled one out and thrust it at George. He stared at it for a moment, then looked up at her and frowned.

'It looks like a pile of mud and stones to me.'

'But you are not looking closely enough!' Kitty traced her fingernail across the photograph. And then he saw it too. The shadow of something buried in the soil.

'What is it?'

'A metal bowl.'

'Great. Look, I ain't got time for this.' He made to stand. 'I'm s'posed to be—'

'Wait! Here. This is even better.' She passed him a photograph of a dirt-encrusted object.

George raised a questioning eyebrow.

'It is a huge buckle. Made of solid gold. This shows it before cleaning, but even here you can see how it is decorated with snakes and birds' heads.' She picked out a faint pattern of twining bodies and curved beaks. She looked up, eyes glittering. '*Opa* says it is priceless.'

In spite of himself, George felt his mouth gape open.

Kitty gave a triumphant smile. 'I thought you would be impressed.'

She handed him one photograph after another. With the Regenbogens' help, he saw through the layers of grime to what lay beneath. A pair of long-handled silver spoons. A pile of gold coins in the remains of a giant purse, its lid studded with jewelled plaques showing men flanked by wolves and giant birds of prey. And a strange, four-sided stone bar with a set of mysterious faces carved at each end. There were weapons and armour too. A set of rusted spears; a lump of sand-clogged chain mail; pieces of a giant shield and fragments of what the old man said they believed was part of a great metal helmet. And then the sword. Nearly three feet long, the iron blade topped with a pommel of garnets and gold.

'But this is my favourite!' Kitty thrust another photograph under George's nose.

He stared at the piece of metal displayed on it. It was shaped like a knife blade but forked at one end and hooked at the other, its surface covered in the same snake-like shapes as the buckle. There were more jewels too, which Kitty told him were deep red garnets – three on either side, with a single, seventh stone at the top of the hook.

George drew in a breath. 'What is it?'

'A dragon.' Kitty's eyes flashed with fire. 'This is its tail.' She pointed at the forked tip. 'And these are its wings.' She traced the curved strips of metal sprouting from the garnets on each side. 'And here is its eye.' She pointed at the single jewel set in what George could see now wasn't a hook but the creature's head. 'And these . . .' She zigzagged her finger across the set of jagged spikes sprouting from the beak-shaped mouth. 'These are its jaws. The dragon was fixed on the king's shield to frighten the enemy. Isn't that right, *Opa*?'

'That is what we think, yes. Magnificent, isn't it?'

George nodded. As he stared down at the coils etched across the surface of the creature's body, the back of his neck prickled at something half-remembered. He shrugged the feeling off and flicked his gaze to the final photograph in Kitty's hand. It showed two men. One of them was Ernst Regenbogen. George guessed from the way the other man was standing he was probably much younger, but it was difficult to be sure because his face was a blur.

'Who's that?'

Ernst Regenbogen took the photograph from Kitty. 'My digging partner, although it is not a good picture of him. He moved as the photographer took it. He was a German archaeology student, but he had lived and studied over here for a while. I liked him. He was young, but he had the makings of an excellent archaeologist.' He shook his head and sighed. 'The war brought a stop to so many things.'

George frowned. 'What d'you mean?'

'His career for one. And the dig too, though the pair of us believed there was still one final piece of treasure left to find.'

'The king's crown!' Kitty clutched the box of photographs to her chest, her eyes shining with excitement.

George's mouth dropped open. 'What king?'

The old man cleared his throat. 'The one we think was buried with all these things inside the ship, though we never found his bones.'

'Who was he?'

'We are not certain, but we think it could be the Anglo–Saxon king, Redwald, High King of what amounted to England in those days.'

Kitty jumped up and plucked a red leather-covered book from the nearest bookshelf. 'Tell him the story, *Opa*. The one about the crown.'

'Come now, Kitty. George does not want to hear about that now. I am sure he has better things to—'

'Please, *Opa!*' Kitty curled her arms around the old man's neck and laid her head on his shoulder.

'Well, all right. As long as you have time, George?'

George licked his lips. 'I ain't sure. You see, I'm meant to be—'

'Guarding some potatoes. Yes, you said, but it will only take a few minutes. Go on, *Opa*.' Kitty thrust the book at her grandfather and sat down cross-legged on the rug in front of him.

'Very well.' Throwing George an apologetic look, the old man opened the book and leafed through the pages until he found the one he wanted. He glanced up at them. 'Are you ready?'

They nodded.

'Then I will begin.'

CHAPTER 8

The Legend of the Dragon-headed Crown

    Long ago, when the earth was still bound by magic and gods kept watch over the affairs of men, a fearsome dragon stalked the land. Wherever it went, it caused chaos, destroying crops, livestock and homes.

    But like all dragons, what it craved most was treasure – glittering goblets, jewelled buckles, precious gold rings. These were the things which kept its blood hot and its fire stoked. And no matter where the treasure was hidden, the snake-necked monster would always sniff it out. Then it would drag it back to its lair beneath the roots of a great, gnarled tree, mound it up and lie on it until its scales glowed like molten gold, its heart burnt like a red-hot furnace and it was ready to wreak havoc again.

The king who ruled over the land became ever more desperate as the dragon laid waste to his kingdom and stole away all his treasures. Then word reached him of a famed dragon-slayer. At the king's invitation, the dragon-slayer sailed to his shores in a great longship, his army of battle-hardened warriors at his side.

The dragon-slayer and his men tracked the dragon and followed it back to its lair. They waited until darkness fell and the beast went off hunting. Then the dragon-slayer slunk into the creature's earth-cave, buried himself in the great golden treasure mound and waited.

The fire-spitter returned from another night of pillage and plunder, its jaws full of yet more precious treasures. It loaded them on top of the gold pile, then curled itself around it and fell into a deep smokeless sleep.

Slowly, carefully, the dragon-slayer crept out from his hiding place among the heap of treasure. He stole to the dragon's side, unsheathed his pattern-welded sword and thrust it into the great gold-hoarder's heart, killing it with one strike.

When the king, who had no children of his own, learnt what the dragon-slayer had done, he took some gold from the dragon's treasure hoard. He asked the wily smith-god, Wayland, to make a crown and promised to the dragon-slayer that he would pass it on to him with his kingdom when the time came for him to die.

So Wayland crafted the crown with all his skill, setting on top of it a great dragon-headed crest. But the smith-god was a great mischief-maker. And while the body of the dragon was *still warm, he took some of its blood and engraved the crown with a powerful charm.*

And the words of the charm were these: 'He who has me has the kingdom.'

When the old king died, the crown – which the people called Kingdom-Keeper – passed to the dragon-slayer. While it was safe in his hands and those of his descendants, the land prospered and all was well.

But the charm was double-edged; if the crown fell into the wrong hands, things would be different. Very different indeed...

'And that is where the tale ends.' Ernst Regenbogen gave George a mysterious wink. He closed the book and handed it back to Kitty.

George frowned. 'But what's the legend got to do with this king? The one you say's buried in the ship.'

Kitty leapt to her feet. 'We think King Redwald is the dragon-slayer's descendant. Tell him, *Opa*!'

The old man raised an eyebrow. 'That is what some people say, Kitty. Though others think it is a story and nothing more.'

George pulled a face. 'Sounds like! I mean, dragons and magic charms and things. They ain't real, are they?'

Kitty snatched up the photograph of the dragon from the shield. 'And this?'

George snorted. 'What does that prove? It's just a bit of old metal.'

Kitty shot him a hurt look. Thrusting the photograph back in the box, she closed the lid and marched back over to the desk.

A bubble of guilt rose up inside George. 'Sorry. I—' He clamped his mouth shut and looked down at the floor.

'It is all right. She likes you really, I can tell.' The old man gave him another wink.

George felt his cheeks go red again. 'So . . . so is there really a crown, mister?'

Ernst Regenbogen hesitated then gave a slow nod. 'My young digging partner' – he tipped his head at the photograph lying on the cushion beside him – 'he thought so. He found a reference to a crown in an old Anglo–Saxon document he unearthed in a German monastery before coming over here. And it seemed very convincing. It claimed that Redwald's people buried it close to where he, his ship and his other treasures lay – for safekeeping, after his son, the new king, was murdered. Of course it does not mean it is the crown of the legend – the Kingdom-Keeper . . .'

George opened his mouth to say something but Kitty cut across him.

'It might be, *Opa*!'

'Hush, *Liebling*. Let George speak.'

George cleared his throat. 'So you didn't find it? The crown I mean.'

The old man shook his head. 'No. We started to look for it, but when it was clear we would soon be at war with Germany, my colleague decided to return home. Not long after, the dig was closed down.'

'Yes.' Kitty sidled back over and sat down on the arm of the sofa. 'And then the war started and *Opa* had to help the others get the finds up to London, didn't you, *Opa*?'

The old man gave a grim smile. 'That is right. We could not risk them being left to the mercy of Herr Hitler and his friends. The treasures were taken first to the British Museum and from there to a secret storage place deep underground.'

'What happened to him? Your partner?'

'He is no doubt busy fighting for the Fatherland, like so many other young men of his age. Such a waste . . .' Ernst Regenbogen looked down at the photograph again and sighed.

The distant sound of clock chimes echoed in through the door. A knot of panic gripped George's stomach. 'What time is it?'

Ernst Regenbogen pulled up his sleeve and looked at the wristwatch on his arm. 'A quarter past two.'

The knot grew tighter still. Bill Jarvis was going to kill him! George leapt to his feet. 'Sorry. I've got to go. Thanks for the tea, mister.' He dashed out on to the landing and down the stairs.

As he reached for the front door handle, a set of light footsteps pattered across the tiles behind him.

'Wait! I can take you there if you like?'

He twisted round to face the girl. 'Take me where?'

'To the burial site. Tomorrow afternoon, maybe?'

He frowned. 'I dunno. Look, I'm not sure if . . .'

Her face fell.

He puffed out a breath and gave a quick nod. It was easier to agree than try and explain.

As he stepped back out into the street, he threw a hurried glance in the direction of the pub. The pony and cart were still there, but there was no sign of Bill Jarvis. He heaved a sigh and sped off towards them. But as he reached the cart, a stocky figure stepped out from behind it, a pocket watch in his hand.

'Where you been, City Boy? And what yer done with my taters?'

George's stomach gave a sickening leap. The back of the cart was empty. Someone – Raymond Scroggins and his gang? – must have pinched the rest of the potatoes while he'd been at the Regenbogens'.

'Well?' Bill Jarvis stood over him, hands on hips, black eyes drilling into him.

George looked at his boots, brain whirring for an excuse. 'I-I-I dunno. I—'

'Too busy sleepen' on the job, yer good fer nothen' little—' Jarvis raised a hand as if to clout him, then jerked it down quickly again as a woman carrying a baby turned into the square. The woman walked past them and shot Jarvis a disapproving stare.

Jarvis scowled and shoved George towards the front of the cart. 'I'll see to yer when we're home. Go on, get up there. I haven't got all day.' Climbing up beside him, he grabbed the whip and cracked it down hard against the pony's bony grey rump.

When they finally arrived back at the farm, Jarvis reined in the pony and pulled up the brake. 'Get down!' He shoved George out of the seat, jumped down beside him and grabbed hold of his shirt. 'You city brats are all the same. Never done a day's honest work in yer lives.' As he yanked George closer, a reek of sour ale flooded his nostrils. George gagged and made to turn away, but Jarvis gripped his chin and forced his head back round.

'Look at me when I'm talken' to yer! How the Government thinks I can keep this place goen' with a bunch of milky-faced weaklings in place of real men, I don't know. That first 'vacuee I had last year was bad enough. But you've been trouble since the day yer arrived. And now...' Keeping a tight grip on George, he reached for his belt and fumbled with the buckle. 'Now yer goen' to pay.'

A hard knot of fear formed in the pit of George's stomach. That last beating had been bad enough, but this time Jarvis was angrier. Much angrier. And there was drink in him too. He struggled against him, trying desperately to break free.

A series of frantic barks sounded from the other side of the barn wall, followed by the scrabbling of claws against wood.

Jarvis threw a look over at it, then glanced back at George, eyes flooding with fresh spite. Digging his fingers inside his waistcoat pocket, he pulled out a small rusty key.

A stab of fear shot through George. 'No, please!' He made a swipe for the key, but Jarvis shouldered him aside. Marching over to the barn, he unlocked the padlock, wrenched the door open and stepped inside.

George scrambled after him into the gloom.

Jarvis plucked a broken broom handle from a pile of

junk. He sized it up with a satisfied smile. 'I'll warm up on yer mangy friend first and teach *you* a lesson after. Come here, mutt.'

There was a clink of chains and a low growl from the corner. Jarvis advanced towards the sound, thumping the broom handle against his thigh.

George curled his fists. He had to stop him. Casting about for a weapon, his eye caught on a rusty shovel hanging from a hook on the wall. He leapt over to it and yanked it free.

Jarvis jerked to a halt in front of the dark shape hunched against the wall. 'Shut yer racket, fleaball.' He raised the stick above his head. 'Now, are yer ready fer yer beaten'? Good! After three. One ... two ...'

THWACK! George slammed the flat side of the shovel against Jarvis's back. The great bully let out a groan and staggered forwards, then pulled up and spun round, eyes goggling like a madman. He lurched towards George, face red with fury, waving the broom handle from side to side.

Stumbling backwards, George threw down the shovel and turned to run. But his way was blocked by a wall of mouldy hay bales. He twisted round, Spud's warning barks ringing in his ears. Jarvis had him cornered.

'Got yer!' He swung the stick back over his shoulder and took aim ...

George dropped into a crouch, hands raised to fend off the blow. There was a loud grunt followed by a heavy thud, then silence. He stayed where he was for a moment, then straightened up slowly, heart pounding, and looked round.

Jarvis lay stretched out on the ground a few feet away, eyes closed, face a nasty shade of grey.

George froze. What if he was dead? There was only one way to find out. He took a deep breath and crept towards him; drawing as close as he dared, he reached out and gave his shoulder a quick prod. Jarvis moaned and rolled over, but his eyes stayed shut.

Still alive then. George let out a sigh. He hated Jarvis, but he didn't want him dead. What had happened to him anyway? He looked about him, searching for a clue. And then he spotted the rake lying half-hidden in the straw. He must have tripped over it and clocked himself one on the handle. But he'd be sure to blame it on George if he got half the chance.

Willing Jarvis not to wake up, George dashed over to Spud and yanked the chain free from the hook. As he worked it loose from around his neck, the dog licked his hand, then pulled back his lips and snarled at his tormentor.

'It's all right. He can't hurt you now.' George ruffled a hand through Spud's fur and led him quickly outside.

A sudden loud squeal made him jump. He spun round. A pair of slimy pink noses were poking through a gap in the fence behind him. The pigs. They wanted feeding. He clenched his jaw. That wasn't his job. Not any more. Still, it wouldn't be fair to make them go hungry. He grabbed the slops bucket and chucked them a few handfuls of potato skins.

'Wait here, boy. I'll be back soon.' He tossed the bucket

aside and headed towards the cottage. Five minutes later he was back again, knapsack hoisted over his right shoulder. He threw a look over at the barn, but there was no sign of Jarvis.

'Come on, boy. Let's go.' He gave Spud a quick pat and headed across the yard. As he passed the cart, he caught sight of the leather satchel lying on the seat. Charlie's hard-earned money was in there: he wasn't leaving without *that*. He climbed up and rummaged inside. The note wasn't there. He'd have to take coins instead. Fishing a spare sock out of his knapsack, he shovelled a pile of shillings and sixpences into it and folded the end over.

As he shoved it inside his pocket, his fingers made contact with the ring. His heart did a quick somersault. In an hour or two's time, he'd be seeing Charlie again. And that was all that mattered for now, wasn't it? Pulling the ring free, he slid it on to his right thumb. Then, with another quick glance at the barn, he slipped out of the yard, Spud at his heels, and hurried away down the track in the direction of town.

CHAPTER
9

The sun pitched down like a furnace, but in spite of the heat, George kept up the pace. If Bill Jarvis woke up, he'd be on them quicker than a spider on a fly. And if he caught Spud . . . His stomach clenched as he glanced down at him. He wasn't going to let that rotten bully hurt either of them ever again. He gritted his teeth and pushed on.

As he reached the crossroads, he saw a figure heading towards them along the track to their left. It was hard to be sure, but it looked like the man he'd seen Jarvis trading with yesterday. He hadn't spotted them yet. Best keep it that way.

'Come on, boy.' He made to set off again, but Spud stayed put, flattening his ears and giving a low growl.

The man jerked to a halt and squinted up the track.

Grabbing Spud by the scruff of his neck, George clamped a hand over his snout and dragged him into the bushes. He squatted down and held his breath.

Silence. Then the sound of the man's boots crunching forwards at the same steady pace as before.

George heaved a sigh. They hadn't been rumbled. Leastways, not yet . . . He kept a tight grip on Spud and waited.

The footsteps drew closer, then stopped again.

George sneaked a quick look. The man was near now – no more than a handful of yards away. It was Jarvis's friend all right. He had the same narrow face and fair hair and he was wearing that heavy old coat too. He must be melting.

The man took a quick look about him, then scrambled up the bank next to the track and into the trees. What was he up to? George waited a moment, then, motioning to Spud to stay put, he slid out from their hiding place and crept over to it. Clambering up the side, he poked his head over the top, and peered into the leafy shadows beyond.

He spotted the man a short distance away, crouched next to a fallen tree trunk. He'd unbuttoned his coat and was busy pulling what looked like an old sack from beneath it.

George frowned. What if he wasn't a member of the Home Guard, but some kind of poacher instead? They skulked about in the woods setting traps and the like, didn't they? It looked as if that was what this one was up to now. He chewed on his lip. He should probably report him to the police, but he couldn't risk it – not after that fight with Jarvis. He shuddered at the memory, scalp prickling with fresh sweat.

The man had untied the sack and was examining its contents. A glint of gold caught the light. George's eyes widened – he hadn't been expecting that! He craned forwards, trying to get a better look. But the man was tying the sack back up again now, hiding whatever was inside from view.

Suddenly the light began to dim. A cold, clammy feeling crept across the back of George's neck. He shivered and took a deep breath, wondering if he was about to have another of his turns. But it couldn't be that because the man had noticed something too. He was on his feet now and looking about him, the sack pressed to his chest, his eyes flashing with sudden fear.

CRAAK!

George stifled a gasp as the shadowy form of a huge bird shot out of nowhere and swooped down on the man, snatching at his hair with its talons and beating the air with its pitch-black wings.

The man fought back, swiping at the bird with his right hand, clutching the sack tight against him with his left. As his fingers made contact with the bird's wing feathers, it lifted off and sheered away. For a moment George thought it had gone. But a few seconds later it was back, powering through the trees again. As it swooped in for a second attack, the man snatched up a fallen branch and swung at it with a cry. The bird spun clear and shot out into the open.

Seizing his chance, the man threw the sack over his back

and tore off into the woods. The bird circled round and dropped down on to the bank a few feet from where George was crouched. It peered into the trees, then, ruffling its feathers, it put its head on one side and fixed George with a black beady eye. He backed away from it nervously. The bird gave another harsh croak, before lifting up suddenly and disappearing away over the tops of the trees.

A wet nose nudged the back of George's leg. He bent down and pulled Spud to him. 'What was all that about, boy?' He lifted his head and blinked. It was brighter again now, but there was still a chill in the air. And something else too. Like someone – or something – was watching them. He shivered and jumped to his feet. 'Come on, let's get out of here.' He patted the side of his leg, signalling to Spud to stay close, and set off at a run.

When they reached the edge of town, George kept his eyes peeled for someone to stop so he could ask the way to the airbase. But there was no one in sight. He was about to take the road that led into the centre when a canvas-roofed army truck rattled into view. He stuck out an arm to flag it down.

As it ground to a stop, the driver poked his head out of the cab window. 'What d'you want, sonny?'

George shaded his eyes. 'Which way is it to the airbase?'

The soldier wrinkled his forehead. 'Why're you asking?'

He flushed. 'I need to get an urgent message to my brother. He's one of the pilots there.'

The soldier looked him up and down, then gave a quick nod. 'You can have a lift if you like. We're going that way ourselves. Hop up back, but look lively. We've got another load of wire to pick up and take down to the coast before the day's out.'

'Thanks, mister! Come on, Spud.' George hurried round to the rear of the truck. As he got there, another soldier appeared above the tailgate and held out his hand. 'Here you are, sunshine.'

George heaved Spud up and bundled him inside. Then, gripping the soldier's hand, he let himself be hauled aboard.

It was stifling inside and thick with the smell of engine grease and men's sweat. Two rows of soldiers sat slumped in the shadows on either side of him, their backs resting against the canvas walls of the truck. As he stepped in between them, one or two glanced up, but the rest kept their eyes closed and their chins tucked firmly against their chests.

The soldier who'd helped him on board sat down and patted the empty space on the bench next to him. As George dropped down alongside him, the truck roared back into life and lurched off down the road.

'Here.' The soldier offered George a dented metal canister. 'Have some water. You look like you could use it.'

'Thanks.' Unscrewing the lid, George took a quick swig; then doing his best to keep his balance, he poured some water into his cupped hand and offered it to Spud.

'So' – the soldier raised his voice above the engine noise – 'you're off to the airbase to see your brother then?'

George handed the canteen back to him and nodded.

'Ground crew, is he?'

'A pilot.'

The soldier frowned and jabbed a finger at his ear. 'You'll have to speak up a bit.'

'A pilot!'

The soldier cocked an eyebrow in surprise. 'What does he fly?'

'I dunno, but I'm hoping it's a Spitfire. He's been in training since he joined up, but he's going on his first mission any day now.'

The soldier took a sharp breath. George glanced up at him. 'What's wrong?'

'Nothing, lad. It's just that it's a tough job fighting the Luftwaffe and the new boys, well, they don't always . . .' The soldier's voice trailed away.

A fresh jolt of fear spiked George's chest. He pulled back into the shadows and stared at his boots. It was bad enough having to listen to Bill Jarvis spouting his opinions about Charlie's chances. He didn't need to hear it from this man too.

As if sensing it was a sore point, the soldier stopped talking and left George to himself. He was glad when the truck finally shuddered to a halt and the man nudged him and told him it was his stop.

George manoeuvred Spud up and over the top of the tailgate and jumped down after him. As his boots hit the ground, the soldier leant out and pointed at a high wire fence away to their right.

'We're turning off here, but if you follow that fence a bit further, you'll reach the main entrance soon enough. And look' – he frowned and ran a hand over the back of his neck – 'take no notice of what I said earlier. Your brother'll be fine, I'm sure he will.' He shot George a quick mock-salute and drew back inside.

The truck rumbled into life again. As it disappeared round the bend, George darted over to the fence and peered through it. On the far side of a large, grassy field stood a bunch of low huts. Beyond them were what looked like a pair of giant Anderson shelters, their hump-shaped roofs painted dark green. Scattered before them stood small groups of fighter planes, their fuselages shimmering silver in the heat. His breath caught in his throat. They were beautiful. More beautiful than anything he'd ever seen. Like a flock of great silver birds, wings outstretched and ready to fly. As he stood there squinting, trying to identify them, the sound of men's voices carried towards him and then suddenly, high above everything, a real bird started warbling fit to bust.

George's heart soared at the thought of seeing Charlie again. He'd probably be surprised at first. Worried, even. But he'd understand when he told him how rotten Jarvis was; he knew he would.

He started. What was he doing, wasting time standing here? 'Come on, boy. Let's go and find Charlie.' He took a deep breath and set off towards the entrance.

CHAPTER
10

There was a barrier across the entrance when they got there. As George and Spud approached it, a stocky man in the blue-grey uniform of the RAF stepped smartly out from the guard hut next to it and stalked round in front of them, a rifle clutched across his chest.

Spud leapt up barking, hackles raised. The man jerked the rifle up and pointed it at him.

'No. Don't!' George dragged the dog back by the scruff of his neck. 'Down, boy! Sorry, mister. He doesn't mean anything by it.'

The guard lowered the rifle and frowned. 'That animal should be on a lead. Anyway, what are you doing snooping around here? Be off with you, laddie, before I call the police.'

George pulled back his shoulders and forced himself to look the man in the eye. 'I've come to see my brother. I've got a message for him.'

The guard's frown deepened. 'How do you know he's stationed here?'

'He told me.'

He shook his head. 'He shouldn't have done that. It's against the rules. What's his name?'

George wavered. The last thing he wanted was to get Charlie into any trouble.

'Come on. Out with it. I won't report him, if that's what you're worried about.'

George drew in a breath. 'Penny. Charlie Penny. He's just finished his pilot's training.'

'A sprog, eh? All right.' The guard held out his hand. 'Give it here and I'll get it to him.'

George took a step backwards. 'It . . . it ain't written down.'

The guard's eyebrows bunched together. 'Civilians aren't allowed the base. Not unless they've been authorized.'

George slumped his shoulders. He threw a glance at the hut. 'Can't you call him then? Get him to come down here instead?'

The guard jutted out his chin and fixed him with a stern stare. 'Some of us have got a war to fight, you know. Now push off back home to your mum sharpish, before I lose my patience.'

'But I can't.'

'Why not?'

'Cos . . . cos she's dead.'

The guard's features softened. 'I'm sorry to hear that, laddie.' He cleared his throat. 'Look, how about if I fetch a pencil and paper and you scribble down what you want to say to your brother now? I'll pass it on to him when my shift finishes at six.'

George's stomach tightened. He hadn't come all this way just to leave Charlie a note. He slid his eyes to the hut and back to the barrier again. 'All right, mister.'

With a quick nod, the guard turned and marched back inside.

George waited until the man was safely out of sight, then clicked his tongue. 'Quick, boy. Let's go!' The pair of them darted beneath the barrier and set off at a sprint towards the base.

An angry shout rang out behind them. George kept his head down and sped on, heart pounding. They were halfway to the aircraft hangars before he dared take a quick look back. There was no sign of the guard. He was probably phoning through a warning. The sooner they found Charlie, the better. He gulped in a mouthful of air and put on a fresh spurt.

As they neared the first group of planes, a low drone of voices sounded away to his left. He wheeled round. A group of young men sat slumped in deckchairs outside one of the huts, some reading, others playing cards or talking. One or two of them wore leather flying jackets, but most were in their shirtsleeves, their blue uniform jackets slung over the backs of their chairs or cast down next to them on the grass.

George held his breath. Was Charlie among them? As he peered over, torn between getting closer and trying his best to avoid them, a hand grabbed him by the arm and spun him round. An airman stood in front of him, mouth open, brown eyes wide with surprise.

'George?'

Before he had a chance to say anything else, George flung his arms round him and buried his face against his chest.

For a blissful few moments all he knew was the smell of wool mixed with Woodbines, the comforting warmth of Charlie's arms and the steady thud-thud of his heart against George's cheek. Then, as Charlie pulled free, the world came crowding back in again, dazzling him with its light and noise.

Charlie stared down at him, his expression of surprise replaced by one of worry. 'What are you doing here?'

George frowned. 'Ain't you glad to see me?'

''Course I am, Georgie, but—'

George's jaw dropped as he caught sight of the Spitfire standing a short distance behind Charlie. 'Gorr! Is that your plane?' He dashed over to it, Spud bounding along behind. A ripple of excitement pulsed through him as he ran his hand along the brown and green fuselage. The panels were smooth and warm to the touch. He'd never been so close to one before. As he stood on his toes, trying to see inside the cockpit, a shadow fell across the bullseye target painted on the fighter's side.

'George, you ain't answered my question.'

A knot formed in George's chest. He blinked and turned to face him. 'I . . . I wanted to come and wish you luck. Before your first mission.'

'Does Mister Jarvis know you're here?'

'Er . . . not exactly, no.'

'What do you mean?'

George drew in a breath and met his gaze. He'd have to tell him sooner or later. It might as well be now. 'I've run away.'

Charlie's eyebrows jerked up. 'You've done *what*?'

George licked his lips. 'It was awful there, Charlie. Me and Spud, we couldn't stand it a minute longer, could we, boy?' He dropped down and pulled Spud to him.

Charlie's eyes flicked to the dog as if noticing him for the first time. 'You mean you've stolen his dog?'

George jumped to his feet. 'No. You don't understand. He was going to beat him. Don't make us go back there. Please!'

Charlie stared at him for a moment then shook his head. 'I'm sorry, George, but you're going to have to.'

George's stomach gave a sickening leap. 'Wh-what? But I can't, I—'

Charlie put a hand on his shoulder. 'You're just a bit homesick, that's all.'

'But he's a dirty rotten bully! He—'

Charlie cut across him, his voice edged with impatience. 'This is war, George. We all have to do things we don't want to. Now listen.' His grip tightened. 'I'm expecting to go up and fight the Luftwaffe anytime now, and I can't be worrying about you while I'm doing that. So I need you to be brave and stick it out, at least until things quieten down here a bit. D'you understand?'

George hung his head and kicked at a tuft of grass with his boot. 'When's that going to be?'

'I don't know, Georgie.' Charlie tilted George's chin up. 'But I'll come and get you as soon as I can, I promise.'

George's eyes blurred with sudden tears. 'What if . . . what if you don't come back?'

A look of doubt stole into Charlie's eyes, and for a few seconds he seemed lost for words. Then he blinked and threw back his shoulders, fixing George with a steady gaze. 'You've still got the ring, ain't you?'

George gave a quick nod and stuck out his thumb.

'Good. Look, here's mine too.' Charlie fumbled beneath his shirt collar and pulled out a length of brown leather cord.

George stared at the wink of gold metal nestled in his brother's fingers.

'*Together Always.* Remember?'

He sucked in a breath and nodded again.

'Good lad. Now we'd better get you off the base before the squadron leader gets wind.' Charlie looped his arm round George's shoulder and steered him away from the plane.

As they set off back across the grass in silence, the sun beat down, sending trickles of sweat running down George's back. He was desperate to tell Charlie about Bill Jarvis. About the beatings and what had happened this afternoon – why it was impossible for him and Spud to go back. But how could he now, after what he'd said?

The guard strode out to meet them as they approached the hut, his mouth set in a thin hard line.

'Leave this to me.' Charlie drew the man to one side and had a quiet word. He threw a stern look at George, then gave a grunt and let them pass.

Charlie stopped at the barrier and looked down at George, his eyes full of fresh concern. 'You haven't had another of those turns, have you?'

George shook his head.

A look of relief washed over Charlie's face. 'You know what to do if you do, though?'

'Take deep breaths and count to five 'til I feel better.'

'That's right.' Charlie ruffled a hand through George's hair. 'You'll be all right, Georgie. We both will. Just make sure and keep a tight hold of that ring, eh?' He shot him a quick smile.

George's throat tightened. He wanted to say something; tell Charlie good luck. But his tongue was thick in his mouth and all he could do was give another nod.

A loud clanging rang out across the field behind them. Charlie started and swung round, eyes wide, face paling.

'What's that?'

'We're being scrambled. I've got to go, Georgie.' He gave him a swift hug, then turned and set off back across the field at a run.

George made to go after him, but the guard stepped forwards and blocked his way. 'Come along, laddie. You've delivered your message. Leave your brother to get on with his job.'

He could only watch helplessly then as Charlie joined up with the other pilots, all of them tugging on their flying jackets and running at full pelt now towards their planes. For a moment George lost sight of him, but then, as the first of the fighters growled into action, he saw him again, clambering from the wing of the Spitfire into the cockpit.

Across the field, Spitfires and Hurricanes were getting ready for take-off, engines exploding into life, propellers spinning, wheels bouncing over the ground. One by one, they powered across the grass before lifting up and disappearing over the hangars and away into the blue.

And then it was Charlie's turn. George curled his fingers over the ring and watched, heart in mouth, as the Spitfire bobbled across the field, following in the wake of a Hurricane. As the plane gathered pace, the engine noise changed from a hum to a growl to a spine-tingling roar, and then it was airborne, nose lifting, wings tilting, wheels sliding out and up beneath it. As it arced round, George saw a gloved hand lift up in the cockpit and wave. Then it sped away over the top of the hangars after the others and was gone.

The knot in George's throat grew tighter still. 'Where're they going?'

The guard frowned. 'I'm not sure.' A sudden *bring-bring* sounded from inside the hut. He jumped to attention. 'Go on, be off with you. And make sure you go straight home. Whatever's occurring, you'll be better off indoors.' He turned and hurried back inside.

George's heart clenched. Home was with his brother. But Charlie was off now, doing what he'd been trained for, fighting for king and country. For George too. As the last of the fighters took off and disappeared from view, he uncurled his fingers and stared down at the ring.

He'd do his best to put a brave face on it, for Charlie's sake. But he couldn't go back to Bill Jarvis's. Not now, not ever. Which meant he'd have to find somewhere else to stay. But where? The only other people he knew were the Regenbogens. Maybe they'd put him up for the night? And after? He wasn't sure. A sudden thought occurred. He could go back to London. Stay with Mrs Jenkins for a few days and get her to write to Charlie and explain about Bill Jarvis. If he knew the whole truth, he'd find George another place right away, he was sure. But he'd worry about that tomorrow . . .

'Come on, boy.' He gave Spud a quick pat on the head.

As he turned to go, a harsh croak made him start. He glanced up, squinting. A bird was circling overhead, its wing-feathers shining blue-black in the sun.

It couldn't be, could it? As he shielded his eyes to get a better look, the bird called again, then veered away towards a line of trees on the horizon.

George shook his head. He had better things to do than waste time gawping at a bloomin' crow. Whistling for Spud to follow, he headed off back along the road into town.

CHAPTER
11

It took what felt like a good hour of walking to reach the town. They were nearing the first of the houses when a low humming noise vibrated against George's ears. He looked up, hoping against hope the call to scramble had been a false alarm and Charlie's squadron was flying back to base.

But the plane, when he spotted it, was on its own, heading towards him up the river valley from the coast. He shaded his eyes. It was too high up to stand a chance of making out any markings, but it didn't sound like a Spitfire; a Hurricane neither. As the plane drew nearer, it changed tack and began to arc slowly back and forth across the sky; almost as though it was looking for something...

A sudden feeling of unease crept over him. What if it

was an enemy spy plane, making the most of things while Charlie and the others were off fighting? But would it really fly out in the open like that and risk the chance of being seen by the Home Guard? George shook his head. There must be some other explanation. There had to be. Best stop worrying about it, and start keeping his eyes peeled for Bill Jarvis instead!

But the only people he saw as they made their way along the narrow streets of the town centre were an old man walking his dog and a couple of boys playing with a tennis ball against the wall of the butcher's shop.

As he arrived outside the Regenbogens', he glanced up, but there was no sign of movement behind the windows. He drew in a quick breath. What if they weren't in? There was only one way to find out. He raised the knocker, rapped once against the door and waited.

Silence.

Heart pounding, he knocked again.

Still nothing.

Please be in, please. He bent down, pushed the flap of the brass letter box back as far as it would go and peered inside. The familiar smell of mothballs pricked his nose. He was about to drop the flap and knock for the third time when a pair of light footsteps pattered along the hall.

'Who is it?' It was the girl.

'It's me. George Penny.'

There was the sound of a bolt being drawn. As the door swung inwards, Spud sniffed the air and gave a loud yip.

Kitty jumped back with a small cry. 'What is that?'

'My dog. It's all right. He won't hurt you, will you, Spud boy?' He bent and gave the dog's ears a quick ruffle. 'Can we come in?'

Kitty hesitated for a moment, then stepped to one side and let them pass.

George shot her a grateful glance. 'Thanks. I—'

She put a finger to her lips. '*Opa* is taking a nap. I do not want to disturb him.' She motioned for him to go through a door on their right.

As he opened it and stepped into the room beyond, he blinked against the glow of early evening sunshine flooding in from the street outside. The door clicked shut behind them.

'What are you doing here? Did you forget something?'

'No. I . . . er . . .' He pushed Spud down into a sitting position and looked sideways, avoiding her gaze.

'What then?'

He heaved a sigh. It was no use. He was going to have to spill the beans. How else would he get her to agree to let them stay? He turned to face her, took a deep breath and began.

Kitty listened wide-eyed as he told her about Bill Jarvis. How rotten he'd been to him and Spud, making George do all the hard work and beating them both for the smallest thing. And how it had got even worse after Jarvis had caught them trying to run away. When he told her about what had happened in the barn, the colour drained from her cheeks.

'Is he all right?'

'I . . . I think so. He got knocked out, that's all.'

'What are you going to do now?'

'I dunno.' His shoulders slumped. 'I went to the airbase to tell Charlie, but then the bell rang and they had to scramble.'

'Scramble?'

'Go into action.' George's stomach knotted again at the thought. He blinked and cleared his throat. 'The thing is, I was wondering . . .'

Kitty raised an eyebrow. 'Yes?'

'Could we stay here? Me and Spud. It would only be for tonight.' He tensed, waiting for her to say no.

Her gaze slid to Spud then back to him. 'I suppose it will be all right.'

He puffed out a breath. 'Thank you.'

She frowned. 'But what about after?'

He gave a quick shrug. 'I'll think of something. Anyway, Charlie'll be back from his mission by then.'

She shot him a doubtful look, then gestured at the floor. 'You can sleep in here. But your dog will have to go in the shed outside. I will fetch him something to eat and drink.'

George reached down and stroked Spud's head. Poor old boy. Still, a shed was heaps better than being chained up in Bill Jarvis's smelly old barn.

Once they'd got Spud settled – with a bowl of water and a bit of bread crumbled up into some leftover broth – Kitty went upstairs again to get George a blanket. While she was gone, he headed back into the room and peered about him.

He'd never seen anywhere like it before – leastways not in someone's house. The walls were lined with glass-fronted cabinets stuffed full of more of the sorts of things he'd seen in Ernst Regenbogen's study: cracked clay pots, bits of shiny black stone fashioned in the shape of axes and arrowheads; and piles of shells and old animal bones.

'It is wonderful, no?'

He spun round. Kitty stood at the door, a blanket and pillow clutched to her chest, eyes shining.

'No . . . I mean, yes . . . I mean . . . So what is it? Some sort of museum?'

'Yes. *Opa* opens it to the public during the week. Though he does not get many visitors. Not now, anyway.' She turned to him, eyes full of envy. 'You are lucky, coming from London. *Opa* says they have the best museums in the world there. You must have been to lots of them.'

A memory bubbled up inside George of the time Charlie had taken him to the Natural History Museum for his eleventh birthday, the summer before last. He'd loved it: seeing all the cases of stuffed animals and birds, the cabinets of rocks and fossils and, best of all, the giant skeleton of 'Dippy' the diplodocus.

He went to tell her, then changed his mind. It was a special memory: his and Charlie's – not for sharing, not even with a friend.

He dropped his gaze and shook his head. 'We didn't have time for that sort of thing.'

Kitty shot him a disappointed look. 'That is a shame. Here.' She thrust the pillow and blanket at him. 'You can make a bed for yourself over there on that rug. Sir Lancelot will watch over you.' She tipped her head to the far corner of the room. George's eyes widened at the sight of a large suit of armour standing in the shadows, its gauntleted hands gripped round the hilt of a huge sword, the tip of which rested between a pair of great steel feet.

'Where did your granddad get that from?'

A look of pride flashed across her face. 'A junk shop. It was covered in rust when *Opa* brought it here, but he cleaned it up and now it is as good as new.'

George's stomach made a loud gurgling noise.

Kitty glanced at it and giggled. 'You sound even hungrier than your dog was.'

George nodded sheepishly. He was famished. Parched too. Apart from the quick guzzle of water from the soldier's flask, the last thing he'd had was the tea and biscuits here, and that had been hours ago.

'Wait a moment.' Kitty darted out through the door, her footsteps echoing away down the hall.

She returned a few minutes later carrying a tray stacked with supplies: a plate of cheese and crackers, a glass of milk, a candle in a holder and a small box of matches. As he took it from her, she spotted the ring.

'What is that?'

He put the tray down on top of a nearby cabinet and tucked his thumb beneath his fingers, cheeks flushing. 'It was my mum's.'

Kitty nodded and gave a small, sad smile. 'I should go now. If *Opa* wakes up he will wonder where I am.'

A squirm of doubt rose up inside George. 'You . . . you won't tell him, will you? About Bill Jarvis, I mean.'

She frowned. 'I do not like lying to him, but . . . all right then.'

'Thanks.' He flashed her a grateful look.

She gave another quick nod and motioned to the window. 'Remember to pull the curtains if you are going to use the candle. Oh, and *schlaf gut*.'

Before George could ask her what she meant, she slipped out through the door and was gone.

After making light work of the cheese and crackers, he drew the curtains, fastening them together in the middle with the small hooks sewn into them, then lit the candle. As he settled down under the blanket, he thought he heard church bells ringing. He stifled a yawn. That couldn't be right, could it? Not on a Saturday. But there was something else about the bells too. Something to do with the war. It was important, he knew, but try as he might, he couldn't think why. He yawned again. Before he could give it any more thought, tiredness got the better of him, his eyelids drooped shut and he drifted off into sleep.

When he woke, the candle had burnt down to little more than a stump.

He sat up with a jolt and looked around him, confused for a moment about where he was. And then, as his eyes fell on the glass cabinets, he remembered. He let out a sigh, gave a cheese-tasting burp and pulled the blanket back over him. He was about to blow out the candle and go back to sleep when a sudden draught caught it. The flame flickered and swayed, casting strange curling shapes up the walls and across the ceiling. He blinked, but when he looked back again the shapes had drawn themselves together into one thick shadowy body. He clutched the blanket to him and watched open-mouthed as it writhed around the room, swallowing up everything it touched in its thick twisting coils. It wasn't possible. It *couldn't* be ... His lungs squeezed tight against his ribs.

Breathe, Georgie. Breathe.

He scrunched his eyes shut, sucked in a deep breath and began to count.

He'd made it as far as three when there was a sudden tearing sound. A shock of ice-cold air slammed into his face. He gasped and flicked his eyes open. The candle had blown out and now, in its place, a patch of silver moonlight slid back and forth across the floor. He scrambled up on his knees and peered at the window. The blackout curtains had broken free of their fastenings and were billowing out into the room.

He frowned. The window hadn't been open before – he was sure of it. Neck hairs spiking, he lifted himself up and crept over to it. Apart from a pale wash of moonlight, the square outside was in darkness. As he made to push the window shut, his eyes snagged on a dark shape tucked in by the steps of the old Shire Hall. It looked like someone was standing there, though the more he peered at it, the harder it became to focus.

He gave a quick shiver and heaved down on the window again. As it inched shut, a loud croak sliced through the air.

He looked up with a start. A large bird was hopping along the Shire Hall roof, silhouetted against the night sky. George's stomach fluttered. The window was still open a fraction, but try as he might, he couldn't get it to close. Giving up on it, he yanked the curtains across, blocking the bird and the Shire Hall from view.

He'd imagined it. He must've. The sooner he fastened the curtains, the sooner he could get back to sleep. But as he struggled with the hooks, they ballooned out again and this time he was certain. There *was* someone out there. They might not be showing themselves, but something – a cold prickling of his skin – told him they were there.

What if it was a thief come to steal something from the museum? He spun round. The suit of armour stood a few feet away. He dashed over to it and grabbed the hilt of the sword. It wouldn't budge. He shot a look back at the window. The blackouts were wide apart, and now a tall black shadow loomed in the frame. Heart pounding, he yanked at the sword again.

It juddered and slid free, the weight of it dragging him forwards. He gripped it tight with both hands and heaved it up. As he swung it round, the window frame rattled and a pinched angry face pressed itself against the glass.

'Put that light out! Don't you know there's a war on?'

The ARP warden! A flood of relief surged through George. He lowered the sword, then frowned. Light? What light? He twisted round. But the warden was right. The candle was burning again, its flame straight as a die.

His breath caught in his throat.

'Did you hear me in there?'

'Er . . . yes. Sorry, mister.'

The face hung there for a moment then disappeared and a few seconds later, a pair of footsteps echoed away down the street.

Wiping his forehead against his sleeve, George propped the sword against the suit of armour and stumbled back to his makeshift bed. He stared down at the candle again and shook his head. It didn't make sense. Maybe it was the cheese giving him bad dreams? Blowing the flame out, he sank to the floor, pulled the blanket up over him again and closed his eyes. A few moments later he was fast asleep.

CHAPTER 12

Sunday 8 September

The sound of a cat yowling in the street outside jolted George awake. He blinked. A shaft of pale daylight was leaking through the gap between the blackout curtains.

As he threw back the blanket, his eyes snagged on the candle stub again and a wave of goosebumps rippled across his skin. It had all felt so real, what he'd seen – or thought he'd seen – last night. He shrugged the feeling off. What did it matter now? There were more important things to worry about – like whether Charlie had got back from his mission in one piece.

He jumped to his feet, walked over to the window and looked out. There was no one about yet. Most of the other houses still had their blackouts in place. As he peered above the rooftops at the early morning sun, a sudden image sprang into his head of a Spitfire caught in a blaze of bullets from an enemy plane and spinning out of control. He gulped in a breath and squashed the thought back down. Charlie would be all right. He'd promised him he would. As long as George still had the ring. He twisted it off and read the inscription again, then slid it back on his thumb. As he turned back into the room, the sight of the suit of armour lurking against the wall sent a fresh shiver through him. He shook his head. He needed some air.

It was as he was reaching for his boots that he caught sight of the feather. It was lying against the skirting board, wedged into a gap in the floorboards. He slid it free and held it up, tracing the tip of his finger along its silky black surface. He glanced behind him, half expecting to see the outline of a bird perched on top of the Shire Hall roof, but there was nothing.

Tucking the feather in his knapsack and slinging the bag over his shoulder, he pulled on his boots and tiptoed out into the hall. He paused for a moment, straining his ears for any sign of movement up above, then crept along it and out through the door that led into the back yard. As he approached the shed, there was an excited doggy yip and the sound of claws scrabbling against wood. He yanked the door open. A pair of dusty black paws thudded against his chest, nearly knocking him off his feet.

He ruffled Spud's ears. 'Good to see you too, boy. Come on, let's go for a walk.'

He was about to steer him back across the yard when he spotted an old leather dog collar and lead hanging from a nail on the back of the shed door. As he wiped the cobwebs off and fastened the collar round Spud's neck, the dog wrinkled his forehead and gave a small whimper.

'Sorry, boy, but it's for the best. If you went running off and Bill Jarvis got hold of you . . .' George shook his head. 'Come on.' Giving a gentle tug on the lead, he led him back towards the house.

The town was showing the first signs of waking as they slipped out on to the street. A few of the houses had their blackouts raised. The sound of a man's voice on the wireless drifted out through the open window of the house next door.

'*In spite of church bells being rung in many towns and villages last night, there was no invasion attempt and the Government would like to reassure the public there is no need to panic.*'

George's eyes widened. The church bells. Of course, that was it! Since the start of the war, Mister Churchill had said they could only be rung as a warning. Was that why Charlie and the others had been scrambled? Because they'd thought the Jerry invasion was coming. Except it sounded as if it had been a false alarm. Which meant, with any luck Charlie was probably back at the airbase right now, tucking into his breakfast with the rest of them. He puffed out a breath and set off down the hill.

As he walked along the street that led to the river, his head was awhirl with thoughts of what to do next. Spending a night at the Regenbogens' was all well and good, but he couldn't expect them to put him up for any longer; not when he hardly knew them. Mrs Jenkins would take him in again for a bit though, he was sure of it. All he needed was enough money for the train fare back to London. His hand drifted to the sockful of coins in his trouser pocket.

'What are you up to, Georgie-Porgie?'

'Wh-what?' He blinked and spun round.

Raymond Scroggins stood in front of him, arms folded, legs splayed. He was doing his best to appear mean, though with his slitty red and black eye and swollen nose, he looked more like he'd gone a round with Desperate Dan and lost.

A smile tickled George's lips.

'What's so funny?' Scroggins's good eye shrank to the size of the injured one.

'Nothing. I-er . . .'

A sly look crept across Scroggins's face. 'You're in big trouble, Georgie-boy.'

George's heart skipped a beat. For a moment he thought Bill Jarvis must have gone and reported him to the coppers. But it wasn't that.

Scroggins's mouth curled into a smug grin. 'I told my father what you did to me yesterday. He says if he catches you trying to bully me again, he's going to arrest you.'

George felt a quick surge of relief followed by a stab of anger. 'Bully? You're the bully round here! Picking on people who can't fight back.'

Spud flattened his ears and bared his teeth in a snarl. Scroggins eyed him nervously and took a step backwards.

'If you mean your little Nazi girlfriend, she had it coming. She and that spying grandfather of hers should be locked up and tried for treason.'

'That's rubbish. They ain't doing nobody any harm. Why don't you just leave 'em alone?' George turned to go, but Scroggins grabbed his knapsack and swung him back round.

Spud leapt up, barking.

'Get away, you mangy thing!' Scroggins bent down, picked up a stone and threw it at him.

Spud yelped and jerked back ripping the lead from George's grasp. Before he could stop him, he put his head down and hared off down a nearby alleyway, disappearing from view.

'Now look what you've gone and done. If you've hurt him . . .' George shoved Scroggins aside and set off after Spud. As he reached the end of the alleyway, he glanced about him. He was standing on the edge of a small gravel yard, bounded on three sides by a high brick wall. 'Spud? Where are you, boy?'

A low whimpering sounded from behind a pile of logs stacked against the back wall.

'It's all right, boy. It's only me.' George crept over to the logs and bent down. As he peered through a gap into the dark space beyond, a crunch of gravel rang out behind him. He made to stand, but before he got the chance, Scroggins barged against him, sending him sprawling face down in the dirt. A few seconds later a heavy weight thudded on top of him, pinning him to the ground.

'Get off me!' George made to roll over, but Scroggins grabbed his left arm and wrenched it up behind his back making him cry out in pain.

'What would that brother of yours think if he could see you now?'

George struggled against him. 'You leave Charlie out of it.'

Scroggins yanked George's arm higher. 'Not that he'd care much, I s'pose.'

George gritted his teeth. 'What d'you mean?'

'Well, if he did, why did he go off and desert you like that? What with you being an orphan and all?'

'He didn't desert me! He joined up to do his bit. He'd make mincemeat of you if he was here now.' George bucked and twisted. But it was no use; Scroggins had him trussed up good and proper.

'But he isn't, is he? He's busy flying around in a nice shiny aeroplane with his posh new friends. They like to think they're so brave, those pilots, but they're cowards, the lot of them! I bet you they flew in the opposite direction last night when they got wind the Jerries were coming. Just like at Dunkirk.'

'What're you talking about?' George made to push him off again, but Scroggins shoved him back down.

'Didn't you hear? When the Jerries bombed our soldiers on the beach, the RAF were nowhere to be seen.'

'That ain't true. They were busy doing all sorts of things to help; keeping the Luftwaffe from attacking the rescue ships for one. Charlie told me.'

'He would, wouldn't he. But *my* big brother knows different.'

'Your brother?'

'He got hit in the back by a bullet from a Jerry plane when he was waiting to be rescued. He's still in the hospital now. They say . . . they say he might not walk again.' Scroggins's voice shrank into what sounded like a stifled sob.

George felt a stab of sympathy. 'Look, I'm sorry about your brother, but—'

'No you're not! But just you wait until it happens to you.' Scroggins gave a loud sniff and pushed him down again. 'Hello? What's this?' A hand wormed its way into George's trouser pocket and yanked the sock of money free. There was a chinking sound as Scroggins shook it up and down next to George's ear. 'Finders keepers!' He sprang up suddenly and tore back across the yard.

'Oi! Give it back!' George scrambled to his feet and pelted after him. As he shot out on to the main street, he collided with a woman pushing a big, black pram. By the time he'd picked himself up off the ground and apologized, Scroggins was well and truly gone. For a second George thought about running to the police station and reporting him. But what was the point? They'd never believe him over an inspector's son.

He heaved a sigh and trudged back down the alley. As he reached the yard, Spud slid out of his hiding place and came bounding towards him, tail raised.

George crouched and hugged the dog to him, burying his face in his fur. What was he going to do now? At least with the money he'd stood a chance of getting back to London. Now all he had left was the ring – and he'd never part with that. He went to run his finger over it and froze. It was gone! He stared in horror at the empty space on his thumb. It must've worked loose in the struggle with Scroggins.

He twisted round, scanning the ground, but the ring was nowhere to be seen. Heart thudding, he retraced his steps, Spud at his heels, probing every patch of weeds and gap in the paving stones as he went. Still nothing.

He hurried over to where he'd tangled with the pram and dropped to his knees. As he raked through the dirt with his fingers, Charlie's face flashed up before him. He'd *sworn* to his brother he'd keep the ring safe. He *had* to find it. Because if he didn't . . . George's eyes filled with water. He blinked hard and scrabbled at the dirt again, his breath coming in ragged sobs.

'George?'

He started. Kitty. What was she doing here? He kept his head bent and carried on scouring the ground.

'What are you looking for?'

'Nothing. I—' He sniffed and shook his head. If he said the words – that the ring was gone – it would make it real, and then what?

A warm hand gripped his shoulder. 'Are you crying?'

He wiped his face with his sleeve and shrugged her hand off. 'Leave me alone. What are you doing following me anyway?'

Kitty hugged her arms across her stomach and drew in a

breath. 'There has been some bad news.'

George reached for Spud's lead and got slowly to his feet. 'What?'

She looked down at the ground. When she spoke, her voice was barely more than a whisper. 'London. It was bombed last night. There were so many planes they thought it was the invasion. It is why they rang the church bells, though *Opa* and I were both sound asleep and did not hear them . . .'

George's heart lurched. So the Jerries *had* attacked yesterday. It was bad enough hearing the news about London. But what about Charlie? He groaned and closed his eyes.

'George? Are you all right?'

He blinked and looked back at her in a daze. 'My brother. That's why they sent him up yesterday. I've got to go over to the base. Find out if he got back all right . . .' He turned to go.

Kitty gripped his arm. 'Wait.'

He tried to pull free but she clung on tight. He spun back round to face her. 'What?'

'Come home with me. We will tell *Opa*. He will help you. I know he will.'

He frowned. 'How?'

'We have a telephone. We can call the airbase instead. It will be quicker.'

He hesitated. He was desperate to go back to the base, but she was right. He'd find out sooner if he went with her. He heaved a sigh. 'I s'pose.'

'Come.' She took Spud's lead from him and set off up the hill towards the market square.

He scanned about him one final time, but it was no use. The ring was nowhere to be seen. Hunching his shoulders and shoving his hands in his pockets, he trudged after her.

CHAPTER 13

There were more people on the streets now. A lot more than usual for a Sunday morning. They stood in small huddles, their faces wearing looks of shock and concern. From the snatches George heard of their hushed conversations, it was clear they were all talking about the same thing.

'Terrible! Hundreds of 'em. Like a plague of locusts.'

'...a firestorm. Not a builden' left standen', so I heard.'

'Those poor people! Bombed out of house and home.'

The words, half murmured, half sobbed, wormed into his ears, filling George with a fresh sense of dread. If there were as many planes as everyone was saying, what chance would Charlie and the others have stood? He curled up his fingers. Best not to listen to them. It was only making him feel worse. He put his head down and hurried on after Kitty.

As they climbed the stairs, the old man came out of the study to meet them. 'George?' He raised a tufty white eyebrow. 'What are you doing here?'

George shifted uncomfortably under his gaze.

Kitty jutted out her chin. 'He has come to stay with us, *Opa*. The man he was living with is a bully. He was going to beat George's dog' – she dipped down and gave Spud a quick pat – 'so he decided to run away.'

George's jaw tightened. 'I wasn't running away. I went to the airbase to find my brother, 'cept he went off to fight the Jerries, and now . . .' He swallowed against the lump forming in his throat again.

'George is worried about him. I said you would telephone the airbase and check to see if he is all right.'

Ernst Regenbogen frowned. 'I am not sure that is a good idea, *Liebling*. It will be a busy time for them. Especially after what happened last night.'

George took a step forwards. 'Please, mister.'

The old man gave a small sigh. 'Very well, I will try.' Turning back into the study, he walked over to the table where the telephone sat and picked up the receiver. He hooked his finger in the dial and spun it round. 'Operator? Can you connect me to the local airbase? Yes, thank you, I will hold.'

As the seconds ticked by, the knot in George's stomach tightened. 'Why don't they hurry up and answer?'

The old man put a finger to his lips as a tinny voice

buzzed into the receiver. 'Hello, I am hoping you can help me. I would like to enquire about one of your pilots. I understand he was in combat yesterday. I wondered if—'

The tinny voice cut across him. George stepped alongside, straining to hear.

Ernst Regenbogen drew in a breath. 'Yes. I realize you are busy, sir, but—'

A surge of impatience swept through George. He snatched the receiver from him and pressed it to his ear.

'My brother, Charlie Penny. He went up to fight the Jerries yesterday. I want to know if he got back all right?'

'I'm sorry.' The voice was crystal clear now. 'But as I've just explained to the gentleman, even if I knew I'm not permitted to give that information out over the telephone.'

'But you've got to tell me. Please! He's all I've got . . .' George gave a choked sob.

'How old are you, lad?'

'Thirteen.'

The man on the other end of the phone hesitated, then cleared his throat. 'Wait a moment.' There was a dull thud and the sound of footsteps marching away.

Kitty pushed in next to George. 'What is happening?'

'He's gone to check.' George rolled his eyes. What was taking him so long?

Ernst Regenbogen squeezed his arm. 'It is difficult, I know, but try and be patient, George.'

George blew out his cheeks. At last, after what seemed like an age, the footsteps came marching back.

'Sergeant Penny, you say? Are you his next of kin?'

A cold flutter ran down the back of George's spine. They were the same words the policemen had used when they'd come to tell them about Mum and Dad.

'Yes. George Penny. I told you before – I'm his brother.'

The man coughed and fell silent.

'Hello? Are you still there?'

'Yes. Look, perhaps you'd better put me back on to the gentleman who made the call.'

'No. He's *my* brother, so you can tell *me*!'

The man cleared his throat. 'Well, if you're sure . . . I'm afraid your brother didn't come back last night.'

A sharp stabbing pain shot through George's chest. 'Wh-what? But where . . . where is he?'

'We don't know. One of the other pilots who went up with him reported smoke coming from Sergeant Penny's plane after he'd engaged with the enemy. The pilot says the Spit went down and—'

'No!' George dropped the receiver and stumbled backwards.

Kitty's eyes widened. 'What is it?' She reached out a hand.

He twisted away from her, eyes blurring. The worst had happened. He'd lost the ring, and now, because of it, Charlie was gone too. He shuddered and sank to the floor, head bowed, arms clutched tight about him.

A whiskery snout poked the back of his hand. 'Not now.' He pushed Spud off. The dog whimpered and slunk away across the room.

The old man's voice sounded behind him. 'I am sorry, sir. He is upset. Yes, I understand. We live over the museum. The number is Woodbridge four-five-three. Thank you, sir. Goodbye.' The receiver clicked back into place.

A firm hand gripped George's shoulder and shook him gently.

'George?'

He kept his head down, fighting back the tears.

'Listen to me. All is not lost.'

'Wh-what?' He blinked and jerked up his head.

Ernst Regenbogen peered down at him, his blue eyes a mix of kindness and concern. 'Charlie is reported *missing*, not *dead*.'

George gulped in a breath. 'I . . . I don't understand.'

'The man on the phone was about to tell you. They found the wreckage of your brother's plane on a beach further up the coast, but there was no body.'

George scrubbed at his eyes. 'But if he bailed out and he's alive, he'd have turned up by now, wouldn't he?'

'Not necessarily. If he is injured and no one saw where he fell—'

George scrambled to his feet. 'But they're looking for him, aren't they?'

Ernst Regenbogen gave a sigh. 'They are doing their best, but it is not easy. They are expecting the Luftwaffe's bombers to return again soon and I am afraid with so many other lives at risk, to go hunting for a single pilot may not be such a priority.'

Fresh tears sprang to George's eyes. 'But . . . but he's my brother.'

The old man put an arm round his shoulder and drew him close. 'I know, George. I know. But the man has promised to call us as soon as they have any news.'

'When?'

He frowned. 'I do not know. He said it would be a day or two at least. Maybe longer.'

George pulled away from him. 'A day or two? I can't wait that long! And Charlie can't either. Not if he's hurt.' He turned towards the door.

Ernst Regenbogen caught him by the arm. 'Where are you going?'

'To the airbase. To make them do a proper search.' He made to wrench free, but the old man was stronger than he looked.

'No! Listen. The RAF – the whole country – is on high alert. They will not let you near the place. And besides, from what you have said of him, I do not think your brother would approve of such a rash action either. Those people have a very important job to do. You will not be helping if you distract them from it.'

George heaved a sigh. Kitty's granddad was right; he knew it. But if Charlie was lying injured in a ditch somewhere . . . He shivered.

'Come now.' Ernst Regenbogen gave him a reassuring smile. 'It is hard, but you must do your best not to think the worst. There is still a chance, and where there is a chance, there is hope too.'

George's shoulders slumped. 'I'm sorry. It's just that . . .' His lips trembled. He looked away again.

'We understand. Don't we, Kitty?'

'Yes, *Opa*.' Kitty reached out and gave George's hand a quick squeeze. 'Shall I go and make us a cup of tea?'

'That is an excellent idea. I will come and help.' As the old man turned to go, he tipped his head at the small furry figure lying hunched against the wall in the far corner of the room. 'I think perhaps an apology is due to someone else too, don't you?'

George's cheeks flushed. He glanced over at Spud and nodded.

The old man cleared his throat. 'Good. Now, once you have made up and the three of you have had a bit of breakfast, you can go for a walk along the river. The fresh air will do you all good, I am sure.' He gave George a quick wink and followed Kitty out into the hall.

George walked over to where Spud lay, head sunk between his paws. The dog lifted his snout as he approached and peered back at him uncertainly.

He squatted down and stretched out his hand. 'I'm sorry, Spud. I won't be mean to you ever again, I promise.'

The dog crept forwards, eyebrows twitching. He sniffed hesitantly at George's fingers, then gave them a quick lick.

George heaved a sigh and pulled him close, pressing his cheek against his soft fur.

At least he still had Spud.

He couldn't face eating much breakfast. He didn't want to go for a walk either, but in the end it seemed better to be doing something rather than sitting around waiting.

As Kitty led them off down the back streets, he made sure to keep his eyes peeled for Bill Jarvis again. The last thing he wanted was to bump into him.

The tide was out when they reached the quayside, leaving the river to weave its way like a sludge-coloured snake between marooned boats and islands of marsh grass. A bunch of gulls wheeled and screeched above them, swooping down every now and again to scavenge for food.

George's nostrils pricked at the smell of seaweed and wet mud; it reminded him of home and summer afternoons with Charlie down by the Thames, hunting for bits of driftwood for the model plane they were building. Charlie had promised they'd finish it before he left to join the RAF, but they never had, and now . . . George's heart shrank up inside him. Now, what if it was too late?

He ran his finger over the space where the ring had been and stifled a groan.

Kitty glanced at him. 'Are you thinking about your brother?'

He nodded.

'I know it is hard, but remember what *Opa* said about having hope.'

'You don't understand. It's my fault he's missing.'

She frowned. 'How can it be?'

He hugged his arms to his chest. 'You remember the ring I was wearing?'

'Your mother's ring? Yes, it is beautiful.'

'It was . . .'

Kitty's frown deepened. 'What do you mean?'

'I lost it.'

Her fingers fluttered to her necklace as if to check it was still there. 'But where? When?'

'This morning. Scroggins came after me when I was out walking. Started having a go at me about Charlie; blaming him and the RAF for his brother getting wounded at Dunkirk. Then he jumped me and took my money – Charlie's money. The ring . . . it . . . it must've come off in the struggle.' His chest squeezed again at the memory.

'So that is what you were looking for when I found you?'

George bit his lip and nodded again.

'Still, I do not see what that has got to do with your brother?'

George heaved out a breath and hung his head. 'Charlie gave it to me before he left to join up. He told me to keep it safe. Said if I did he'd come back to me. 'Cept . . . 'cept I didn't, did I? And now he's missing and—' He gulped as fresh tears pricked his eyes.

Kitty reached out and took his hand. 'It is not your fault. How could it be? Besides, you only lost the ring this morning.'

She meant well. George knew that. But what did it matter *when* he'd lost the ring. The fact was he'd broken his promise to Charlie to keep it safe, and now he was missing – or worse . . . He turned away from her and looked out across the shimmering brown mud, doing his best to hold the tears at bay.

Kitty cleared her throat and pointed to the top of the steep wooded bank opposite. 'That is where *Opa* and the others found the ship burial.'

George drew in a breath and squinted out at the distant grass-topped ridge poking above the trees.

She shot a quick look back at him. 'I could take you there now, if you like?'

George kicked at a tussock of grass growing next to the path. A puff of sandy brown dust rose into the air. He shrugged. 'I s'pose. How far is it?'

Kitty glanced up the river and frowned. 'It will take about an hour, maybe a little longer. That is if we do not get stopped at the pillbox.'

'Pillbox?'

'It is a sort of guard post, on the other side of the bridge. *Opa* says they have put a pair of Home Guardsmen there to keep a lookout in case the enemy comes.'

A sudden memory of the strange plane he'd seen yesterday leapt into George's head. He looked up, half expecting to see it fly into view, but except for a few gulls the sky was empty. He shrugged. It couldn't have been a Jerry plane anyway. If it was, the Home Guard would have reported it and it'd be all over town by now. Especially after what had happened last night.

He kicked at the grass tussock again. 'I can't see the guards being bothered with us. So, are we going, or what?'

Kitty opened her mouth as if to say something, then clamped it shut and set off along the path at a brisk walk.

George flushed. He'd been rude again. He hadn't meant

to be. She and her granddad had been kind to him. And they were right. The only thing he could do now was to wait and hope.

A sharp yip jolted him out of his thoughts. Spud stood in front of him, ears pricked, tail wagging, straining against the lead.

'All right, boy, all right. I'm coming.' Throwing another glance at the ridge, he hunched his shoulders and let Spud tug him up the path after her.

CHAPTER
14

They followed the path for about a mile, skirting round boatyards and passing wooden jetties, until finally a bridge came into view.

As they approached it, George spotted the pillbox. It was set halfway up a bank on the opposite side, a low concrete building with slits in the walls, which he guessed were for keeping a lookout from and firing on the enemy.

Kitty glanced at it nervously. 'What if they *do* try and stop us?'

'Why should they? We ain't Nazis, are we?'

'No, but—'

'Well then. Come on, boy.' George scrambled up the last bit of path and out on to the bridge.

But the guards didn't appear, and there was no sign of

them when they reached the other side either.

Kitty frowned. 'That is odd. I am sure *Opa* said there was always someone on duty here.'

George shrugged. 'Maybe they've gone for lunch.'

She raised an eyebrow. 'Lunch?'

'Look, how should I know?' He jerked his head at a fork in the road. 'Where to now?'

She gave a loud huff and marched past him, taking the road to their right.

As they rounded the first bend, she gestured at a bramble-lined path leading away into a patch of dense woodland. 'This way.' She wrapped her skirts round her legs and headed off down it.

Spud tugged on the lead, eager to follow.

George eyed the brambles warily. 'Hold on, boy.' Picking up a stick, he beat the worst of them back and set off after her into the shadowy gloom.

They'd been going about ten minutes, stopping every so often for George to clear the way, when Kitty pulled up suddenly.

'We must be careful here. There is a drop.' She pointed ahead to where the path hugged the edge of a steep-sided pit.

As they balanced past it in single file, George took a quick look down. The bottom was a good fifteen feet beneath them, littered with rocks and the trunks of dead trees. He licked his lips. Fall down there and you wouldn't be getting out again in a hurry.

Once they'd cleared it, they picked up pace again, weaving in and out of the trees. At last, just when George had given up hope of ever seeing proper daylight again, the woods thinned and gave out on to a ridge of open ground. A tree-covered slope fell away to their right with glimpses of the river below. Ahead of them, halfway up the ridge, stood an old brick hut with a rusty corrugated iron roof. Beyond it, in the distance, was a large grey-white building, its windows framed by clumps of greenery.

Kitty nodded at it. 'That is where the lady who owns the land the mounds are on lives.'

'Mounds?' George frowned. 'You mean there's more than one of them?'

Kitty shot him a mysterious look. 'You will see soon enough. But we must be careful. We are not really supposed to be here. If they catch us, they will report us to the police.'

George's breath caught in his throat. The coppers! That was the last thing he needed. 'Maybe we should—'

But she was already hurrying up the slope. Reluctantly, he set off after her. Once they'd passed the hut, she slanted off to the left, giving the house a wide berth until they'd put it safely behind them. Then, arcing back round, she headed straight again, making for a clump of trees and bushes at the top of the ridge.

George puffed out a breath and called after her, 'How much further?'

'Not far. Another five minutes.'

The sky darkened as they reached the trees and a breeze got up, rippling through the leaves. Spud gave a low whine and dropped to the ground.

'It's all right, boy. It's just a bit of wind.' George gave his muzzle a quick stroke. But as they pushed their way in amongst the tangle of twigs and branches, he couldn't help feeling uneasy too.

When they reached the open again, Kitty jerked to a stop and let out a breath. 'We are here.'

George pulled up alongside her, bringing Spud to heel.

They were standing on the edge of a field – but a field like no other he'd seen before. Rising up in front of them were a collection of large grassy mounds, their tops covered in fronds of dense green bracken. As a sudden gust of wind combed through the bracken, the mounds seemed to shiver as if something lurking beneath had woken and was beginning to stir.

George's skin prickled.

'It is marvellous, no?' Kitty spun round, face beaming.

He blinked and gave a quick shrug. 'They look like a bunch of overgrown molehills to me.'

She clicked her tongue against her teeth. 'You should not say that, George Penny. It is disrespectful.'

'Why?'

'Because this is a burial place.'

'But I thought your granddad said they didn't find any bones when they dug up the ship?'

She frowned. 'That is true, but *Opa* says the soil might have eaten them away. Besides, they found traces of bodies in two of the other mounds.'

In spite of himself, George felt his eyebrows rise. 'So were there ships in them too?'

'They found some iron nails in the second mound they dug, but nothing like what they discovered in the main mound.'

'Where is it then?'

'Over there.'

George shaded his eyes and peered at where Kitty was pointing. Halfway along the field, someone had cut what looked like a massive trench into the ground, piling up steep banks of sandy soil on either side of it. He pulled a face. 'Looks like a bomb's hit it.'

Kitty jutted out her chin. 'The dig was closed down before *Opa* and the others had the chance to bury it again. All they could do to protect it was cover it with a layer of bracken. Anyway' – she gave a sniff – 'you do not seem to be very interested, so . . .'

George felt his cheeks redden again. 'Sorry. I didn't mean anything by it. I'd like to take a closer look, honest.'

She wavered, then, with another quick sniff, she stalked off towards the trench. He set off after her, tugging Spud behind.

As they reached the trench, he gave a low whistle. There was enough space to fit two London buses into it, nose to tail with room to spare. He drew up alongside her and stared across it, trying to imagine a dirty great ship being sunk down inside.

'So how did those Anglo–Saxons, or whatever you call 'em, get it up here, then?'

Kitty arched her eyebrows. 'They pulled it up from the river, of course.'

'The river? But that's way back down there.' He jabbed a thumb over his shoulder.

'They used tree trunks as rollers, and dragged the ship over them. That is what they think, anyway.' She pressed her lips together in a know-it-all sort of way.

George puffed out a breath. 'Sounds like bloomin' hard work. Why not just dig an ordinary man-sized hole and stick the king in that?'

'Because he was *the king*. Besides, he needed his ship to get to the afterlife.'

'The afterlife?' George rolled his eyes. What was she on about?

She let out a sigh. 'The place where the king's soul could live on after he had died. Like Heaven, except they did not call it that. It is why they buried him with his treasure and all those other things. So he could take them with him.'

George's chest knotted as a fresh memory of his parents slid up inside him. Mum and Dad's only real treasure had been their rings and they'd left those behind. But now the rings were gone too, and Charlie with them. And then another thought curled into his head. If Charlie was dead and they couldn't find his body, how would he ever get to the afterlife? A sudden chill breeze lifted George's hair. He started. What was he doing, thinking such things? He glanced about him, shivering. He should never have let Kitty bring him here.

Spud pressed himself against George's shins and gave another whimper. George ruffled a hand through his fur and shot a look up at the sky. The white fluffy clouds from earlier had gone, replaced now by a lowering blanket of grey. The breeze had strengthened too and was tugging hard at their clothes and hair. As a rumble of thunder sounded in the distance, the wind grew more powerful, whirling pieces of bracken up out of the trench and above their heads.

Kitty clutched George's arm. 'What is happening?'

'Some kind of storm, from the looks of it. Best take cover.' He pushed her towards the trees, dragging Spud behind him.

They were nearly there when a flash of white light ricocheted around them. Spud gave a piercing yelp and leapt backwards, tearing the lead from George's hand. Before he got the chance to grab hold of it, he whipped round and streaked away across the mound field, faster than a bullet from a gun.

'Come here, boy!' George made to go after him, but Kitty yanked him into the shelter of the trees.

'No! It is too dangerous.'

'I have to. He's my friend.' He twisted free and dashed out into the open again. Cupping his hands round his mouth, he yelled Spud's name. But the wind spun his voice round and blew it back at him. Where had he gone? He scanned about him, but there was no sign. He put his head down and set off in between the mounds.

As he threaded his way round them, another lightning bolt ripped through the sky, and for a moment he could have sworn the mounds were moving again; rippling and sliding like the back of some giant underground snake.

He blinked and shook his head. A trick of the light. It must be . . .

He pushed on, but as he rounded the next mound, the wind slammed against him, lifting him off his feet and throwing him to the ground. He lay there for a moment, all the breath knocked out of him. Then, as he hauled himself up on to his hands and knees, a small black shape hurled itself across the gap between the two furthest mounds.

He got to his feet and ploughed after it, but Spud – if it was Spud – bolted off in the opposite direction, heading for the shelter of a large windswept tree.

George held his breath and battled towards it. As he drew closer, it loomed over him, its spiky-leaved branches snatching at the air like the tongues of a thousand darting snakes. He peered beneath them, into the damp, mossy blackness beyond.

'Spud? Are you in there, boy?'

Silence apart from the creak of storm-tossed boughs and the roar of the wind at his back.

His chest tightened. If he lost Spud too, he wouldn't be able to bear it. He sucked in a breath and stumbled forwards. As he entered the woody darkness, the noise from the storm faded. The only sound now was the pounding thud of his heart in his ears. He blinked against the shadows and stuck his hands out in front of him, feeling his way through the thick, dank air.

And then he saw it: a tall dark figure standing next to the tree's gnarled trunk.

He froze. 'Who's there?'

The figure lifted its head slowly and drew in a long, rattling breath. For a moment George thought it was going to speak. But when it breathed out, it was a feeling – not words – that spilt from its lips. A feeling deep, dark and full of fury, like a hundred thunderstorms rolled into one. What you felt when someone took something precious from you; something you'd give your life to get back.

A tide of ice-cold panic surged through George. He turned to run, but his boots were stuck fast by the tree roots. He tried desperately to yank them free, but it was no use; they wouldn't budge.

And now the figure was on the move, walking towards him, step by measured step. And though its face was hidden in shadow, George could feel the white-hot anger of its gaze.

In desperation, he bent down and tore at his bootlaces, but the knots grew tighter still.

He cast around him looking for something to defend himself with, but there was nothing. Only a few twigs and a scattering of needle-like leaves.

He lifted up and turned to face it, curling his fingers into fists. 'Keep away from me!'

The figure took another ratchety breath and jerked to a stop. It shot out its right hand and pointed at him, a flash of gold glinting on its outstretched finger.

George's heart shrank up inside him. 'Who are you? What d'you want?'

But still the figure gave no reply.

A loud *craak* echoed behind him. He twisted round. A great black bird was sitting on a nearby branch, head cocked, eyes bright and unblinking. George clenched his jaw and spun round to face the figure again. But whoever – or whatever – it was, it had gone.

The bird gave another harsh croak and dropped to the ground. It hopped towards George, wings outstretched.

'Get out of here!' He made to shoo it away, but the bird stood its ground. Then, with a rustle of black feathers, it lifted up into the gloom and was gone.

A sudden finger of light poked through the thick net of branches above him. As he blinked and looked about him, an excited bark rang out away to his right. He turned just in time to see a bundle of black fur springing towards him.

Relief washed through him. 'Spud! I thought I'd lost you!' He crouched down and hugged him tight, blotting out all thoughts of what had gone before.

'Come on, boy. Let's go and find Kitty.' He was about to jump up again when he remembered the tree roots. He shot a nervous glance at his boots, but they seemed somehow to have freed themselves. Heaving a sigh, he got to his feet and scrambled towards the daylight, Spud nipping at his heels.

As he burst out into the open, he squinted against the sudden brightness. The storm had passed. Except for a few spiked leaves scattered across the ground, there was no sign it had ever happened. He gulped in a draught of grass-sweet air.

A figure in a blue and white checked dress came running towards them. 'George! Where have you been?'

'I-I don't know. I went to look for Spud and—'

Kitty skidded to a halt and gave a delighted cry as Spud leapt up and licked her on the cheek. 'I am glad you are both safe.' She ruffled the dog's ears and flashed George a smile, then frowned. 'You look like you have seen a ghost.'

He glanced behind him. A sharp breeze rippled through the tree's dark leaves, making them whisper and rustle like birds' wings. And then it was still.

He shivered and drew a quick breath. 'I . . . I'm fine.'

Kitty shot him a puzzled look.

'Honest.'

'All right, if you are sure. Listen!' She gripped his sleeve. 'I have found something!'

'What?'

She led him round to the other side of the tree and pointed to the ground.

He frowned. 'What am I s'posed to be looking at?'

She squatted and traced the shape of a small square hole in the space between two tree roots. 'Someone has been digging here. In other places too.' She tipped her head at the piles of sandy soil dotted in front of them.

'It's probably just some animal. A rabbit, or one of them moles.'

She clicked her tongue against her teeth. 'An animal does not use a spade.' She ran her fingers along the set of neat slice marks that formed the sides of the hole.

'Your granddad and the other archaeologists, then?'

'Yes, but it has been freshly dug.' Kitty scooped up some of the soil and let it trickle through her hands. 'Feel this.' She pulled him down beside her and pressed his hand into the earth at the bottom of the hole.

His fingers brushed against a set of shallow dips and ridges. 'So what?'

'Something was buried here. Whoever made this hole found it and dug it up.'

An image of the poacher slid up inside George's head. He sank back on his heels, his frown deepening.

'What is wrong?'

He shook his head. 'It's probably nothing.'

'Tell me. Please!'

He hesitated, then took a deep breath and told her about what he'd seen as he and Spud were making their getaway yesterday afternoon from Bill Jarvis's farm. When he got to the bit about the mysterious object inside the poacher's sack, Kitty gasped and clutched his arm.

'He's a treasure thief, I am sure of it!' She jumped to her feet. 'We must go back and tell *Opa* so he can report it to the police.'

George snorted and stood up. 'The coppers ain't going to be bothered about some old poacher digging up a bit of metal in a field. They've got more important things to worry about.'

Kitty wrinkled her forehead. 'You are right.' She turned away, then twisted back again, eyes shining. 'There is only one thing left to do. We must investigate ourselves!'

'What?'

'You saw where this poacher left the track?'

'Yes, but—'

She shot him a sly look. 'You are not scared of him, are

you, Saint George?'

He drew himself up to his full height and thrust his arms across his chest. 'Don't call me that, and no I ain't!'

'Come on, then! What are you waiting for?' Before he could stop her, she snatched up the end of Spud's lead, then turned and hurried off towards the trees.

CHAPTER 15

As they made their way down to the road again, thoughts of what had happened beneath the tree crowded back into George's head. He'd imagined it. He must've done. It'd been dark in there and he'd been worked up too, what with Charlie going missing and all that talk of dead people and the like. Or maybe he'd had another of his turns? What about last night in the museum? Had that been one too? He shivered. If that's what they were, it meant they were getting worse. Much worse. He sucked in a breath. One thing was for sure though. The bird *was* real – he had the feather to prove it.

'George?'

'Wha-what?' He blinked and looked up.

Kitty had pulled up a few yards ahead and was staring

back at him with wide eyes. 'I think there is someone in the pillbox.'

'It's all right. I told you before. They're not going to bother with the likes of us.'

But he was wrong. As they approached the bridge, a man in a baggy Home Guard uniform stepped out from behind the pillbox, rifle raised.

'Halt!'

Kitty gave a small cry. Dropping Spud's lead, she jerked up her hands.

The guard slid down the bank and marched towards them. He came to a stop in front of them and jabbed the gun at George's chest, motioning him to raise his hands.

Spud slunk in front of him, ears flattened, teeth bared.

The guard's eyes narrowed. He swung the gun down and trained it on the dog, finger stroking the trigger.

George glared at him. 'Hey! What d'you think you're doing, mister?' He bent and yanked Spud behind him.

'Wait!' Another guard had appeared out of nowhere. He looked older than the first one and wore a corporal's stripe on his left sleeve. He pushed his companion's gun muzzle to one side and signalled to him to pull back.

The first guard gave a grunt, then turned on his heel, climbed up the bank and disappeared back inside the pillbox.

The corporal fixed them with a hard stare, then with a clipped 'Go!' he waved them away with the back of his hand.

George was about to say something when Kitty grabbed

him by the arm. 'Yes, sir. Thank you, sir.' She scooped up Spud's lead and tugged the pair of them after her.

When George turned and looked back a few moments later, the guard had gone. He frowned. 'They were a bit heavy-handed, weren't they?'

She nodded. 'Perhaps they have not finished their training? They forgot to ask for our identity cards too.'

'You're right. Looks like that first one got issued with the wrong uniform. Did you see how baggy his trousers were? And what about those scrapes that corporal had on his knuckles? A right pair of bruisers, if you ask me.'

Kitty pulled a face. 'Bruisers?'

He sighed. 'It don't matter. Come on, let's get going.'

But instead of making for the river path, Kitty took the road ahead.

George called after her. 'Are you sure you're going the right way?'

'I think so, yes. This road leads back to the town. From what you have said, the road to your farm should join up with it before we get there.'

He caught her up, frowning. 'It ain't *my* farm.'

Kitty flushed. 'No. Sorry.'

They carried on in silence for a bit, George's head filling with fresh worries about Charlie and what he had seen beneath the tree.

He recognized the turning as it came into view. Spud did too and gave a low whine.

George threw the dog a nervous glance. It was enemy territory for the pair of them. But he could tell from the look on Kitty's face that she wasn't going to take no for an answer.

'It'll be all right, Spud. I promise.' He patted his head. 'Here, I'll take him.' He took the lead from Kitty and set off up the road.

Keeping his eyes peeled for any sign of Jarvis, he led them up the hill to the crossroads, then down the track where he'd seen the poacher head into the woods. As he reached the spot, a chill breeze ruffled his hair. He frowned and glanced about him.

Kitty pulled up next to him. 'What is it?'

'Nothing.' George shook his head and pointed to the bank. 'He was up there when the bird attacked him. Then he disappeared off into the trees.'

Kitty's eyes widened. 'Back to his camp.'

He shrugged. 'Maybe. Or maybe he was just trying to get away from the thing.' His skin prickled. He knew what that felt like all right.

She peered into the shadows. 'Well, there is only one way to find out.' She planted her right foot on the bank and began to climb.

Heaving a sigh, George wrapped his hand round Spud's lead and clambered after her.

When she reached the top she gave a small cry. 'There is a path. Look!'

He scrambled up to join her. A thin trail snaked ahead of them into the gloom.

Kitty made to leap forwards, but George pulled her back. 'Me and Spud'll go first. If anyone can sniff out danger, it's him.' He pushed past her and set off along the trail.

The further in they went, the closer the trees grew and the darker and more stifling it became. They'd been going ten minutes, maybe more, when Spud pulled up short and sniffed the air.

'What is it, boy?' George squatted down next to him and followed his gaze. There was a break in the trees away to their left, and beyond it what looked like a small clearing. He turned and pressed a finger to his lips. 'Wait here.'

Kitty nodded.

George grabbed Spud by the collar and set off, keeping low and threading his way in between the trees. When he reached the edge of the clearing, he dropped down behind a fallen log and peered cautiously over the top of it.

A large swathe of mossy grass stretched in front of him, fringed on all sides by trees and prickle-leaved bushes. In the centre was a small mound of charred sticks and branches, the remains of a half-cooked rabbit suspended across them from a makeshift spit. But there was no one about, leastways not as far as he could see.

He turned to give Kitty the all-clear, then started. 'Gorr! What d'you mean creeping up on me like that?'

'His camp! I told you so.' Kitty shot him a triumphant look and slid past him.

'Wait!' He snatched at her skirts. 'Where're you going?'

'To investigate.'

'But what if someone comes?'

'Spud will be our guard dog, won't you, boy?' She ruffled Spud's ears, then stepped out into the open.

Giving another quick check around him, George drew in a breath and darted after her. As they crept past the campfire, his foot struck an ash-covered lump. He turned it over with the toe of his boot. A half-cooked potato. And another.

He looked up and frowned. Where had Kitty got to now? Then he spotted her. She was standing in front of a sagging green tent pitched in the shadow of an ancient-looking tree.

Beckoning him over, she lifted the tent flap and disappeared inside.

He held back for a moment, then followed. As he dipped in alongside her, his nose wrinkled at the smell of mouldy canvas and rotting leaves.

'He has been sleeping here.' Kitty pointed to the low camp bed lying against the back wall. An upturned crate stood next to it, a candle stub and a cut-throat razor on top of it.

George was about to pick up the razor when Spud gave a sudden yip and pushed past him into the gap beneath the bed.

'Come here, boy.' George bent down and tried to drag him back out, but the dog wouldn't budge.

Kitty crouched down and peered into the shadows. 'I think he has found something!' She slid on to her stomach and crawled in after him. A few moments later she reappeared, dragging a dusty sack behind her. She scrambled to her feet and shook it up and down. 'There is something inside.' She fumbled at the knot. '*Ach!* I cannot undo it.'

'Give it here.' George snatched it from her and worked it loose.

Kitty's eyes shone back at him in the gloom. 'We should take it outside.'

'Wait.' Thrusting the sack back at her, he lifted the tent flap and took a quick look about him. 'All right. All clear.' He ducked out into the daylight, Kitty and Spud following close behind.

He gestured at the sack. 'Open it then.'

Kitty took a deep breath and slid her hand inside. As she pulled the object clear, George frowned. It was filthy dirty, covered in a crust of brown sand studded with stones. The shape of it reminded him of a pastry-cutter; the sort his mum used to make jam tarts with, except bigger. Much bigger, and with a sticky-out bit poking up from the rim.

'It looks like a bit of old junk to me.'

Kitty sighed. 'That is because you have no imagination.' She lifted it up and gasped.

'What?' He drew in closer to get a better look. And then, as she tilted it to the light, he saw it too: a flash of gold-coloured metal.

'King Redwald's crown. It must be!' Kitty's voice quavered. 'That man *is* a treasure thief.'

'Let me see.' As George's fingers closed round the object, something sharp spiked his skin. He cried out and let go, shoving his hand under his armpit.

'What is wrong?'

'The ruddy thing cut me!'

'Show me.' Kitty tugged his hand free and forced open his fingers.

A crescent-shaped cut, about two inches long, arced across the centre of his palm. As they stared down at it, a line of fresh blood leaked out and spread across the surrounding skin.

Kitty clicked her tongue against her teeth. 'It needs a bandage. Here.' Reaching in her dress pocket, she pulled out a handkerchief and tied it across his palm. 'This will do for now. We can clean it when—' Her voice tailed away suddenly.

George looked up, following her gaze. A large bird was circling above the clearing, its wing feathers splayed like two sets of great black blades. A cold worm of fear slid across his chest.

Kitty frowned. 'You said there was a bird before.'

He was about to reply when a low growl sounded behind them. He whipped round. Spud had sunk into a crouch, hackles raised, eyes fixed on the trees behind them.

Holding his breath, George scanned the shadows. And then he heard it too. A distant sound of feet crunching through leaves. 'Someone's coming.' He snatched up Spud's lead.

'Wait!' Kitty bundled the object back into the sack. 'We must take this to *Opa*.'

The crunching sound grew louder . . .

George seized Kitty by the hand and dragged her across

the clearing, Spud bringing up the rear. They were nearly at the trees, when a cry went up behind them.

Kitty made to turn, but George shoved her forwards. 'Don't look! Run!'

As they tore off into the gloom, he ignored his own advice and shot a quick glance back, hoping against hope the man wasn't following. But he was, and gaining on them too. It was the poacher all right. He'd recognize that hollow-cheeked face anywhere.

'Faster!'

Kitty jumped and put on a fresh spurt of speed.

The three of them zigzagged between the tree trunks doing their best to lose their pursuer, but he kept on coming, drawing closer all the while.

It was when George looked back a second time, he saw he had a gun. A spurt of sick shot up his throat. Gulping it down, he ploughed on after Kitty, Spud panting at his side.

At last the bank came into view. Racing towards it, they launched themselves down it and hared off along the track, arms and legs pumping.

But still the poacher came.

As they reached the crossroads and turned out on to the main road, a sharp stab of pain ripped along George's ribs. He staggered on, clutching his stomach, but it was no use. The pain was tearing him in half. He had to stop. He groaned and slumped to his knees.

Kitty skidded to a halt and called back to him. 'George! Get up!'

'I can't. *Go!*'

She wavered. 'But—'

'I said go!'

'No. I am not leaving you.' She jutted out her chin and marched back up the road towards him.

He gave another groan.

The poacher's boots came crunching closer. Any moment now he'd round the bend and find them and it would all be over. George sucked in a breath and closed his eyes.

A sudden rumbling noise echoed in his ears. He lifted up his head and twisted round.

An army truck was rattling up the hill towards them, sending up clouds of dust as it came. As it reached them it creaked to a halt. A man thrust his head out of the passenger window.

'Hello again.'

It was the soldier George had sat next to in the back of the truck yesterday.

The man glanced at Kitty, then back at George and frowned. 'Is something wrong?'

George got to his feet and gulped in another breath. 'There ... there was a man. He was following us.'

The soldier shaded his eyes. 'I can't see anyone.'

George turned to look. He was right; the road behind them was empty.

Kitty pushed in front of George, chest heaving. 'He ... he is telling the truth, sir, I swear it!'

'And he had a gun too.'

Kitty spun back to look at George, eyes wide with fear. 'Did he? I did not see . . .'

He nodded, his mouth drying again at the thought.

'A gun, you say? So why was he after you?'

Kitty shoved the sack behind her back. 'He is a poacher. He has a camp back there in the woods.'

'A poacher, eh? Well, I'm afraid we don't have the time to go chasing off after the likes of him now. Not with Hitler and his Nazis on the warpath. You'd best get home both of you, before your parents start to worry.'

'But you don't understand, mister—'

'Sorry, son. Like I said, we've got more important jobs to be doing.' The soldier banged the door with the flat of his hand. 'Let's get going, Fred. Those sandbags aren't going to shift themselves.' The engine started up again and the truck jolted away up the road.

'Why did they not listen to us?'

George shrugged. 'Too worried about sandbags from the sounds of it.' He jerked his head at the sack. 'Why didn't you tell them about that? If it *is* old Redwald's crown, then like you said, it makes the poacher a thief too.'

Kitty hugged it against her. 'I told you. It is better that we take it to *Opa*. He will know what to do.'

'If you say so.' George glanced at the sack and frowned. One thing was sure, whatever the thing inside it was, the poacher had been desperate to get it back. He threw another look over his shoulder. There was still no sign of the man, but that didn't mean he wasn't out there somewhere, watching them from a distance. He shivered. The soldier was right. The sooner they got back indoors, the better.

CHAPTER
16

As they reached the front door, George pulled up short. What if the man at the airbase had been wrong and news of Charlie had come in while they were out? He gazed up at the windows with a growing sense of dread.

Kitty scooted past him up the steps. She pushed open the door and glanced back at him. 'Are you coming?'

Steeling himself, he followed her in. They were halfway up the stairs when a worried-sounding voice called down to them.

'Is that you, Kitty?' The familiar figure of Ernst Regenbogen limped into view.

Kitty lifted the sack and beamed up at him. 'Wait until you see what we have found, *Opa*.' She darted up the last few stairs and dashed past him into the study, Spud skipping along at her side.

George trudged after her, eyes fixed firmly on his boots.

When he got to the top of the stairs, the old man reached out and rested a hand on his shoulder. 'Still no news about your brother, I am afraid.'

George's heart fluttered against his ribs. No news was better than bad news. That's what Mum used to say. But when she and Dad never came back that day, it'd turned out no news was the worst sort of all.

'What did you do to your hand?'

'Nothing.' He shoved it into his pocket. 'It's just a scratch.'

'Hmm. Well, we must make sure and clean it. But first let us go inside and the pair of you can tell me what all the excitement is about.'

George frowned. Kitty might be excited, but that wasn't how he felt. Keeping his head down, he plodded into the study.

Kitty stood at the desk, her hand resting on top of the sack. She looked up when they came in, her mouth curving into a mysterious smile. 'Ready, *Opa*?'

The old man gave a puzzled nod.

She slid the object free. 'Here.' She drew in a breath and offered it up to him, hands trembling.

Taking it from her, he shuffled to the window and held it out in front of him. As the patch of exposed metal caught the light, his eyes widened into two blue 'O's.

'*Ist es wirklich wahr?*'

Kitty flew to his side and clutched his arm with both hands. 'Yes, *Opa*. It *is* true! It is the king's crown, I am sure of it!'

'Calm yourself, child. We must not go jumping to conclusions.' He set the object down carefully on top of the desk. 'Now, tell me.' He fixed her with a sharp-eyed gaze. 'Where did you find it?'

She drew in another breath and told him everything. About their trip to the dig site and the fresh holes around the tree. Then about the poacher; how they'd gone in search of his camp and found the sack stashed away in his tent, though George noticed she stopped short of telling him about the gun.

When she had finished, Ernst Regenbogen took a deep breath. 'We will have to tell the police, of course.'

'Yes, *Opa*, but not until you have had a chance to study it properly.'

The old man's forehead furrowed. 'You are right, *Liebling*. We must be sure of what we have here first. Will you fetch me my cleaning tools please?' He pulled out the chair and sat down at the desk.

George heaved a sigh of relief. That was a close shave. The last thing he needed was for the coppers to come calling and start asking a bunch of awkward questions.

'Yes, *Opa*!' Kitty scurried over to one of the bookshelves, opened a drawer beneath it and pulled out a worn leather bag. She darted back and set it down in front of him.

'Thank you.' Ernst Regenbogen undid the catch, reached

inside and pulled out, in turn, an assortment of brushes, a thin-bladed knife and a small trowel. 'Now.' He glanced down at his watch and back up at them. 'It is past four o'clock. You must be hungry. You should go and find something to eat. And make sure you clean that cut properly too, George. We do not want it getting infected.'

Kitty pouted. 'But—'

Ernst shot her a stern look. 'Do as I say. It is delicate work and I must go slowly, so you will not be missing much.' He picked up the knife and fixed his gaze back on the object. 'Where to start?' He ran a finger across the piece of metal sticking up from the rim. 'Here, I think.'

Kitty's shoulders drooped. She turned and stomped towards the door. George threw a final look at the object and trailed out after her, tugging Spud behind him.

She marched into the kitchen, took a bowl from the cupboard and filled it with water. 'For Spud.' She shoved it at him.

'Thanks.' He set it on the ground and watched as the dog drank from it noisily.

Kitty nodded at the handkerchief on his right hand. 'You should do as *Opa* says.'

George pulled off the handkerchief and ran his palm under the tap, washing the dried blood and dirt away. He frowned. 'That's odd.' He held his hand up to the light. The cut appeared to have healed, leaving nothing more than a faint, purplish scar.

Kitty followed his gaze. 'Perhaps it was not as bad as it looked.'

'Maybe . . .' He curled his fingers over it and glanced up at her. 'Look, I know you want that thing we found to be the king's crown. And your granddad does too, but what if it ain't?'

'It will be.' Kitty pursed her lips. Reaching for a knife, she turned her back on him and busied herself with cutting and buttering the bread and making the tea.

George puffed out a breath. 'Come on, Spud. Looks like we're not wanted here.' He plodded out on to the landing and back into the study.

Ernst Regenbogen sat hunched over the object on the desk. He was so busy brushing and scraping that he didn't even hear the pair of them come in. George slunk over to the sofa, dropped down on it and closed his eyes. In spite of the old man's scratchings and brushings, he was so tired it didn't take long for him to drift into sleep.

'George! Wake up!' A hand gripped his wrist, shaking him awake.

He blinked and sat up with a jolt. 'Wh-what is it?'

Kitty's eyes gleamed back at him. 'Come and see!' Pulling him to his feet, she steered him past where Spud lay fast asleep on the rug, and over to the desk.

Ernst Regenbogen looked up as they approached, his face lit up by a broad smile. 'I have been busy while you have been napping.' He drew back in his chair and held out his hands.

The object rested on the desk in front of him, its surface now cleaned of the layers of mud and grit. It was a crown all right, its gold-coloured surface covered in the same twisting patterns George had seen on the photograph of the belt buckle, except even more beautiful. His jaw dropped.

Kitty nudged him. 'See! I told you! And look, there is a dragon too. Can you see it?'

He frowned. 'I dunno, I—'

She pushed in alongside him. 'Let me show you. It is here on the front of the crest.' She snatched up the knife and hovered the blade over the piece of metal sticking up above the rim. 'This is its body, look. And here are its head and jaws.' As she spoke, she traced the tip of the knife along the snaking curve of metal up to what looked like a bird's beak lined with sharp, triangle-shaped teeth. 'And these are its eyes.' She turned the crest towards the light. Two small ruby-red stones glinted back at George. 'They are garnets, the same as the dragon on the king's shield.'

George let out a low whistle.

'*Opa* says it is made of solid gold.'

'Yes.' The old man lifted up the magnifying glass lying beside him and ran the lens across the crown's surface. 'And of the finest workmanship too.'

'But that is not all. Show him the runes, *Opa*.'

George pulled a face. '*Roons?* What's that in English?'

Kitty giggled. 'It *is* English, silly.'

He flushed and shoved his hands in his pockets.

Ernst Regenbogen looked up at Kitty sharply and frowned. 'Now, *Liebling*. Do not speak to your friend like that.'

Kitty bit her lip and stared down at her shoes.

The old man gave George an apologetic smile. 'I am sorry, George. Forgive my granddaughter. She is a little over-excited. Let me explain.' He cleared his throat. 'Runes are a type of ancient writing. They were used by the Anglo–Saxons, and the Vikings too. Whoever made this crown chose to inscribe it with letters from the runic alphabet.' He angled the crown away from him and tracked the tip of his little finger over a line of faint marks zigzagging across the back of the crest. 'Do you see?' He held up the magnifying glass.

George peered through it and nodded. 'So . . . so what do they say?'

'We do not know yet. We thought you would like to help us find out.'

George threw him a puzzled look. 'How?'

Ernst Regenbogen lifted up from his chair. 'With this.' He reached over and pulled a slim, dusty-looking book down from the shelf next to the desk. 'My special rune translator.' He gave George a quick wink. Clearing a space for the book on the desk, he opened it and flicked through it until he found the page he was looking for. 'Here.' He tapped his finger against the diagram of a large chart divided into two columns.

In the left-hand column was a list of stick-like shapes, including some George recognized from the markings on the crown. The right-hand one contained a matching list made up of ordinary letters of the alphabet and one or two strange-looking ones he'd never seen before.

'But first we need to fortify ourselves.' The old man

turned and gestured to a tray sitting on a nearby table stacked with tea things, a plate of bread and butter and a small pot of honey.

After Ernst Regenbogen had made a fresh pot of tea and they had eaten and drunk their fill, they crowded round him at the desk again, watching as he hovered the magnifying glass over the runes and painstakingly copied them down on to a piece of paper.

'There!' He sat back. 'It is difficult to be sure, but I think that is what is inscribed.'

ᚺᛖ · ᚦᛖ · ᚾᚨᚱᛦ · ᛗᛖ · ᚾᚨᚱᛦ · ᚦᚨᛏᛖ · ᚷᚨᛏᛈᛞᚠᛖ

George gazed at the line of spiky shapes and frowned. They were clearer written in ink, but they still didn't make any sense.

'So, George, are you ready?' Ernst Regenbogen motioned to the book.

George swallowed and gave a quick nod. He raised his finger and ran it down the left-hand column of the rune translator until he came to what looked like the first rune. His eyes darted across to the opposite column. '"H". Least I think so.'

Ernst Regenbogen peered at the page. 'Yes, you are quite right. Well done!' He scribbled it down on the piece of paper. 'Now your turn, Kitty.'

She slid alongside George, took a quick breath and scanned a finger down the page.

And so they continued, taking it in turns to look up the

matching letters, while the old man wrote them down.

When they'd finished, George stared down at the paper and frowned. The words they had spelt out made no sense:

$$he \ þe \ hæfþ \ me \ hæfþ \ þone \ cyningdom$$

He shook his head. 'It looks like a load of old gobblede-gook to me.'

Ernst Regenbogen chuckled. 'Not gobbledegook. Anglo–Saxon.'

'So what does it mean?'

'I am a little rusty, but . . .' The old man ran his eye over the words, muttering them to himself as he went. 'Yes. I think I have it now. "He who has me . . ."'

'Has the kingdom.' Kitty's voice chimed in excitedly as her granddad spoke the last three words. 'Oh, *Opa*! It is Wayland's charm.'

Ernst Regenbogen poked his glasses up on to his fore-head and sat back speechless, shaking his head in wonder.

'The Kingdom-Keeper!' Kitty flung her arms round George's neck and hugged him tight. 'You have found it, George. You have found the dragon-headed crown!'

George felt his cheeks redden again. He pushed her off of him. 'What're you talking about?'

Her eyebrows arched in surprise. 'The legend. You must remember it? The one about the king and the dragon-slayer?'

George snorted. 'But that's just a fairy story.'

Ernst Regenbogen swivelled round in his chair. 'Legends may be stories, George, but there are always grains of truth buried within them – if you know where to look. And one thing we do know' – he slid his glasses down on to his nose again and peered back at the crown – 'the Anglo–Saxons used runes on objects because they believed it gave them special powers. I think the person who made this crown – whoever they were – wanted to do the same.'

George was about to say that just because a bunch of dead Anglo–Saxons believed something had special powers, it didn't make it true when he remembered the ring. He bit his lip as the ache started up in his chest again.

Kitty picked up the crown and held it out, eyes shining with wonder. 'What are we going to do with it, *Opa*?'

'We must hand it in to the authorities. It will need to be stored somewhere safe until the experts can take a proper look at it.' The old man's face clouded over. 'Though with Hitler raining his bombs down on us, goodness knows when that will be. Now, *Liebling*' – he lifted up out of the chair again – 'we must go and prepare tea. It has been a long day and you need more than a honey sandwich or two to sustain you. We will leave you to stand guard, George.' He patted him on the back and limped over to the door.

Kitty traced a fingertip along the dragon's curling body. She gave a fluttering sigh then set it down on the desk and looked up at George. 'The dragon-headed crown is a great treasure. Greater even than the treasures that *Opa* and the other archaeologists have already discovered. And you were the one who found it. When the war finishes, it will go on display at the British Museum with your name next to it. "George Penny, the boy who discovered King Redwald's crown: the ancient and long-lost Kingdom-Keeper.'"

George blew out his cheeks. What did any of that matter when Charlie was still missing? Heart cramping, he took a deep breath and stared blurry-eyed at the floor.

Kitty hesitated for a moment, then giving his arm a quick squeeze, she turned and walked towards the door.

He waited until she'd gone before throwing a quick look back at the crown. A finger of light was sliding across its surface. As it hit the crest, the dragon's garnet eyes pulsed with a strange red fire. The scar on his hand began to ache. He clutched it to him, nursing it against his chest until slowly the sensation faded. When he looked again the light had gone throwing the crown back into shadow.

He shivered. Then, pulling the sack over it, he turned and walked across to where Spud lay, still snoozing. But as he sank down next to him and fondled his ears, he couldn't stop the feeling curling up inside him that the runes were a warning: a warning he mustn't ignore.

CHAPTER 17

The three of them were eating a supper of pea and carrot soup at the small table in the kitchen when a loud *rat-tat-tat* echoed up the stairs.

Spud sat up, ears cocked.

Kitty lowered her spoon. 'Who could it be, *Opa*?'

'I do not know.' Ernst Regenbogen wiped his lips with his napkin and frowned. 'We are not expecting anyone.'

The knocking came again.

A flicker of fear darted up inside George's chest. It'd been the same thing when the coppers had come with the news about Mum and Dad. Him and Charlie, sitting down to a tea neither of them felt like eating. Then the sudden sharp rap of knuckles on wood and the twist in his stomach as he saw the two policemen's helmets through the glass in the front door.

The man at the airbase had said they'd phone. But if it was bad news, what if they decided to send someone instead?

He heaved a sigh. If it was, he might as well face it now. He pulled back his chair. Spud scrambled up, eager to join him.

Ernst Regenbogen put a hand on his arm. 'It is all right, George. I will go.'

'But—'

'Please.' The old man shot him a stern look. He rose to his feet and limped out on to the landing. A few moments later they heard his feet on the stairs.

George waited until he'd reached the bottom, then slipped out after him, Spud at his side. The front door rattled open and the sound of men's voices drifted up from below. Ernst Regenbogen's first, then another man's, gruff and firm.

Kitty slid alongside him. 'Who is it? Can you tell?'

He shook his head. 'I ain't sure.' He peered over the banisters into the gloom.

Ernst Regenbogen's voice echoed up the staircase, louder now. 'But I am not a spy, Sergeant. I have lived here happily for several years. You can ask anyone—'

'I'm sorry, sir, but we have our orders.'

'*Opa! Nein!*' Kitty pushed past George and raced down the stairs two at a time. Spud gave an excited bark and made to follow.

George seized him by the collar and dragged him back

into the kitchen. 'Sorry, boy, but you'll only make things worse.' Pulling the door tight shut, he hurried down the stairs after Kitty. As he reached the bottom step, he jerked to a stop. Two policemen were standing in the shadows by the front door.

'Leave my *Opa* alone!' Kitty pushed past her granddad and planted herself in front of them, hands on hips, legs apart.

The shorter of the two men, who wore the stripes of a sergeant on his sleeve, took a step forward. 'Now see here, missy.' He cleared his throat. 'There's no use in making any trouble. Your granddad has to come with us. And that's final.'

'But it is true what he says. He is not a spy! He loves this country. He would never do anything to harm it.'

The taller copper loped past the sergeant. He stooped and shoved his thin, pale face up close to Kitty's. 'We can't be too careful. There might not have been an invasion last night, but it's coming all right. And we don't need people like *him*' – he jabbed a finger at Ernst Regenbogen – 'giving it a helping hand.'

A spurt of anger shot through George. 'Leave him alone!' He curled his fingers into fists and dashed down the hallway, skidding to a stop next to Kitty.

'Shh, sonny.' The sergeant threw George a warning glance, then took a step towards his companion. 'Come on now, Sidney. No need to take it out on the girl. She's just a child – of no interest to us.' He gripped him by the shoulder.

The tall thin copper gave a loud snort and straightened up.

The sergeant dropped his hand to his side and looked back at the old man. 'It's for your own good, sir. After what happened in London last night, there's a lot of scared angry people out there. You being German, you can hardly blame 'em if—'

'But you can't arrest him. He ain't done nothing wrong!'

'And who asked you, pipsqueak?' The tall thin copper snatched hold of George's arm and pulled him close. 'Hey! Wait a minute.' His eyes narrowed. 'Blond hair. Blue eyes. Skinny build. He fits the bill for that runaway evacuee Bill Jarvis came in and reported earlier. The one who stole the money off him. George Penny, wasn't it?'

The sergeant raised a bushy eyebrow. 'I believe you might be right, Constable.'

George's chest fizzed with fresh anger. 'I ain't no thief!'

Ernst Regenbogen cleared his throat loudly and took a step forward. 'You are mistaken, officer. This boy is the son of a friend of mine. He has been staying with us over the weekend while his father is away on business. He is coming here shortly to collect him and . . .' He glanced at Kitty and coughed again. 'I am sure he will be happy to look after my granddaughter too. Now please, if you are going to arrest me, can we get it over with?'

Kitty clutched his sleeve. 'No, *Opa*. You do not have to go with them.'

Ernst Regenbogen reached for her hand and gave her a sad-eyed look. 'Yes, Kitty, *Liebling*. I am afraid I do.'

George leapt in front of him. 'But she's right, Mister Regenbogen. You don't. Tell them, Kitty. About the crown.'

Kitty's eyes widened. 'The crown, yes!' She turned back to face the sergeant. 'My grandfather, he . . . he has found something very precious. It was stolen, but he rescued it. He was going to come to the police station after supper to hand it in.'

The sergeant grunted. 'This is no time for joking, missy.'

'She ain't joking. I can prove it . . .' Before they could stop him, George wheeled round and sprinted back along the hallway and up the stairs.

As he reached the landing, a muffled bark sounded from behind the kitchen door. 'Sorry, boy, you'll have to wait.'

He darted into the study. The crown was on the desk where they'd left it earlier. He snatched it up, but as his skin made contact with the metal, a spike of hot pain shot through him, forcing him to release his grip.

He winced. The cut must have opened up again. He stared down at his palm, but the scar was just the same. He licked his lips and reached for the crown with his other hand, but the pain came again, only this time it was worse. Much worse. Like a red-hot poker burning into his flesh. He cried out and yanked his hand away. Uncurling his fingers, he peered down at it, but there was no trace of a mark. He looked back at the crown, eyeing it nervously. There was nothing for it – he'd have to get the coppers to come up here instead. Gritting his teeth, he headed out on to the landing and clattered back down the stairs.

Kitty shot him a puzzled look as he approached. 'Where is it?'

He swallowed and shook his head. 'It . . . it wouldn't let me pick it up.'

She raised her eyebrows. 'What?'

'Quiet! The pair of you.' The thin copper turned to the sergeant. 'These kids are trying to make monkeys of us, sir. The sooner we get the old man shipped off to the internment camp, the better.'

The sergeant gave a quick nod of agreement. He turned and fixed George with a stern stare. 'Wasting police time is an offence, young man. Now stand back the pair of you and let us do our job.'

'No! Wait. I will fetch it.' Kitty made to dash off, but the tall copper caught her and swung her back round.

Ernst Regenbogen put out a hand. 'Please, officer!' He drew himself up to his full height. 'Let me deal with this.'

The sergeant hesitated, then gave another nod. 'All right, Sid, do as the gentleman says.'

The other copper scowled and relaxed his grip.

Ernst Regenbogen turned and pulled Kitty to him. 'I must do what the law asks of me, *Liebling*.' He raised a wrinkled hand and smoothed it over her hair.

'Then I am coming with you!' She flung her arms round him, pressing her face against his chest.

He loosened her fingers and gently pushed her away from him. 'Listen to me.' He glanced over at the two policemen and lowered his voice so only George and Kitty could hear. 'A camp is no fit place for a child. But you cannot stay here by yourselves. You must go to the rectory and tell Reverend Griffiths what has happened. He is a good man and will find you both somewhere to stay until I can make other arrangements. And if he needs any money for your keep, Kitty, you know where to find it.'

'But . . .' Kitty stared up at him, brown eyes brimming with tears.

'Come now.' He stroked her cheek and forced his mouth into a small smile. 'Be brave like I know you can be. We are Regenbogens and you must never forget it.'

'Yes, *Opa*.' She drew in a breath and wiped her face with the back of her hand.

'Good girl.' The old man turned to George and grasped him by the shoulder. 'Look after her, will you, George? And make sure you both do as I say, won't you?'

George clenched his jaw and nodded.

The sergeant stepped over to them and gave a quick clear of his throat again. 'You can bring your granddad his things tomorrow morning. We won't be shipping him up country until the afternoon.' Turning on his heel, he opened the front door and stepped outside.

The tall copper shoved Ernst Regenbogen in the back. 'Come on, old man. Let's go!'

As he pushed him through the door, Kitty cried out and tried to follow.

George grabbed her by the arm. 'It ain't no use.'

'Let me go!' She made to twist free, but he held her fast.

A few moments later, the door banged shut and there was silence.

Kitty pulled away from him, eyes flashing. 'It is your fault. We could have stopped them if you had just shown them the crown.'

'I told you, I tried, but—'

'It would not let you!' She spat the words back at him like they were bullets. 'I thought you were our friend, but you are as bad as the rest of them.'

'That ain't fair! Look, it's true. I'll show you. Come on.' He reached for her hand.

'Leave me alone!' Batting him away, she turned and stalked back down the hallway. She'd almost reached the stairs when her legs buckled and gave way beneath her. '*Opa*! My *Opa*!' She lurched sideways against the banisters and crumpled to the floor.

George dashed over and squatted down next to her. 'It's all right, Kitty. He'll be all right.' He put a hand on her arm. 'Look, if we can't take the crown to the coppers, we'll make them come back here and—'

She shivered and shook her head. 'You do not understand.'

'Understand what?'

She looked up at him, lips trembling, face white as chalk. 'It is just like before, with Papa.' Her eyes welled with fresh tears.

'What d'you mean?'

'He went away too, and I . . .' Her voice shrank to a choked sob. 'I never saw him again.'

'But you will, won't you? We'll lick old Hitler and you'll go back home and he and your mum, they'll be there waiting for you.'

'No, they will not. They cannot, they . . .' She raised a shaking hand and pressed it to her mouth.

George frowned. She wasn't making any sense. 'What? Tell me.'

'My parents, they are . . .' She gripped the banisters with both hands and gave a juddering sigh. 'They are *tot*.'

'*Tot?*'

She looked up at him, eyes full of torment then slumped forwards with a groan. When she spoke the word in English, it was a whisper.

'Dead.'

A knot formed in George's throat. 'But . . . but when you said before they were back in Germany, I thought you meant . . .'

She shook her head, then groaned again and gave in to a wave of shuddering sobs.

The knot in George's throat grew bigger. He swallowed against it. He was desperate to say something: anything to make her feel better – but there weren't any words. So instead, dropping down on the floor beside her, he slipped his arm round her shoulders and sat with her until at last the sobbing stopped.

She lifted up her head then and looked at him, her cheeks red, and wet with tears. 'I am sorry.' I should have told you. But it hurts. It hurts so much.' She gulped in a breath and reached for the star pendant, clutching it tight against her.

He squeezed her arm. 'It's all right.'

She gave a small sigh. 'No. It is not. You are my friend and I want you to know the truth.'

CHAPTER
18

George sat there and listened as Kitty told him about her parents. How they had met while they were both working at the University in Munich. How they'd fallen in love, married and then had her. Of family trips to the boating lake in the park near their home. Of helping her mother bake lebkuchen biscuits and being read to by her father every night before she went to bed.

But then – her eyes clouded suddenly – Hitler and his anti-Jewish Nazi party had come to power and Jews everywhere had begun to be persecuted. Kitty's parents had both lost their jobs. They had been forced to find work in a factory and move to a tiny apartment in the worst part of the city.

During one terrifying night in early November, two

years ago, there had been riots in towns and cities across Germany. Jewish houses and businesses had been destroyed; shop windows smashed in; synagogues – the places where Jewish people worshipped – burnt down. In some towns, Jews had even been beaten up and killed.

'After Kristallnacht – that is what they called it later because of all the broken glass on the streets – my parents were very frightened. Everyone knew the Nazis were behind the riots. And then Papa was arrested.'

'Arrested?'

'They put him in a camp. Mama wrote letters to the authorities to try and get him released, but it was no use. And then she lost her job in the factory.'

'So what happened?'

'Friends did what they could for us, but it was hard for them too. I wanted Mama to sell this.' She held out the gold star pendant. 'But she refused. It was my grandmother's, you see. She left it to me in her will.' Kitty curled her fingers back round the pendant and pressed it gently to her lips. 'Then Mama heard about the Kindertransport plan.'

'Kinder-what?'

'The transports. I told you about them, remember? They offered Jewish children lucky enough to have their names put on the list the chance to escape and come to Britain. Because Papa was in a camp and *Opa* was living here in England, they agreed to take me. I did not want to go – to leave them – but Mama insisted. She hid the necklace inside the heel of my shoe so the Nazis would not find it and take it from me at the station.' She bit her lip and looked away.

'What about them, your mum and dad?'

Kitty tightened her grip on the pendant and forced herself to meet his gaze again. 'When the guards in the camp found out Papa had been a professor, they decided to make an example of him. They worked him hard. So hard he . . .' Her eyes filled with fresh tears. She took a deep breath and went on. 'They said he had died of natural causes, but a friend who'd been in the camp with him and managed to get released later told Mama the truth. Not long after, she got sick. But she could not afford the medicine she needed and so she died too.' The star pendant slid from her grasp. She gave a ragged choking sound and pressed her hands to her face.

George stared at her open-mouthed, hardly able to believe what she'd just told him. Hitler marching into Poland and France and those other places was bad enough. But what he and the Nazis had done to Kitty's parents and all those other innocent people . . . He shuddered, remembering again what Charlie had told him the day he'd signed up. That he had to go. Do his best to help try and stop him, even if it meant getting injured – or worse.

George swallowed. Charlie was right. They had to beat Hitler, whatever the cost. Because if the Nazis won, life wouldn't be worth living. Not for anyone.

Kitty gave a loud sniff. 'I . . . I think I would like to go upstairs now.'

He nodded and helped her back to her feet. When they

reached the landing, he thought she might ask him to show her what he meant about the crown. But she walked straight past the study and disappeared into a room at the far end of the hallway without a backward glance.

As he stood there, wondering whether to go after her or not, a low whimper wound out from beneath the kitchen door. A twist of guilt curled up inside him. Poor Spud – he'd forgotten all about him. He darted over to the door and yanked it open. A black shape leapt up at him, drenching him with wet doggy licks.

'Sorry, boy.' Giving him a quick hug, George glanced back up the hall, but the door to Kitty's room stayed firmly shut. He picked up Spud's lead from the table and fixed it to his collar. 'Come on. Let's go for a walk.'

He shot a look into the study as they passed it. The crown sat in the shadows where he'd left it, the dragon crest silhouetted against the fading light. George stared down at his hands and frowned. Had he imagined the whole thing? He clenched his jaw. The only way to find out was to try picking it up again. But not now. Later. Once he'd taken Spud for his walk.

When they got outside, he took a deep breath and looked about him. The square was empty. They were probably all indoors listening to the latest news on the wireless. His stomach tightened. Would the Jerries come back and bomb London again tonight? And what about Charlie? If he was lying out there injured somewhere, could he survive another night in the open? A cold shiver ran through him.

Forcing the thought back down, he peered along the street. Best not go too far – he didn't want to risk bumping into those coppers again. Besides, he'd promised Mister Regenbogen he'd look after Kitty. To the river and back would do. He tugged on Spud's lead and set off at a brisk pace down the hill.

As he neared the junction, he spotted two men loitering in the doorway of an old warehouse. He was about to hurry on when he felt a sharp jerk on the lead. He looked down. Spud sat crouched on the pavement, ears back, teeth bared.

'Come on, boy.' He pulled on the lead, but the dog wouldn't budge.

George glanced back at the men. The taller one had his back to them, but the other one . . . His stomach knotted at the sight of the ferrety-looking face peering out from the shadows. Bill Jarvis! They had to get out of sight and fast.

There was a narrow passage running down the side of the warehouse. He clamped a hand round Spud's muzzle and dragged him into it, then took a deep breath and poked his head out into the street again.

The familiar mean tones of Bill Jarvis's voice snaked towards him. 'So yer want the job doen' tonight, eh?'

The other man replied in a voice too low and muffled-sounding for George to hear.

Jarvis grunted. 'All right. But you'd better make it worth my while.'

There was a chinking sound and the rustle of paper as the taller man reached in the pocket of his coat, then held out his hand.

Jarvis snatched the money and began to count it. The other man pulled back his sleeve and glanced at his wrist, then turned his head and looked quickly out into the street.

As the evening sunlight fell on his sharp cheekbones and pale hair, George stifled a gasp. The poacher! What shady business were he and Jarvis up to now?

Jarvis gave a satisfied grunt and stuffed the money into the pocket of his grubby old farm breeches. 'Are we done?'

The poacher drew back into the doorway and nodded.

'Good. Then I'll see yer at midnight at the place we agreed.'

The other man mumbled something in reply, then hunched his head and turned to go.

George shrank back into the alleyway and pulled Spud to him. A set of footsteps started up and paced quickly away down the street. He held back, praying the second man would head in the same direction as the first.

But the footsteps came their way instead. George's mouth went dry. Heart thumping, he ducked into the shadows and held his breath. As the man drew closer, Spud twisted free and gave a low growl.

The footsteps ground to a stop.

'Who's there?' Bill Jarvis's crooked shadow loomed across the entrance to the alleyway.

George grabbed Spud's muzzle again and froze. If either one of them made a sound now, he'd be on them quicker than a fox on a hen.

There was a loud hocking sound and a glob of something wet and glistening landed on George's right boot. He gritted his teeth, willing Spud to keep still. Finally, after what seemed like an age, Jarvis moved off. George waited until his footsteps had died away, then slumped down and hugged Spud tight. What if Jarvis and the poacher had spotted him before he'd seen them? It didn't bear thinking about. And what job could Jarvis be doing for the man?

A distant clock chimed the hour. Seven strikes. He'd better get back to the house – he shouldn't have left Kitty on her own like that, especially what with her being so upset 'n' all. And anyway, they ought to go and see the vicar like her granddad had said. Checking the coast was clear, he tucked Spud in behind him and set off back up the hill.

But when he got indoors again, there was no sign of Kitty. She must have gone to bed. George didn't blame her; he was fair worn out himself. They might as well stay here tonight. They'd be safe enough. They could go over to Reverend Griffiths' first thing tomorrow.

He let Spud off the lead and slipped into the kitchen to fetch them both a drink. His heart jolted at the sight of the bowls of half-eaten soup and the pulled-back chairs. So much had happened since he'd first met Kitty and her granddad. Good stuff like rescuing Spud and getting away from Bill Jarvis. But bad stuff too. The Jerries bombing London. Getting attacked by Scroggins and losing the ring. And then the news about Charlie . . . His chest squeezed again. He drew in a breath and let it out slowly. And now Mister Regenbogen, carted off by the coppers like some kind of criminal. As for the crown and that business up at the mounds . . . His skin prickled. He still didn't know what to make of all *that*.

A wet nose nuzzled the back of his leg. Spud peered up at him with questioning brown eyes.

'Sorry, boy. You're thirsty.' George filled a bowl from the tap and put it down on the floor in front of him. He was probably hungry as well. His eye caught on a plate of scraps the old man had set aside earlier. He gave Spud them too.

Helping himself to a glass of milk, he tiptoed down the corridor and into the study. The sun had disappeared below the rooftops, filling the room with long shadows. He walked over to the desk and stared down at the crown. He was tempted to try picking it up again. But what if the same thing happened? He flexed his fingers. Best leave it until Kitty was around to see.

Tugging off his boots, he dropped down on the sofa. He swung his legs up and lay back against the cushions. He'd sleep here tonight. He didn't fancy the idea of being back down in that museum again. A few moments later, Spud appeared at the door. He padded over, tongue lolling, and dropped down beside him on the floor.

'Good dog.' George reached out and raked his fingers through the dog's dusty fur.

He lay there for a while, listening to the sounds around him: the buzz of a fly against the window pane; the creak of the floorboards as the air began to cool; the steady breathing of his loyal friend, Spud.

As his eyelids drooped and darkness rose up around him, the sounds grew louder and merged into one, beating against his ears like a set of giant wings. A shadow fell across him. He looked up. A great bird was circling above him. He watched open-mouthed as it spiralled steadily closer, its steel-tipped wings blocking out the light. He knew he should run; find cover. But his feet felt as if they were bolted to the ground, and try as he might he couldn't lift them.

The bird was almost upon him now, its head angled down, its hooked beak ready to strike.

And then he saw it.

A ring. *His* ring, caught up in the bird's razor-sharp talons.

He had to get it . . . he had to . . . As the bird swept down on him, George jumped up and made a swipe. The bird gave a piercing cry and veered sharply away. When it swung round again, the ring had gone. And now its talons were pointing straight at him, ready to rip his face to shreds.

He tried to dodge it, but the bird was everywhere. Switching and swooping; dipping and diving; dazzling him so he didn't know which way to turn. And then, with an ear-splitting screech, it pinned back its wings and dived.

WOOF!

'Wh-what?' George jolted up and looked about him, hands and face clammy with sweat. It was a dream. Another stupid dream. He puffed out his cheeks. He was about to lie back down when a low whine sounded from across the shadow-filled room.

'What is it, boy?' He slid off the sofa and crept towards where Spud sat hunkered on all fours in front of the open door.

He reached out to pat him, but the dog dipped away and slunk out on to the landing. George hesitated. It was probably nothing. Still, best to check. He took a deep breath and followed him out. Spud stood hunched in the darkness at the top of the stairs, ears twitching, a menacing growl coming from the back of his throat. George tiptoed over to him, held his breath and listened.

Silence, except for the mad drumming of his own heart.

He shook his head, but as he made to turn back he heard it too. A scraping sound followed by a heavy thud, like a pair of boots hitting a wooden floor.

He froze. There was someone in the museum downstairs. A thief. It must be! Taking their chance while Kitty's granddad wasn't here. Well, they weren't going to get away with it. Not if he could help it.

But he needed a weapon to defend himself with. Slipping back into the study, he ran his fingers along the bookshelves until he found what he was looking for – the smooth round surface of the axe head. He snatched up the stone and weighed it in his palm. It was heavy enough. It could wing whoever it was if his aim was true.

As he steeled himself, a creak of wood sounded behind him. His stomach lurched. Gripping tight hold of the stone, George spun round and prepared to strike.

CHAPTER 19

'No. Don't. It's me!' A figure crouched in front of him, hands raised, eyes glittering with fear.

'Kitty?' George dropped the stone to his side.

Lowering her hands, she raised herself to her feet again and blew out a breath. 'What are you doing?'

'Shh! There's a thief.'

Her eyes widened. 'Are you sure?'

'Yes. Downstairs, in the museum.'

'What are you going to do?'

'Scare them off, if I can. And if they get nasty . . .' He held up the axe head again.

She shivered. 'All right. Wait a moment.' She darted over to the desk and came back a few seconds later clutching a glass paperweight.

George gave her a quick nod and the pair of them slid out on to the landing.

Spud was still in position at the top of the stairs, back arched, eyes fixed on the hallway below.

George bent and whispered in his ear. 'Stay here, boy. I'll call if I need you.' He patted him and glanced back at Kitty. 'Ready?'

She nodded.

He took a deep breath and set off down the stairs. As he reached the bottom, he peered along the hall into the gloom. The museum door was ajar. Signalling to Kitty to wait, he sucked in another breath and crept forwards, socks slipping on the tiles. When he reached the door, he pulled back against the wall and listened. There was someone in there all right. He could hear them moving things around. He turned and beckoned to Kitty.

She darted towards him, eyes wide, fingers gripped round the paperweight.

'Ready?' He mouthed the word.

She nodded.

Muscles tensing, George took another step forwards. He was about to push on the door, when a loud bang on the other side made him jump. It was followed by an angry-sounding mutter and the creak of footsteps. Coming their way . . .

Before he had a chance to act, Kitty was yanking him back down the hallway and bundling him into a cubbyhole beneath the stairs.

As she darted in behind him, the museum door juddered

open. They held their breath and waited. The footsteps paused, then started up again, padding towards them down the hall. George raised the axe head in readiness.

And then it happened.

A piercing howl ripped through the air, followed by a sudden thundering of paws.

George leapt out just in time to see a black, wolf-like shape sail through the air and land half way along the hall. With a shocked cry, the intruder lurched backwards, then turned and dashed towards the front door. As he fumbled to open it, the wolf-shape slunk towards him, head down, hackles raised. The thief glanced over his shoulder, eyes flashing white with fear. The creature drew back on its hind legs snarling. Then, with another blood-curdling howl, it sprang.

'Nooooo!' The man gave the doorknob one final yank. As the door rattled open, he threw himself through it, the wolf hard on his heels. There was a stifled scream followed by a sharp ripping noise, then the sound of boots pounding off into the distance.

George dropped the axe head and raced down the hall to the open door. A four-legged shadow stood at the bottom of the steps. As he crossed the threshold, it turned its head. A pair of bright eyes winked back at him and a brown snout nosed the air.

'Spud! Are you all right, boy?' George clattered down the steps and pulled the dog into a hug.

'Has he gone?'

He glanced up. Kitty stood at the top of the steps,

peering out into the darkening street.

'Quicker than a rat down a drainpipe, thanks to this fella.' George hugged Spud tight again. The dog gave a pleased-sounding yip and dropped a ragged piece of cloth into his lap.

Kitty jumped down the steps and crouched beside them, frowning. 'What is that?'

George picked the cloth up and examined it. 'The seat of his trousers from the looks of it!' He pulled a face as a whiff of manure and stale beer pricked his nose.

'Wait! Look. He has dropped something too.' Kitty bent over and fished a shiny object from the gutter.

As she swung the battered pocket watch in front of him, George's heart gave a sudden lurch. 'It's Bill Jarvis's.'

Kitty's eyes widened. 'But why would he come here? Unless . . .' Her eyes grew wider still. 'Maybe those policemen told him about you?'

George shook his head. 'I don't think it's me he was after.'

She shot him a puzzled look. 'What then?'

He drew in a breath and puffed it out again. 'I think . . . I think it's the crown.'

'But how could he know about it?'

'Cos the poacher told him.'

Her frown deepened. 'I do not understand.'

He let out another sigh. 'You will when you've heard.' Kitty slipped the watch into her dress pocket and sank down alongside him.

When he'd finished telling her about the meeting

between Jarvis and the poacher, she shuddered and drew her arms about her. 'So the poacher kept on following us after the army truck had gone?'

'He must've.'

'But how does he know Bill Jarvis?'

'I saw them together a couple of days ago, near the crossroads, the first time me and Spud tried to get away from the farm.'

'You did not say before.'

He shrugged. 'It didn't seem important.'

'What were they doing?'

'Trading.'

She looked at him blankly.

'Jarvis was selling him some of his rotten potatoes – I spotted a few in the ashes back at the camp. The poacher must've worked out he was a wrong'un and thought he'd get him to do his dirty work for him.'

'Dirty work?'

'You know. Paying him to come and steal the crown. One thing's for sure, he's desperate to get his hands on it again.'

Kitty's forehead furrowed again. 'What does he look like?'

'Jarvis?'

'No. The poacher.'

'You saw him back at the camp didn't you?'

She shook her head. 'I was too busy trying to get away.'

'Tall, fair hair. A bony-looking face. But why—'

She drew in a sudden breath.

'What's wrong?'

'You remember we told you about *Opa*'s digging part-ner. The archaeology student who believed there was a crown?'

George's mind flitted back to the blurred-faced man in the photograph she had shown him yesterday. He pulled back and stared at her. 'What? You don't think it's him, do you?'

She frowned. 'I . . . I do not know. But your description fits and he knows all about it – the crown I mean.'

'But I thought your granddad said he went back to Germany before the war started?'

'Yes, but what if he has come back to look for it?'

George jerked up his shoulders. 'But why? I mean, if he was caught, they'd probably shoot him.'

Kitty pulled a face. 'I suppose so, but—'

'Look, it can't be him. It's more likely a crook who heard about the ship burial and thought he'd dig himself up some treasure while everyone else was busy with the war.' A sudden thought struck him. 'Wait! Jarvis agreed to meet the poacher at midnight.'

'So?'

'So if he don't turn up, I reckon the real thief'll come back for the crown himself.'

She shivered. 'We must go to the police and tell them what has happened. We can give them the watch.' She took the scrap of cloth from him. 'And this too.'

He shook his head. 'They won't believe us. You saw what those two were like earlier, wanting to pin the blame on your granddad when he ain't done nothing wrong. They'll probably say I stole the watch off Jarvis, same as the money.'

A sudden rushing sound filled the air. Spud yelped and leapt to his feet. George glanced up and froze. A great black bird had landed on the top step above them and was busy rearranging its feathers with its beak.

'*Husch! Geh schon!*' Kitty jumped to her feet and dashed up the steps, flapping her dress, but the bird refused to move.

'I said, *go!*' As she made to run at it again, George sprang up and blocked her.

'Leave it.'

'But it might go inside.'

'I don't think so.'

'How do you know?'

He swallowed. 'I . . . I think it's here because of me.'

It sounded mad, but as the bird fixed its bright black eyes on him, he knew it was true.

CHAPTER
20

K itty stared at him, mouth open, eyes round as dinner plates. 'What are you talking about?'

Gripping hold of Spud's collar, George threw the bird another look. It sat there on the step unmoving, head on one side, as if waiting for an answer too.

He licked his lips. 'You remember the bird back at the poacher's camp?'

Kitty glanced at it, eyebrows raised. 'You mean it is the same one?'

'Yes. And I think you were right. It *was* the one that dive-bombed the poacher too – yesterday, when I saw him in the woods with the sack.'

'But why?'

He shrugged. 'The size for one thing.'

'No, I mean why would it want to attack the poacher?'

'I dunno, but it was here last night as well. And up at the mounds.'

Kitty frowned. 'So you think it is following you?'

Before George could reply, the bird hopped closer and gave a loud croak.

A sudden chill waft of dank-smelling air pricked his nostrils and for a moment he was back there under the tree, staring into the shadows at something . . . someone . . . A prickle of sweat spiked his scalp. He shivered and looked away.

Kitty tugged at his sleeve. 'There is something else. I can tell. And what did you mean about the mounds?'

He shook his head. 'It's nothing.'

'I thought we were friends?' She had that look on her face again; like she wasn't going to take no for an answer.

He heaved a sigh. 'All right.' Shooting another quick glance at the bird, he sank down on the bottom step and pulled Spud to him.

Kitty dropped down beside him and tucked her hair behind her ears. 'Well?' She looked at him expectantly.

He ran a hand across the back of his neck, cleared his throat and began.

He started off telling her about the tree; how he thought he'd seen Spud making for it, then, when he'd got beneath it and couldn't find him, he'd panicked. 'And that's when I saw it . . . him.' He shivered again as the memory of the tall dark figure rose up before him.

'Who?'

'The man. Least I think it was.'

'Did he say anything?'

'No. Just pointed at me. But he was angry. Really angry.'

'How do you know?'

'I could feel it.' He shuddered, remembering the terrible feeling of ice-cold rage. 'And there was something else too . . . on his finger. A ring.'

Kitty's eyes grew wider still. 'What did it look like?'

He swallowed. 'I don't know. I didn't get close enough, but it was gold, I think.'

She drew in a breath. 'What happened next?'

'Nothing. He . . . he disappeared and the bird came, and then I heard Spud barking and you arrived.' He bit his lip. 'I thought afterwards it was a turn.'

She frowned. 'A turn? What is that?'

He felt his cheeks redden. Should he try and explain? No – it was too embarrassing. Best keep it simple. 'Er . . . nothing. I mean, I must have imagined it.'

A strange look crept across her face. 'I do not think so.'

'What?'

Her eyes glittered back at him in the gloom. 'There is something I must tell you. I did not say before, because I thought you would mock me. But . . . well . . .'

Now it was his turn to look puzzled. 'Go on.'

'There is a story—'

He rolled his eyes.

'No. Listen. *Opa* told me. It was before he and the others started work on the dig. The lady who lives in the big house claimed one of her guests woke one night to see a line of ghostly Anglo–Saxon warriors riding across the mound field. They were carrying flaming torches in their hands. The woman told her it looked like a funeral procession for someone important. Someone who died long ago. That was why she asked *Opa* and the others to come and dig there. People thought she was mad. But then' – Kitty's eyes shone brighter still – 'they found the treasure.'

'So what are you saying?'

'That . . . well, what if it was a ghost you saw too?'

A finger of ice slid up George's spine. Could she be right? No, it was daft to even think it.

Craak!

He started. 'Bloomin' crow!' He shot the bird an angry look.

'It is not a crow. It is a raven.'

He shrugged. 'Crow. Raven. What does it matter?'

Kitty pursed her lips. 'But it *does* matter. It matters a lot.'

'What d'you mean?'

'The people of those times believed ravens were messengers between the gods and the world of the living and the dead.'

Another fairy story! George jumped to his feet. 'Look, I've had enough of this. All I want is for them to find Charlie and . . . and for this rotten war to stop so we can go back home and be like we were before.' He kicked angrily at the step, shoved his hands in his pockets and turned away.

Kitty leapt up beside him and pulled him back round, eyes shining. 'I want the same for me and *Opa*, but this is important. I know it is!' She took a deep breath. 'Look.

What if we are both right? What if this bird *has* been following you? And what if it is trying to give you a message too?'

'A message from who?'

'The ghost.'

He gave a loud snort. 'The ghost? So what does it want?'

'You said the bird attacked the poacher?'

He nodded.

'What if . . .' Her eyes widened. 'What if the ghost wants the crown?'

'The crown? But why?'

Her eyes sparked with sudden fire. 'What if it is the king's ghost? Redwald?'

George stared at her in disbelief. It was bad enough thinking there really was a ghost – but this?

But she hadn't finished yet. 'Remember what the legend says. If the crown is safe, then the kingdom will prosper. But if it falls into the wrong hands . . .'

'So if this . . . this ghost doesn't get the crown back, we're going to lose the war? Is that it?'

She flushed. 'I know it sounds impossible, but—'

He shook his head. 'You must be off your rocker.'

A whoosh of feathers sounded above them and something sharp spiked the top of George's scalp. 'Ouch!' He raised a hand to his head and looked up. The raven was circling above him, black claws extended. It gave another loud croak, then flew down and landed on the pavement in front of him, fixing him with its beady eyes.

A fresh chill rippled along his spine. He puffed out a breath. 'All right. Say for a moment it's all true. What d'you expect *me* to do about it?'

'You have to return the crown. Before . . .' Kitty raised her hand and curled her fingers round the star-shaped pendant at her throat. 'Before it is too late.'

'But why me?'

'I do not know. The ghost must have its reasons.'

'So tell me, how am I going to take the thing back when I can't even pick it up?'

'Show me!' Turning, Kitty dashed up the steps and disappeared back inside the house. George licked his lips and eyed the raven again. It cocked its head and blinked back at him.

'Come on, boy.' He grabbed hold of Spud's collar and tugged him inside.

When they got to the study, it was thick with shadows. Kitty made a beeline for the desk. George pulled up alongside her and stared at the dark shape in front of them.

She gave him a gentle nudge. 'Go on. Try.'

He wavered for a moment, then put out his hand. As his fingers brushed the metal, he closed his eyes, waiting for the pain to strike.

But nothing happened. He snapped his eyes open and drew back his hand.

Kitty peered back at him. 'What is wrong?'

'I-I dunno.' He reached out and touched the crown again. Still nothing. He lifted it up gingerly and ran a finger across the dragon crest. 'It don't make sense. Why is it letting me touch it now?'

She frowned. 'I do not know.'

They stared at it in silence. He was about to put it down again when she let out a sharp breath. 'What if the crown really was made by Wayland?'

'That's just a story.'

'Yes, but remember what *Opa* said. How all stories have a grain of truth in them?' Her eyes flashed silver in the gloom.

'Yes, but he didn't mean—'

She wasn't listening. 'What if when you cut your hand, some of the dragon's blood Wayland used to make the charm got into the wound?'

'What are you trying to say? That it's got some sort of *power* over me?'

'Why not?'

George tilted the crest towards him and frowned. He didn't know what to think any more. He glanced back at Kitty. She stood, head bowed, pressing her pendant to her lips. What if she was right after all? What if this was the crown from the legend? And what if it had been King Redwald's ghost he'd seen beneath the tree? But how could it be? Everyone knew there was no such thing as ghosts. Well, everyone except Kitty and those two mad women she'd told him about earlier.

A bolt of hot pain shot up his arm. He cried out and dropped the crown down on the desk.

Kitty clutched at his sleeve. 'What happened? Are you all right?'

'I think so.' He sucked in a breath and forced himself to look back at the crown. As his gaze fell on the crest, the dragon's eyes seemed to pulse again with a faint red glow. He gritted his teeth and turned to face her. 'OK. I'll do it.'

'What?'

'I'll take the bloomin' thing up there and stick it back in the ground.'

She gripped his arm. 'You will?'

'I just said so, didn't I?'

'When?'

'The sooner the better from the sound of it.'

A flicker of mischief lit up her eyes. 'I thought you didn't believe in fairy tales, George Penny?'

He flushed. 'I don't. Pass me my bag, will you?' He jerked his head to where the knapsack lay next to the sofa.

Kitty picked it up and handed it to him. As George reached inside it, his hand brushed against the feather. He shoved it quickly to the bottom and pulled out his things, laying them down on the desk.

'What is that?' Kitty pointed at the two halves of the album.

His chest tightened. 'It's cigarette cards. Planes of the RAF. It was a present from Charlie, but Jarvis went and ruined it.'

She frowned. 'I am sorry. Perhaps it can be repaired.'

He shook his head. 'It won't be the same.' His chest cramped again. Nothing would be. Not if Charlie didn't come back. Not if they lost the war either.

He turned back to the crown and jabbed it with the tip

of his little finger. The metal felt cold to the touch. He heaved out a sigh. None of it made any sense, but if burying it again would make Kitty happy . . .

The clock in the hallway chimed the hour. Seven . . . eight . . . nine.

George pulled on his jersey. Then, wrapping the crown in his pyjama shirt, he slid it inside the knapsack and hoisted it on to his back. 'Come on, boy.' He bent down and fastened the lead to Spud's collar.

'Wait!' Kitty slipped out through the door. She was back a few moments later, a red cardigan buttoned over the top of her dress, a pair of brown sandals on her feet. 'Here.' She thrust a small black torch and a penknife into his hands. 'We might need these.'

'We?'

'I am coming with you.'

'You don't have to.'

'Yes, I do.' She pursed her lips and jutted out her chin, and he knew then it would be hopeless to try and get her to change her mind.

CHAPTER 21

They wolfed down a slice of bread each and took a quick swig of milk, then headed back downstairs.

George glanced up as they stepped out on to the pavement. The moon was already high in the darkening sky.

'We won't use the torch until we're clear of town, in case the warden's on the prowl.' He tightened his grip on Spud's lead. 'Ready?'

Kitty drew in a breath and nodded.

'Come on, then. Let's go!'

As she pulled the door shut, there was a rustle of feathers behind them. George wheeled round just in time to see the raven jump from its perch on the window sill and lift up above them. It circled once over their heads before flying off down the street, its great wings slicing like blades through the cool night air.

Kitty's eyes gleamed back at him. 'Look, it is showing us the way.'

George made a huffing sound. 'We don't need no bloomin' bird telling us what we already know. And make sure you keep to the shadows, in case there's a copper about.' He yanked the knapsack tight against his back and headed down the hill.

When they reached the river, the tide was lapping against the shore. George bent and gave Spud a quick pat.

'Good dog. Here, let's let you off this for a bit.' He unhooked the lead and shoved it in the side pocket of the knapsack.

They set off along the path, George and Spud in front, Kitty bringing up the rear. They had almost reached the bridge when Kitty grabbed George's sleeve.

'I thought I heard something.'

'Where?'

'Back there, in those bushes.'

He glanced over to where she was pointing. The bushes were swaying from side to side, their branches caught in a sudden chill breeze.

He shrugged. 'It's only the wind. Look, if you want to go back—'

'No!' She hoisted her shoulders and marched past him.

A wave of relief rippled through George. He was glad she hadn't changed her mind. Truth to tell, he wasn't keen on the idea of going back up there in the pitch black, even with Spud for company. He threw another quick look behind him and hurried after her.

It was as they were climbing up on to the road that led over the bridge that he saw the light. It was coming in quick pulses from a spot about halfway along the parapet, reflecting out across the river in the direction they'd just come.

Spud arched his back and gave a low whine. Clamping a hand across his snout, George ducked out of sight behind the bridge wall and signalled to Kitty to do the same. He waited for a moment, then raised his head slowly and peered back to where he'd seen the light.

A man was squatting in the shadow of the parapet, holding what looked like a long black torch in his right hand. As George watched, he lifted it up and signalled again.

Kitty poked her head up alongside him. 'What is he doing?'

George frowned. 'Sending a message to someone down-river, from the looks of it.

'Do you think it might be one of the guards from the pillbox?'

'Maybe. Still, better to be safe than sorry.' He unhooked the knapsack from his back and rummaged inside for the penknife. Pulling it free, he poked it into his trouser pocket and shot Kitty a tight-jawed look. 'Just in case.'

They waited for what seemed like an age. At last the man finished his signalling and slipped back across the bridge, heading in the direction of the pillbox.

'Looks like you were right. We'd better go carefully. We've had it if he spots us.'

Kitty nodded. They waited for a moment, then crept forwards, staying low and keeping to the shadows as best they could.

As they slunk beneath the pillbox, George peered up at the slits in its walls. There was no sign of anyone. No sound of them either. He frowned. Maybe the man had gone off on patrol. Best keep a lookout though; leastways until they reached the cover of the woods.

The trees arched above them, blotting out the moon and casting a net of shadows across the road. Every time they stumbled, or stopped to catch their breath, the raven flew back to them, urging them on with a ratchety croak.

But then, as they reached the path that led into the woods, it deserted them, swooping up over the trees and away into the gathering night.

Kitty stared after it. 'Where is it going?'

George shrugged. 'I dunno. We don't need it anyway.' He peered in amongst the trees. 'Let's risk the torch. We can turn it off when we get closer to the big house.' He pulled it out of the knapsack and flicked the beam on.

It was slower going than in the daylight. There were tree roots everywhere and they had to stop more than once to free each other's clothes from low-hanging branches and spiked holly leaves.

George pulled up as the edge of the pit came into view. 'Me and Spud'll cross first, then I'll shine the torch back so you can see what you're doing. Come on, boy.'

He set off, Spud following close behind. When they reached the other side, he turned and pointed the beam back along the narrow trail.

'Just take it slowly.'

Kitty nodded. Scraping her hair behind her ears, she took a deep breath and set off. She was three quarters of the way there when the strap on her sandal snagged on a tree root. She bent to free it, but as it came loose, she lost her footing.

She stumbled and slid sideways, toppling into the darkness with an ear-piercing scream.

George's stomach lurched. 'Kitty!' He scrambled back down the path, Spud barking excitedly at his side. Heart pounding, he swept the beam back and forth across the tangle of rocks and branches at the bottom of the pit. 'Quiet, boy! Kitty! Where are you?'

Please be all right. Please!

A strangled groan echoed up from somewhere down below. He jerked the beam in the direction of the sound.

And then he saw her.

She was clinging with both hands to a tree root, a foot or two below the top of the pit; arms taut, her legs dangling.

'Hold tight.' George dropped down on all fours and propped the torch against a stone, directing the beam down on her head.

She puffed out a breath. 'Quick! My hands are slipping.'

He stretched out and made a grab for her left hand, but it was no use. She was too far away.

'Can you get a bit closer?'

'I . . . I think so, yes.' She screwed up her face in a look of determination and edged her hands slowly along the tree root, one after the other until she was almost beneath him. She looked up again, hair and face damp with sweat. 'Try now.'

He stretched again. This time his hand found her wrist. He clung on to it and thrust out his left arm. 'Take my other hand.'

She swiped and missed. 'It is no use. You will have to get closer.'

He inched forwards, extending his arm as far as it would go.

She grunted and reached again. As his fingers made contact with her other wrist there was a loud splintering sound. She gave a panicked cry.

'It's all right. I've got you!' Slowly, surely, keeping a tight grip on both her wrists, George hauled Kitty towards him. As her head and shoulders appeared, he reached across her back with his right hand, clutched a fistful of her cardigan and swung her up on to the path.

They lay there, chests heaving, gasping for air.

A wet tongue rasped the side of George's face. He lifted up and ruffled Spud's ears. 'It's all right, boy. We're all right.'

Kitty took a deep breath and sat up slowly, a dazed look in her eyes. 'Thank you.' She leant forwards, ran a hand over her left foot and winced.

'Are you OK?'

'My ankle.' I think I have sprained it.'

George hauled himself into a squat and shone the torch over it. 'It don't look too good. D'you think you'll be able to walk on it?'

'I am not sure. Maybe with some help.'

He nodded. Sliding his hand round her waist, he heaved her up on her feet.

She hobbled forwards biting down on her lip. 'It is all right, but we will have to go slowly.'

'Put your hand on my shoulder. When we get past the pit it'll be easier.' He shone the torch over the edge. The tree root she had been hanging from had broken in two and was dangling limply over the rocks below.

He shivered. It'd been close. Too close.

They set off, George taking the lead, Kitty limping behind. As they cleared the pit and the path widened, he drew alongside her so she could use him as a crutch. They stumbled on, stopping every few minutes to give her a chance to rest her ankle. When they reached the edge of the wood, George pulled to a stop and glanced behind him. 'Spud? Where are you, boy?' He peered back into the trees, but there was no sign.

Kitty followed his gaze. 'Where did he go?'

He frowned. 'I don't know. I thought he was following us.'

'Perhaps you should go back and look for him?'

'What, and leave you here on your own?'

'I will be all right.'

'But I promised your granddad.'

Kitty twisted round to face him, eyes flashing. 'I do not

need you to look after me, George Penny! I have travelled halfway across Europe on my own and—' She stopped and gave a sudden choked cry.

'What? Is it your ankle?'

She shook her head and took a step backwards, pointing at something behind him. As he made to turn, a gloved hand clamped the back of his neck. George flung the torch to the ground and struggled to break free.

'George, no! He has a gun!'

A sharp metallic click sounded in his right ear.

'Yes, and if you do not do as I say, I will have no choice but to use it.'

CHAPTER
22

George jerked his head round just in time to catch a glimpse of the man's fair hair and narrow face before a circle of cold metal dug against his cheek. His stomach turned over. It was the poacher!

'Keep your eyes to the front and put your hands above your head, both of you.'

The poacher's voice was posh, but there was something odd about it too. Foreign-sounding . . . like the way the Regenbogens spoke.

George's stomach jolted again. What if Kitty was right after all? What if he *was* her granddad's digging partner?

He threw her a quick glance. Her eyes were wide and startled-looking, her cheeks pale as paper.

'Wh-who are you?'

The man tightened his grip on George's collar and forced him forwards with the muzzle of the gun.

'Where are you taking us?'

'Somewhere where I can keep a close watch on you.'

'Are . . . are you going to kill us?'

The pressure of the gun lessened. The man gave a quick clear of his throat. 'Not unless you give me a reason to. Now, take a lesson from your friend here and keep quiet unless you are spoken to.'

George shot Kitty another look. 'Are you all right?'

She gave a quick nod and dipped her head down.

George grimaced. Where was Spud when they needed him?

As the man marched them off up the grassy slope, the hut they'd passed earlier in the day came into view. Steering them over to it, he drew back the bolt, yanked the door open and pushed them inside.

George peered about him, nose wrinkling at the mildewy smell. It looked like some kind of workman's hut: a pile of tarpaulins in one corner, an old wheelbarrow and a spade in another.

'Sit down.' Their captor jerked his pistol at the tarpaulins.

George spun round to face him. It was the poacher all right. 'Stop ordering us about, will you?'

An uncertain look flashed across the man's face. Close up, he didn't look much older than Charlie. George took a step forwards.

The man tightened his grip on the gun. 'I am warning you . . .'

Kitty tugged on George's sleeve, her voice tight with fear. 'Do as he says.'

George puffed out his cheeks and helped her over to the pile of tarpaulins. 'Now what?'

'Now we wait.' The man pulled back the sleeve of his overcoat, glanced at his watch and frowned. Then, without another word, he turned and stepped back outside, slamming the door behind him. A few seconds later there was the sound of the bolt being rattled across it, and a pair of footsteps marching away.

Kitty hugged her arms to her and gave a small groan. 'I was right. It *is* him.'

George licked his lips. 'Your granddad's digging partner?'

'Yes. Hans Ritter.'

'Are you sure?'

She gave a quick, wide-eyed nod. 'He came to the house once to look round *Opa*'s museum. I was ill with the mumps. I was meant to stay in bed, but when I heard them speaking in German, I crept out on to the landing and spied on him over the banisters.'

'Did he see you?'

'No. I did not want to get into trouble with *Opa* so I kept out of sight. But he must know it was us at the camp.'

'He ain't said anything about it yet, has he? Maybe he didn't get a proper look. I don't understand though. Why risk his life coming back here for the sake of getting hold of some old crown?'

Kitty sat bolt upright. 'But it is not some old crown. It is the Kingdom-Keeper. It is why the king wants you to bring it back to him.' She gripped hold of his arm, her eyes darting anxiously to the knapsack on his back. 'We must not let Ritter get it, George, or he will take it to Germany and it will be too late!'

'All right! All right! But we've got to find our way out of here first.' He jumped up and scanned the walls, searching frantically for an opening they could try and make bigger somehow with the spade. But apart from a small knothole in the door, there was nothing. Anyway, even if they did manage to get past their guard, with Kitty's sprained ankle, they wouldn't stand a ghost's chance of getting away.

An image of King Redwald and his band of ghostly warriors sprang up before him. George pushed it down again. This wasn't the time for fairy stories. He slumped down on the tarpaulin next to Kitty and let out a sigh.

They sat there in silence, Kitty fiddling with her pendant, George fingering his penknife and wondering what Charlie would do in his place.

Suddenly Kitty jerked up her head. 'Someone is coming!'

George held his breath and listened. She was right. Voices. Men's voices. He scrambled up, crept to the door and squinted through the knothole. A bunch of shadowy figures were approaching.

Kitty drew alongside him, supporting herself with what looked like an old bean stick. 'Can you see them?'

He blinked and focused again, but it was no use; the hole wasn't big enough to get a proper view. He shook his head.

The voices grew louder. Nudging him aside, Kitty pressed her ear to the hole. She listened for a few moments, then gave a small moan and pulled back, eyes wide with fear.

'What?'

She opened her mouth to speak, but nothing came out. And then, as the voices grew louder still, George understood why she was so afraid. Because it wasn't English the men were speaking; it was *German*. His chest tightened. 'Jerries!'

She nodded.

'What're they saying?'

She took a deep breath and put her ear to the hole again. 'Ritter is telling the others about the crown.'

Another man's voice broke in. Steel-tipped and stony-hard. A voice used to giving orders.

She shivered. '*He* is the one in charge. He is angry. He wants to know why Ritter does not have it.'

Their captor spoke again. Quieter, more nervous-sounding.

Kitty held her breath, then whispered, 'Ritter says it is in *Opa*'s museum. That he has paid a local man to get it back.'

George curled his fingers. 'That'll be Jarvis.'

'He says he has arranged to meet him here at midnight.'

George grimaced. 'He'll be lucky. Bill Jarvis ain't stupid. He won't show up empty-handed.'

The second man spoke again, his voice full of tight menace. George's scalp prickled.

'Wait!' Kitty grabbed hold of George's sleeve. 'The one in charge is furious. He is asking more questions. And now . . . now Ritter is telling him. Oh!' She stumbled back, hand clutched to her throat.

'What?'

'He *does* know it was us that took the crown from the camp. What if . . . what if he guesses I am *Opa*'s grand-daughter?'

George frowned. 'But I thought you said you never met?'

'It is true, but—'

'So, if they make us talk, we'll say we took it to the museum because we thought it was the best place for it. That we knew the man who lived there would know what to do with it.'

Kitty chewed at her lip. George could tell she wasn't convinced; but what choice did they have?

The man in charge was speaking again. Kitty rammed her ear back against the knothole.

'What's he on about now?'

'The crown. It is not the only thing they are here for.'

'What else?'

She flapped her hand at him to be quiet, listened some more, then gave a stifled gasp.

'What is it? Tell me!' He grabbed her by the shoulders.

She looked back at him, eyes full of terror. 'They are here to . . . to prepare the way for the others.'

'What others?'

'The ones who are coming by plane.'

'You mean more bombers?'

'No. Soldiers. Parachutists!'

'What?'

She shuddered and hugged her arms about her. 'It is the invasion, George. The real one. It is coming here. Tonight.'

CHAPTER 23

A flurry of thoughts and memories spiralled up inside George: of the strange plane he'd seen zigzagging across the river and the two Home Guardsmen who'd been in such a hurry to chase them away; and the man – Ritter, it must've been – back there on the bridge sending signals down the river. But before he had the chance to tell Kitty what he was thinking, there was a rattle of metal and the door swung open.

They leapt back as the silhouette of a man in a long dark coat filled the frame.

'What are you doing here?' It was the one in charge. Like Ritter, he spoke perfect English, but his voice was older-sounding and the words spat from his mouth like the *rat-tat-tat* of a machine gun.

George's stomach gripped tight. This man was dangerous. More dangerous than Ritter. If he suspected they knew about the invasion plans, he'd have them shot on the spot . . . A trickle of sweat ran down the side of his cheek. As he raised his hand to wipe it away, a voice – Charlie's voice – echoed in his ears:

When the enemy's got you in his sights, Georgie, you've got to come out fighting. If he sees the whites of your eyes, you're done for.

He gritted his teeth. Charlie was right. He was scared. Scared stiff. But he wasn't about to let on. Not to a bunch of rotten Nazis.

'Answer me!'

George sucked in a breath and took a step forwards. 'It ain't any of your business.'

The man gave a sharp, guttural laugh. 'No? Well, we will see about that.' He turned and barked an order in German.

'*Jawohl*, Hauptsturmführer Adler.'

Hans Ritter appeared at the officer's right shoulder. The older man waved a gloved hand. Marching stiffly past him, Ritter pulled a long black torch from his pocket, flicked it on and angled the beam on to George and Kitty.

Adler followed him in, yanking the door shut behind him. He stepped into the beam of light, folded his arms across his chest and fixed them with a pair of gunmetal-grey eyes. 'If Schütze Ritter here is to be believed, the two of you have – what is that quaint English expression? – tried to put a fly in our ointment already today.'

Mustering all the courage he could find, George forced himself to return his stare. 'Sorry, mister, I don't follow you?'

'Really?' The hauptsturmführer cocked an eyebrow. 'Well, let me help you then. I understand you have stolen something; something that does not belong to you.'

George's right hand drifted to the strap of his knapsack. He blinked and jerked it down quickly before Adler had the chance to notice. 'We ain't stolen anything.'

'No? Well, that is not what Schütze Ritter says, and though it is a close call' – Adler shot the younger man a scornful look – 'I think I know which one of you I prefer to trust.'

A rush of anger flooded up inside George. 'But it ain't yours!'

'Ah!' Adler flared his nostrils. 'So you *do* know what I am talking about? Well, the good news is that the article in question will soon be safely back in our possession, will it not, Ritter?' He threw the younger man another sharp look.

Ritter snapped to attention. '*Jawohl*, Hauptsturm-führer!'

George clamped his lips together. That's what *they* thought! He shot a glance at Kitty, but her head was down, her gaze fixed firmly on the floor.

Adler narrowed his eyes. 'Now, I will ask you again. What are the two of you doing here?'

George shifted his feet. 'We . . . we were taking our dog for a walk.'

Adler raised an eyebrow. 'Your dog, eh? So where is it now?'

'He ran off. We were about to go and look for him, weren't we?' George turned to Kitty.

She gave a quick nod and looked down at the floor again.

Adler gestured to Ritter. The two men drew into a huddle and began a whispered conversation.

Kitty jerked her head up and threw George a panic-filled look. He pulled the knapsack tight against him and tried to force a smile. But it wouldn't come. He peered over at the two men. What was Adler going to do with them? Keep them prisoner or – he glanced at the gun poking from Ritter's pocket – something else? He swallowed. One thing was certain – they needed a plan, and fast.

He dropped his gaze and stared blindly at the ground, sieving his mind for ideas. He could try and bargain with them. Confess he'd got the crown. Offer it to them if Adler agreed to let him and Kitty go. But once the Jerries had got it, what was to stop them going back on their word? He shook his head. It had to be something else – something that gave them a chance to raise the alarm about the invasion plan.

A sudden thought sparked inside him. He didn't have to tell them the whole truth; but he could tell them *part* of it. Then there might be a way . . . He glanced back at Adler. Would it work? He didn't know, but it was their only hope.

He took a deep breath and called out to him. 'If you think Crooked Bill Jarvis is bringing you the crown, you've got another think coming.'

Hauptsturmführer Adler jerked up his head. 'Who?' Grabbing the torch from Ritter, he stalked over and fixed George with a wolfish stare.

George pulled back his shoulders and held his gaze. 'The man who's meant to be stealing it back for you. You see, it turns out he's afraid of dogs.'

Adler's eyes shrank to two black points. 'What are you talking about?'

Kitty elbowed George sharply in the ribs. He slipped her what he hoped passed for a reassuring look and turned back to face the two men.

'He scarpered before he had a chance to get his mitts on it.'

'Scarpered? Mitts? *Was ist das?*'

'Sorry. I forgot you don't speak *proper* English, do you? It means he ran away before he could get his hands on it.'

'Is this true, Ritter?' Adler rounded on his comrade, jaw muscles twitching.

The younger man's face wore a confused look. 'I-I do not know, sir. The man I hired for the job *is* called Jarvis, but as I told you, he is not due to deliver it here for another' – he glanced at his watch – 'hour and a half.'

Adler swung round to face George again. 'So if this man, this Bill Jarvis, does not have the crown, then where is it?'

George curled his fingers into fists. Time to feed him the bait.

'It's locked away. Somewhere safe. In a place no one would even think of looking. Me and my friend, we're the only ones who know where. We . . . we could go and fetch it for you if you like, mister?' As he spoke the words, a pulse of burning heat shot from the knapsack and spread across his back. He clenched his jaw and did his best to steady his gaze.

Adler's eyes narrowed. 'What? And alert your British bobbies too? I do not think so! Know this; if you try to play games with me, it will end badly for both of you.'

A tide of panic rose up George's chest. 'I don't . . . I mean I won't . . . I mean . . .'

Adler studied George for a moment, then sniffed and gave a quick nod. 'Perhaps the two of you can be of some use to us after all. Here is what I propose. *You*' – he jabbed a finger at George – 'will return to the town. My man Ritter here will accompany you. You will retrieve the crown from wherever you have hidden it and hand it to him. And remember; he knows what it looks like, so do not think to fool him with an inferior object. In the meantime, to be sure that you do not go back on your word' – he swung his gaze from George to Kitty – 'we will keep your friend hostage.'

George's stomach clenched. That wasn't what he'd planned. But what choice did he have? If he confessed to having the crown now, they'd shoot them both for sure.

Adler bent forwards and traced a gloved finger down the side of Kitty's quivering cheek. 'No need to fear, little one. If this brave boy gives us what we want, then we will let you both go . . . eventually.' He turned to George and gave him a hard-mouthed smile. 'However, if you try to double-cross me' – his eyes glittered like two chips of granite – 'I am afraid, pretty Miss . . .' He shot Kitty another look and frowned. 'What is your name, young lady?'

Kitty tensed and looked down quickly.

Adler grabbed her chin and forced her head up again. 'Answer me!'

She shivered. 'My name is . . . is—'

'Mary. Her name is Mary MacTavish. She's an evacuee like me. 'Cept she's from Scotland.'

'Scotland?' Adler raised an eyebrow. 'Is that so?'

Kitty kept her eyes fixed straight ahead and gave a quick nod.

He dropped his hand. 'Very well, Mary. Now, where was I?' He wrinkled his forehead into a mock frown. 'Ah, yes! So if your friend here decides to double-cross me, I am afraid you will pay the price for his treachery.'

Kitty shuddered and looked away again.

George's chest tightened. 'What d'you mean?'

Adler's lips curled into a sneer. 'I think you know perfectly well what I mean.'

'But you can't. That's . . . that's—'

'Do not tell me what I can and cannot do.' Adler's voice cut across him, razor-sharp. 'Now, you have a choice. Either go and fetch the crown. Or stay here and we will see if Mister Jarvis turns up with it after all. And if he does not and you still refuse to help us, Ritter will take young Mary and his pistol for a little target practice. Is that not so, Ritter?'

Ritter's eyes widened for a second. Blinking quickly, he reset his jaw and pulled his arm into a sharp salute. '*Jawohl*, Hauptsturmführer Adler!'

Kitty gave a small choked cry.

'It's all right.' George gripped her arm. 'They can't hurt you. I won't let 'em.'

Adler snorted. 'Brave words. But words on their own will not be enough.' He clamped a hand on George's right shoulder. 'So, what is it to be, little man?'

George twisted away from him and stared down at the floor. He'd tried his best, but somehow his plan had backfired. All he could do now was go back to the Regenbogens' house and pretend to find the crown and hope, once he handed it over, he could somehow persuade Adler to let them both go.

Another pulse of heat shot out from the knapsack. He grimaced. If it kept doing that, he wouldn't be taking it anywhere . . . He slumped his shoulders. The only other thing was to put up a fight and try to get away. But what chance would they have against a bunch of Nazis?

And then, just as he was about to give up all hope, it came to him. What if he could find a way to shake Ritter off and double back up to the big house to raise the alarm? It was risky, but if he kept his wits about him, it might just work.

He took another breath and raised his head. 'All right. I'll go.'

Kitty threw him a puzzled look, but he ignored it and concentrated on meeting the Nazi's gaze.

'You have seen sense. Good! What time is it, Ritter?'

The younger man checked his watch again. 'Twenty to eleven, sir.'

Adler frowned. 'Not long to go now. You are to be back here by one, or else . . .' He tipped his head in Kitty's direction. Then, beckoning to Ritter, he yanked the door open and stepped outside. The younger man threw them a quick glance and followed Adler out into the night.

As soon as he was out of sight, Kitty clutched George's sleeve. 'They must not get the crown. You have to take it back to the burial site, before it is too late.'

He rolled his eyes. 'There's more important things to worry about right now, like getting shot of Ritter and raising the alarm.'

'But after that. We have to make sure it is safe. Remember what the runes say.'

He frowned. 'I don't see what difference it's going to make.'

The heat came again; stabbing into him like a set of red-hot claws. He gave a small groan and slid the knapsack off, face scrunching up in pain.

Kitty stared at the bag, then back at him. 'See! You have got to do it, George. Promise you will. Please!' She tightened her grip on his arm, eyes blazing with fresh fire.

'But what about you?'

She pulled back her shoulders and jutted out her chin. 'I will be all right. Like *Opa* said, I am a Regenbogen!'

He hesitated for a moment, then drew in another breath and nodded. 'All right. I promise.'

'Thank you!' Giving him a quick hug, she reached in her dress pocket and pulled out Bill Jarvis's watch. 'Here. So you can keep a check on the time.'

A shadow darkened the door. George pocketed the watch quickly as first Adler, then Ritter, stepped back inside.

The older man stalked over and thrust George and Kitty apart. 'You have had quite long enough to say your farewells.' He gestured angrily at his comrade. 'Take the boy away!'

'*Jahwohl*, Hauptsturmführer!' Clicking his heels together, Ritter grabbed George by the arm and marched him to the door.

As he bundled George forwards, a voice called from the darkness, 'You can do it, Saint George. I know you can!'

George turned to catch a final glimpse of Kitty, but Ritter blocked his way leaving him no choice but to grip the knapsack to him and stumble out into the night.

CHAPTER
24

A small group of men stood huddled outside the hut. They looked like a bunch of boatmen in their black caps and dark, workaday jackets and trousers – except boatmen didn't walk about in the middle of the night with boot-black on their faces and signalling lamps in their hands. They jerked their heads up and stared at George as he passed. One of them called out something in German and the sound of harsh laughter ricocheted through the air.

George twisted round. Ritter spun him back again and led him away down the slope. As they neared the bottom, George's heart gave a sudden jolt. What if Spud turned up now? He wouldn't stand a chance against Ritter and his gun. He licked his lips and chased the thought away. He had to stay focused. Work out how he was going to get free.

He glanced down to where the path led off into the woods. The German might have the gun, but he didn't know the lie of the land. If he could lead him by the pit, he might have a chance. Sliding the knapsack back over his shoulder, he turned towards it.

Ritter yanked him to a stop. 'Where are you taking me?'

'It's a shortcut. It'll save time. Twenty minutes, at least.'

His eyes narrowed. 'You had better be telling me the truth.'

'I am, mister. I mean, sir.'

Ritter rubbed a hand across his chin and peered into the undergrowth. 'All right. Let's go.' He jerked the gun at him.

George stumbled down on to the path, and into the trees. As he did, a beam of light flared up behind him. His chest tightened. The torch. If Ritter spotted the pit . . .

He slipped his hand in his pocket and fumbled for the penknife. He had to be ready to act. Do anything it took . . . As his fingers curled round the handle, a cold snake of fear wound its way up his chest. What would it be like to have to kill a man? Or what if . . . what if it was him who got killed instead? He shook his head. Think like that and you'd be beat before you got started.

Keeping his eyes fixed on the path, he slid the knife out and prised the blade free with his thumb. The trees had begun to thin out on his left. They must be approaching the pit. He threw a glance at Ritter. If his plan was going to work, he needed to try and distract him.

He took a deep breath. 'You're one of them diggers, ain't you?'

'What?' Ritter's eyebrows arrowed up in surprise.

'The lot that found that old ship here, last summer.'

Ritter's pace slowed. 'How do you know about that?'

George snatched a look to his left. The path fell away into blackness. If he could keep him talking a few seconds longer . . . He gripped the knife tighter. 'There's . . . there's a photograph. The old man who looks after the museum showed it me. He told me you and him were digging partners. That the pair of you went looking for the crown.'

'Digging partners, yes. Friends too.' For a moment Ritter's face wore a distant look, as if remembering happier times. 'I learnt a lot from him, even though . . .'

'You mean, even though he was a Jew?'

Ritter's cheeks flushed. 'That is enough!' He jabbed the gun into George's ribs and shoved him forwards. 'Keep moving.'

A dribble of cold sweat trickled down the back of George's neck.

You're almost there, Georgie. Don't let him put you off now.

He drew in another breath. 'So if you didn't find the crown before, how come you managed it this time?'

'You ask a lot of questions. Still, what can it matter if I tell you now?' Ritter cleared his throat. 'When I got back to the Fatherland, I undertook further studies. It was only then I realized the answer had been staring us in the face all along.'

George frowned. 'What do you mean?'

'The legend. I am guessing the old man told you about

it? It talks about the dragon's treasure hoard being buried beneath a tree.'

'Yes, but—'

'If you have been up to the site, you will know there is really only one possibility.'

'But it's just a story.'

'Maybe so. But that is where I found it.'

Goosebumps rippled across George's arms and neck. He pulled the knapsack tight against his back. 'What are you planning to do with it anyway?'

Ritter sighed. 'It is not me you should be asking, but the *Führer*.'

George juddered to a stop and spun round, mouth gaping. So it was Hitler Ritter had come to steal it for. Did *he* believe in what the runes said too? He must do. Why else would he go to so much trouble to get his hands on it?

Ritter blinked. 'I have said too much.' He cast a quick look about him, as if half expecting his leader to appear out of the shadows and start screaming at him for giving away his secrets. 'Come on.' He motioned at George to get moving again.

But he stood his ground.

'If your *Fewer*, or whatever he's called, fancies himself as King of England, he should know the job's taken.'

'Silence! Now do as I say.' Ritter yanked George round. As he pushed him forwards, his hand made contact with the knapsack. 'Wait a minute! What is this?' He probed the bag with his fingers and gave a small cry of surprise.

A knot formed in George's throat. He whipped round smartly before the German could get a proper hold.

Ritter stared back at him, eyes glittering with astonishment. 'So, you have had it with you all along.' He shoved the torch under his arm and thrust out a hand. 'Give it to me.'

George backed away up the path, left hand gripping hold of the knapsack strap, right hand still concealing the knife.

'I said give it to me, or—'

A loud snarling noise ripped through the air, followed by a sudden sharp cry. Ritter slid the torch back down into his hand and jerked up the beam.

'*Mein Gott!*'

George wheeled round. Halfway along the path, the figure of a boy sat cowering, his arms raised in defence against a furry black shape hunkered down in front of him. As the light fell on him, he dropped his hands and stared back blindly, lips quivering, face ashen pale.

'Get him off me, please!'

George's heart skipped a beat. Scroggins! What was he doing here? And Spud too.

He glanced back at Ritter. 'It's my dog. He—'

At the sound of George's voice, Spud gave a quick yelp and sprang round.

The German's eyes flitted to the dog and back to George again. 'The bag. Now!' He raised the gun up and took a step forwards.

Spud gave a low growl and sloped along the path towards him, head down, teeth bared.

Ritter eyed him nervously. 'Keep him back, or I will shoot.' He lowered the gun muzzle, training it on Spud.

'Come here, boy!' George made a grab for Spud's collar and missed.

'This is your last chance.' Ritter slid his finger on to the trigger.

George thrust the penknife up and held it out in front of him. 'No! Don't!'

A sudden harsh call sounded above them. He looked up just in time to see a great black bird swoop down and sink its claws into the back of Ritter's scalp.

Ritter gave a startled cry and staggered forwards. Tossing the gun and torch to the ground, he batted at the bird with both hands. But it clung on, beating its wings against him. Then, with a loud rasping croak, it stabbed him in the forehead with its razor-sharp beak.

With another sharp cry of pain, Ritter lurched to the left, lost his footing and toppled backwards into thin air. There was a crump, a groan, then . . .

Silence.

Heart pounding, George dropped the knife down to his side and snatched up the torch. He bent forwards and shone it into the blackness below. Ritter lay in a gap between the rocks at the bottom of the pit, arms outstretched, eyes tight shut. George played the beam across him. He was still breathing, but he was out for the count.

A small furry head butted the back of George's hand. He drew in a breath and sank to his knees, burying his face against the dog's warm neck. 'I thought I'd lost you good and proper this time, boy.'

A set of footsteps crunched towards him. He sprang back up, torch raised.

Scroggins shielded his face with his hands. 'Put that thing down, can't you? You're blinding me.'

George dropped the beam and frowned. 'What're you doing here?'

Scroggins slid his hands down and shot him a guilty look. 'Following you.'

George caught his breath. So it was *him* Kitty had heard back there on the river path. 'Why?'

Scroggins ran a hand over the back of his neck. 'I-I don't know. I saw the two of you outside Kitty Whatsername's house earlier. You looked like you were up to something, so I came after you, but then I lost my way and went round in circles until that dog of yours leapt out on me and pinned me down.' He threw Spud an uneasy look.

George gave the dog an approving pat. 'Serves you right.'

The other boy flushed. 'Where's your bird gone?'

'He ain't *my* bird.' George scanned about him, but the raven had disappeared.

Scroggins slid to the edge of the pit and peered in. 'Who is he, anyway?'

George flicked the penknife shut and dropped it back in his pocket. 'A *real* Nazi. And there'll be plenty more of 'em if I don't get help right now.' He drew the knapsack tight against him.

'What do you mean?'

'The Germans are coming. Here. Tonight.'

Scroggins gaped. 'Wh-what? But how do you know?'

'I wouldn't, except for Kitty Regenbogen. And now she's—' In spite of himself, George's bottom lip trembled. 'She's their prisoner.'

'But—'

'Look, I ain't got time for this.' George gave a quick whistle. 'Come on, boy.' As he turned to go, the toe of his boot struck something half buried in the leaves. He kicked them aside and directed the torch beam down. Ritter's pistol. He picked it up and examined it. A Luger: he could see that now. Heavy too, but it was a better defence than a penknife. He shoved it into the waistband of his trousers.

Scroggins grabbed him by the sleeve. 'Where are you going?'

'I told you. To raise the alarm. There's a house back up there. With any luck, the lady who lives there'll have a phone.'

'I'll come with you.'

George raised his eyebrows. The old cocksure Scroggins had gone. This new one seemed to be doing his best to try and be his friend. He shrugged. 'Suit yourself.' Shining the light ahead of them, he set off through the trees.

As they reached the edge of the wood, he glanced out across the open ground. If they kept low and skirted wide of the hut, with a bit of luck they wouldn't be spotted. He pulled Jarvis's watch from his pocket and ran the torch beam over the scratched face. Twenty to twelve. That left just over an hour to get help and keep his promise to Kitty too.

But what if, in the meantime, Adler and the others found out she was German, and had understood every word of what they said? That she was Jewish too. They might kill her then, anyway. He clenched his jaw. He mustn't think like that. He had to stay focused – get up to the big house and raise the alarm; that was the best way to save her; to save everyone.

He switched off the torch and shoved the watch back in his trouser pocket. Then, signalling to Scroggins to stay close, he sped up the slope, Spud bounding along at his side.

CHAPTER
25

They kept out of sight of the hut, giving it as wide a berth as possible. As they crested the hill, the shadowy bulk of the house loomed up before them. George powered towards it, boots crunching across the gravel drive. He skidded to a stop when he reached the grand-looking entrance porch and scanned the windows, chest heaving. Was anyone up? He frowned. With the blackouts in place it was impossible to tell.

Scroggins drew up alongside him gasping for breath. 'Wh . . . what are we going to do now?'

'Ask to use the telephone and call your dad.'

'Father?' Scroggins blinked. 'But . . . but he'll give me a whipping if he finds out I'm up here with the likes of you.'

George snorted. 'He's got more important things to

worry about than that.'

Scroggins hunched his shoulders. 'I s'pose. What if they're all in bed?'

'They won't be in a second.' George darted beneath the porch and yanked the bell-handle. A distant jangling echoed somewhere inside. He held his breath and waited.

Nothing, except the dying tinkle of the bell. He hammered against the door with his fist.

'Hey. Steady on!' Scroggins tugged on his jersey. 'We don't want to go upsetting them. The owner's a friend of my father, you know.'

George rounded on him. 'I don't care if she knows the King and Queen – we've got to get her up and sharpish.' He stepped back from the porch and peered up at the windows again, but the blackouts stayed firmly in place.

Scroggins cleared his throat. 'What if she's out? Father says she goes away quite a lot.'

George's stomach quivered. He hadn't bargained for that. But it wouldn't stop him. Not with Kitty and the rest of the country depending on him.

He took a deep breath and flexed his fingers. 'We'll just have to break in then, won't we?'

Scroggins eyes widened. 'What? But you can't do that. It's against the law. If Father finds out he'll have my guts for garters.'

A ball of anger fizzed up inside George. 'You're lucky you've still got a dad.'

Scroggins swallowed. 'I'm sorry. What happened to your parents anyway?'

'They were killed in an accident.' George blinked and looked away.

'Oh. I . . . I didn't realize.'

'No.' He turned back and fixed him with a hard stare. 'There's a lot you don't know about me. And about Kitty too. Calling her a Nazi, when her dad was put in a camp and killed by them. Saying those things about my brother when he's been up there risking his life to keep us all safe.' George's chest cramped as he spoke the words. He gave a small moan.

Scroggins gripped his arm. 'Are you all right?'

'I'm fine!' He jerked away, eyes smarting.

Scroggins gnawed on his lip. 'I'm sorry. I shouldn't have said those things. Or taken your money either. It's just that, well, it's been hard, what with Doug being wounded and everything.'

'Your brother?'

Scroggins nodded and hung his head.

George puffed out a breath. He could tell him about Charlie going missing. But what good would that do? He gripped Scroggins by the shoulder. 'Look, we're on the same side, ain't we?'

Scroggins raised his head sheepishly and met his gaze. 'Yes. Yes we are.'

'Good. So let's do what we have to do and get help fast.' Reaching behind his back, he fished out the Luger.

Scroggins threw the gun a nervous-looking glance. 'What are you going to do with that?'

'You'll see.' George slipped over to the nearest window.

Handing Scroggins the torch, he held the gun by the barrel and swung it sideways, smashing it against the pane. A shower of broken glass flew through the air, scattering across the gravel at their feet. George made to reach through the jagged hole.

'Wait!' Scroggins shrugged off his jacket. Winding it round his arm, he punched out the remaining fragments of glass, undid the window-latch and pulled it open.

George gave a low whistle. 'You're good at this, Raymond. Done it before?'

Scroggins flushed. 'No, I—'

George flashed him a quick grin. 'I was pulling your leg, stupid.' Ramming the pistol back in his trousers, he unhooked the bottom of the blackout and climbed inside.

As he thudded down on the floorboards, a smell of beeswax and soot tickled his nose. He lifted up and poked his head back through the open window.

'Hand me the torch, will you?'

Scroggins thrust it at him. Flicking it on, George pushed the blackout aside and swung the beam around the room.

He was in some kind of grand parlour with comfy chairs and thick patterned rugs scattered across a polished wood floor. At the far end stood a stone fireplace. A portrait of a dark-haired woman in a blue dress hung above it. The owner. It must be. George drew closer and ran the light across her face. With those pursed pink lips and that steady brown gaze, she looked like a no-nonsense sort of person – definitely not the type to believe in ghosts.

A heavy thunk sounded behind him. He spun round. Scroggins crept towards him, boots crunching on bits of broken glass.

'Where's Spud?'

'Waiting outside.'

George skimmed the torch beam across the small tables and cabinets dotted about the room. There were plenty of fancy vases, glass bowls and the like, but no sign of a telephone.

'It'll probably be out in the hall. That's where we've got ours.' Scroggins slid past him, making for a door on the far side of the room.

George hurried over to join him. A long tiled hallway stretched away in front of them. Halfway down it stood a small wooden table, a black telephone perched on top of it.

Scroggins shot George a quick smile. 'Told you so.'

'D'you know the number?'

''Course I do!' Scroggins pushed past him and pounded down the hallway, boots clattering against the floor-tiles. As he reached for the receiver, he glanced back at George and frowned. 'What shall I say?'

'The truth. That there's a bunch of Nazis camped up near the ship burial. That they've taken Kitty Regenbogen prisoner and that if they don't hurry up and do something, the whole German army'll be parachuting down on top of us and marching into town.' As the words echoed back at him, a wave of panic surged up inside George. He swallowed hard, doing his best to keep it at bay.

'What if he doesn't believe me?'

'You'll have to make him then, won't you?' He gave Scroggins a quick nod, then turned and slipped back through the parlour door.

As he stepped into the room, there was a faint rustling sound and a draught of cold air lifted his hair. George shivered and glanced over at the window. It was nothing. A bit of wind sneaking in through the open blackout, that was all. He pulled out the pocket watch and scanned the torch beam across it. Quarter past twelve. His stomach flipped. There was no time to get the crown up to the burial site now. He had to get back to Kitty and fast.

But as he took a step towards the window, a fresh bolt of pain shot into his back and coursed up his spine. He gave a sharp cry and dropped the torch. It hit the floor with a dull thud. The light flickered and went out.

The sound of hurried footsteps echoed down the hallway. A few seconds later, Scroggins raced in through the door and skidded to a stop in front of him. 'What's wrong?'

George drew a shuddering breath. 'It's all right . . . I-I'm all right.' But as he straightened up and made to set off again, a second bolt ripped up his spine, clamping his skull between white-hot teeth. He crumpled to his knees with a groan.

'You don't look it.' Scroggins bent over him, eyes wide with concern.

George sucked in another breath and got to his feet. 'Go and make that call, will you?'

Scroggins wavered, then darted back into the hall.

George yanked the knapsack against his back. 'All right. All right. You win.' He curled his fingers into fists and took a step forwards. The burning pain didn't return.

And finally then he was sure what Kitty had said must be true. The crown *was* the Kingdom-Keeper and it was down to him, George Penny, to save it.

Scroggins's voice echoed back down the hallway. He was talking to the operator. Asking to be put through. Any minute now he'd be speaking to the inspector and then help would come.

George steeled himself. As for him, he had a promise to keep. He'd let Charlie down when he lost the ring. He wasn't going to let Kitty down too.

CHAPTER 26

As George's boots crunched down on to the gravel, a pair of bright doggy eyes shone up at him.

'Come on, boy. We've got some digging to do.' He gave Spud a quick pat and set off at a run back along the drive and up on to the ridge, following the route he and Kitty had taken that afternoon.

As he cleared the trees and stepped out in to the mound field, his heart sank. A mist had come down, sinking the mounds beneath a dank, grey tide so only their tops showed above it, like a chain of low, dark islands.

George shivered. He didn't rate his chances of finding his way to the tree quickly in this lot. A sudden pulse of heat rippled across his back. He gritted his teeth and fixed the lead to Spud's collar. He was about to set off again when a loud croak tore through the air. He jerked back his head and watched open-mouthed as a winged shape swept towards them.

The raven. He frowned. What was it up to now?

The bird circled above them. Once. Twice. Three times. Then it dipped down and flew off in front of them, cutting a path through the mist with its wings.

With an excited yip, Spud sprang after it, yanking George behind him.

It was easy to follow the bird at first. But as they ploughed on, the mist thickened around them, and George began to fear that if it got any worse, he would lose sight of the creature for good. But instead of deserting them, the bird stayed close, calling to them and doubling back when the mist was at its worst.

And then, as they rounded the side of yet another mound, the raven glided down and landed on the ground in front of them. As George pulled up, wiping beads of moisture from his cheeks and eyelashes, a sudden breeze blew in and the mist cleared to reveal a dark mass of twisted branches and spiky black leaves looming up before them. His heart jolted. The tree. At last! Now all he had to do was dig a quick hole and stick the crown in it, and then he could get back down the hill and save Kitty.

He squatted down and pulled out his penknife. He was about to slid out the blade and start digging when he felt a sharp tug on his fringe. He gave a start and looked up. The raven sat in front of him, its head cocked to one side.

'Get off me, you bloomin' thing!' He shooed it away,

but it hopped back again and made another lunge.

'All right. Where then?'

The bird turned and hopped in beneath the branches of the tree.

George licked his lips. He didn't want to go back in there again. What if the ghost-king was waiting for him? His scalp prickled at the memory of the dark figure coming towards him; its voiceless rage and the sudden glint of gold from the ring as it raised its finger and pointed at him.

The ring! He gave a choked cry. What if it wasn't the king? What if . . . what if it was—

'Charlie!' He let go of Spud's lead and stumbled forwards into the darkness, heart racing, head spinning.

The further in he went, the thicker the shadows grew. They crowded round him, clutching at his throat, forcing the breath from his lungs, until at last, chest heaving, he dropped to his knees. He stared blindly into the blackness.

'I'm sorry, Charlie. I didn't mean to lose it. Honest I didn't.' He slumped forwards, tears streaming down his cheeks, his breath coming in ragged gasps.

A sudden surge of pain shot through him. Except this time it was coming from deep inside him, gripping his heart, threatening to tear it in two.

What did it matter about burying the crown? Charlie was dead and nothing was going to change that. Now or ever.

He lifted his head, sobbing, and ripped the knapsack from his back. He was about to toss it to the ground, when a familiar voice sounded in his ear.

'Keep fighting, George. You've got to keep fighting.'

He blinked the tears away and peered about him, straining to see. 'Charlie?'

A low sighing sound filled the air and a soft breeze ruffled his hair. He closed his eyes and for a moment he was back at home, curled up on the sofa next to Charlie, listening wide-eyed to one of his stories about famous fighter pilots from the last war.

Then the breeze faded and was gone.

He drew in a breath. Charlie was right. He had to carry on. Do his best to make sure he and Scroggins's brother and all the others hadn't fought in vain.

He scrubbed at his eyes with the back of his hand and looked up. The raven was perched on a root in front of the tree's gnarled trunk. As George met its gaze, it dipped its head and jabbed its beak into the ground.

George got to his feet and picked his way over to where it sat. Loosening the strings of the knapsack, he tugged the crown free and set it on the ground. He glanced up at the raven again. It stared back at him, unblinking.

A dark furry shape nosed alongside him. 'It's all right, boy. I've got to do this on my own.' George nudged Spud gently away. Sucking in a breath, he slid out the knife blade and sliced it into the soil.

Once he'd made the first few cuts, it was easy to scoop the earth out with his hands and it wasn't long before he'd dug what looked like a crown-sized hole.

As he lifted up the crown, a finger of moonlight shone down on to the crest through the tree's branches, and for a second the dragon's eyes burnt with the same red fire as before. George shivered and peered about him, but there was nothing. Even the raven had disappeared. Lowering the crown into the hole, he covered it over and pressed the soil down firmly with both hands.

He sat back frowning. Had he done the right thing? Only time would tell.

Time! He snatched out the pocket watch and peered at it. Ten to one. His stomach clenched. In ten minutes' time Adler was going to shoot Kitty!

Checking the Luger was still safely tucked into the back of his trousers, he slung the knapsack over his shoulder, grabbed Spud's lead and scrambled to his feet. 'Come on, boy! Kitty needs us!'

When they got back out into the open, the mist had cleared. George heaved a sigh of relief and set off at a sprint, weaving a path between the mounds. They were halfway across the field when Spud jerked to a halt, nose raised, ears twitching.

'What is it, boy?' George cocked his head and listened hard. And then he heard it too.

A low rumble, like distant thunder.

He glanced about him. A wind had got up and was rippling across the bracken-covered backs of the mounds. The rumbling noise sounded again, closer this time. And now the ground was shaking too. Spud pressed against his legs, shivering.

Gripping tight hold of the lead, George tore across the rest of the field, twisting and turning past the remaining few mounds. As they reached the cover of the trees, he stopped for a moment and threw a quick glance over his shoulder. The thunder had faded. The wind too. But now there was something else: a throbbing ache in his right hand.

Grimacing, he switched the lead to his other hand and held out his palm. The scar from the crown was twitching, as if something was stirring beneath the skin. He blinked and flexed his hand. This time when he looked, it was still.

Before he had a chance to make any sense of it, he felt a sharp tug on the lead. He frowned. Spud was right. They had to get back to the hut, and fast.

There was no sign of Scroggins when they reached the house. If he'd got any sense he'd hole up inside and wait for the coppers to come. *If* they came . . . George's chest tightened. Shaking off the thought, he put his head down and sped on.

As they neared the top of the slope, he dropped down and slunk forwards until the front of the hut came into view. He frowned. Where had Adler's men gone? And what about Kitty? Was she still inside?

He licked his lips. There was only one way to find out.

'Ready, boy?' Taking a deep breath, he leapt up and dashed towards it, Spud at his side.

The door was bolted when they got there. Keeping a close look about him, he tiptoed up to it and put his eye to the knothole.

He couldn't see Kitty at first. And then, as his eyes got used to the gloom, he spotted her hunched in the corner, knees drawn up to her chest, head bowed.

He was about to call her name when he felt a sharp tug on his trouser leg. He looked down. Spud sat bolt upright, both ears cocked. George held his breath. Voices. Adler's and another man's. Heading this way. They were coming for Kitty. They must be.

He had to stop them. But how?

A thought flashed into his head. If he could trick Adler into believing he'd returned ahead of Ritter with the crown, then distract him somehow, it might buy enough time for help to arrive. But he'd have to get him to think he'd come up from the town, or he'd smell a rat. And he needed to get rid of Spud too. He glanced back at the door. He was desperate to let Kitty know he hadn't deserted her. But there was no time for that now. He had to go.

Taking a tight grip of Spud's lead, he scrambled up the slope again, then skirted along it and doubled back down towards the woods. As they reached the first of the trees, he peered in among them, willing Inspector Scroggins and his men to appear. But there was no sign.

He gnawed at his top lip. He'd just have to stick to his original plan and hope they were on their way. But to make it work, he needed something that would fool Adler into believing he had the crown. Tying the end of Spud's lead to a tree branch, he bent down and scoured the ground until at last he found what he was looking for. A lump of rock about the same size. He weighed it in his hand. It was heavy enough too. Stuffing it into the knapsack, he tied the string into a double knot and held it out in front of him. It wasn't perfect, but it would have to do.

As he slipped the bag back over his shoulder, Spud whined and strained on the lead.

George's stomach knotted. 'Sorry, Spud. You've got to stay here. If those Nazis see you, it'll be curtains for all of us.' He bent and ruffled his ears. 'I'll come back for you soon, boy, I promise.' He shivered. His voice sounded sure, but it was the last thing he felt. Pulling his jersey down over the Luger, he took a deep breath and set off back up the slope.

CHAPTER 27

As George neared the back of the hut, he heard more voices. Kitty's – low and scared-sounding – then Adler's, clipped and steel-edged. Any minute now, he might pull out his gun and shoot her. There wasn't a moment to lose! He steeled himself and darted forwards.

'Halt!' A figure leapt out in front of him, pistol raised and pointed at his chest.

George froze. Ritter! 'B-but how . . .'

The ghost of a smile flickered across the German's face. 'I have learnt to become almost as good at climbing as I am at digging since I joined the army.' He eyed the knapsack. 'So, you still have the crown?'

George swallowed and gave a quick nod.

'Let me have it and maybe I can persuade my commanding officer to release you.'

George clutched the bag tight against his shoulder and backed away. 'No. Not unless you let my friend go too!'

The door to the hut flew open with a bang.

Hauptsturmführer Adler stepped out into the moonlight. He shot a quick look about him, then fastened George with an iron-hard stare. 'So you are back, little man. And all alone too! I would have expected you to go for help.'

'I . . . I tried, but I got lost in the woods and . . .' George let his voice shrink to a whisper, doing his best to get the Nazi to believe him.

'Hmmm. I wonder if you are lying to me? No matter.' Adler gave a dismissive wave of his hand. 'Tell me, how did you manage to escape? Ritter is having trouble remembering after his knock on the head.' He flicked the younger man an angry look.

A burst of relief flooded through George. So he didn't know about Scroggins and Spud. That was something anyway.

'I dunno . . . I—'

Ritter pointed at George's knapsack. 'He still has the crown, sir!'

Adler shot a glance at it and took a step forwards, eyes narrowing. 'That is something Ritter *has* been able to tell me. That you had the crown on you all along.' He clicked his teeth. 'I warned you against playing games. Now hand it over!'

George balled his fingers into fists and stood his

ground. 'No. Not until you let Ki— I mean Mary go.'

A look of cold amusement rippled across Adler's face. 'You have got courage, I will give you that.' He hesitated for a moment, then gave Ritter a quick nod.

The younger man slipped past him into the hut. He emerged a few seconds later, dragging Kitty behind him.

When she saw George, she cried out and made to break free, but Ritter held her back.

Adler gave a hollow-sounding laugh. 'Your friend has spirit too. A shame she is just a girl. We could use her sort fighting for the Fatherland.'

'Never!' Kitty puckered her mouth and spat.

'No, Kitty. Don't!' George leapt forwards.

The muscle in Adler's jaw twitched. 'You told me her name was Mary?' He swivelled his gaze back to Kitty. She reached up and clutched nervously at the necklace round her throat. The Nazi's eyes shrank to two steely slits. He stalked over to her and tore it free. 'What is this?' He snapped his hand open and stared down at the star-shaped pendant. 'The Star of David. *Ein Judenmädchen!*

Kitty tossed back her shoulders and stared back at him defiantly. 'Yes, I am Jewish and I am proud of it!'

He shot up an eyebrow. 'And a German-speaking one too. I wonder . . .' He stroked a finger across his lips. 'You wouldn't by any chance be related to that dirt-grubbing Jew Ritter told me about, would you?'

A look of terror flashed across Kitty's face.

Adler's mouth pressed into a tight smile. 'I thought so!' He swung the necklace from side to side, then thrust it at

Ritter and fixed George with an ice-cold stare. 'So, I am guessing that if your little Jewish friend here is as good at eavesdropping as both of you are at lying, you will know it is not only the crown we have come for?'

George's throat gripped. Where had the coppers got to? A few more seconds and it would be too late.

'We don't know nothing, mister. Honest we don't. Here. You can have the crown. Just let us go.' He swung the knapsack from his shoulder.

'George, no!' Kitty struggled to get free again, but Ritter held her fast.

'Enough!' Adler jerked up his hand. 'Your time has run out.'

George's stomach lurched. 'Wh-what d'you mean?'

'What I say. You have a weapon, Ritter?'

Ritter's cheeks paled. 'My knife, sir, but—'

'Good. Take the girl away and kill her. Then come back for the boy.'

'No! You can't!' George leapt to Kitty's side.

'Silence!' Adler shoved him away. 'Now do as I say, Ritter. It is an order!'

Ritter shook his head. 'I am sorry, sir. I cannot do it.'

Adler's face twisted with sudden rage. 'What? You dare to disobey your commanding officer?'

Ritter swallowed. 'They are children, sir. They have done nothing wrong. I . . . I will not—'

Adler shot him a look of disgust. 'I knew you were weak from the moment we first met.' Thrusting his hand beneath his coat, he pulled out a pistol and trained it on the other man. 'Raise your hands.'

Ritter blinked. Taking a step backwards, he lifted his arms slowly above his head.

'When the *Führer* hears of your disobedience, he will want to make an example of you, I am sure. In the meantime, there is no place for a traitor in our ranks.' Adler rammed the gun against Ritter's chest. 'Get in there.'

'But sir, you do not have to do this.'

'Quiet, or I will shoot you here and now!' Adler jostled Ritter into the hut and slammed the door. He rattled the bolt across it, then turned and locked his eyes back on George and Kitty. 'It looks as though I will have to do the job myself.'

As the words left his mouth, a low droning noise thrummed above them. Adler jerked back his head and stared in the direction of the river.

George followed his gaze. At first he saw nothing except wooded slopes and the glimmer of water beyond them. But then, as the noise grew louder, he spotted them: a bunch of Messerschmitts, and behind them a line of other, bigger planes. All heading their way.

Kitty gasped and clutched his sleeve.

Adler pressed his mouth into a grim smile. 'So . . . it begins.'

CHAPTER
28

The Nazi undid the top button of his coat and pulled
out a pair of binoculars. As he raised them to his eyes,
George caught sight of a badge pinned on the inside of his
collar. It was a bird. An eagle; silver-grey wings spread in
flight, steel talons gripped round a ring – a ring with the
crooked arms of a swastika fixed inside it.

George shuddered. He threw another glance up at the
sky. There were more of the bigger planes now. Twenty at
least, powering towards them like a swarm of huge black
beetles, each one of them, he guessed, packed full of
German soldiers, waiting to parachute down . . .

Adler jerked down the binoculars and turned back to
them, eyes glittering with triumph.

A jet of hot anger shot through George. 'You'll never

win. There's an airbase up the road. They'll be here in a second, just you wait!'

Adler snorted. 'My men knocked out the local radar station earlier, so your brave RAF boys will have no idea of our plans. Besides, our Luftwaffe has been keeping them busy again in the skies above London.' He trained his pistol back on them. 'Now, who is going to be first?'

Kitty gave George a panicked stare. He bit his lip. If help was coming, it wasn't going to be in time for them. There was only one thing left to do – he'd have to use the Luger. He reached for the gun, then slid his hand back to his side. Taking on Ritter had been one thing, but a cold-blooded killer like Adler? It was mad even thinking of it – unless he could distract him . . .

'Wait! You want the crown, don't you?'

Adler glanced at the knapsack, then sneered back at him. 'It is mine for the taking.'

'That's where you're wrong.' George thrust the bag out in front of him.

Adler's forehead bunched into a frown.

'Come on. See for yourself!'

Kitty gave a small groan and slumped to her knees.

Seizing hold of the bag, Adler flipped open the flap and worked at the ties. The knot held fast. He cursed. Ramming the gun in his pocket, he tore off his gloves and tried again.

A trickle of sweat ran down the side of George's face. He had to act now! As he reached for the Luger, Charlie's voice echoed in his ears: *Keep your nerve, George.* Bracing himself, he yanked the gun out and swung it round, gripping it tightly with both hands.

At the same moment, Adler ripped open the bag and dug his hand inside. A look of astonishment stole across his face. '*Was ist das?*'

'Stop, or I'll shoot!'

Adler froze.

George did his best to hold the Luger steady. 'Put your hands up.'

Adler hesitated, right hand still gripping the knapsack, then slowly did as he said.

The sound of plane engines grew louder still, but George kept his eyes firmly fixed on the Nazi. 'Kitty, get his gun.'

Kitty sprang up and limped over to Adler. Shooting him a nervous look, she drew the gun from his pocket and slung it as far away from them as she could.

Adler cocked his right eyebrow. 'You are cleverer than I thought. So, where have you taken it?'

George tightened his grip on the Luger. 'Back where it belongs.'

Kitty stared at him, eyes wide and shining. 'You mean . . .'

George gave a quick nod.

Adler's jaw twitched. 'You are either very brave . . . or very foolish. Unfortunately for you, I fear it is the latter.' In one swift movement, he jerked out his arm and swung the knapsack at George's head.

Kitty screamed a warning. George ducked, but the Nazi

had him on the back foot. He grabbed George round the middle. Wrestling the Luger from his grip, he spun him round and pointed the muzzle of the gun at his chest.

'So' – he wiped his forehead with the back of his sleeve – 'it would appear I am back in command again. Now, show me where you have hidden the *Führer*'s crown, or when our troops land I will give the order for your little town to be razed to the ground.' He jabbed a finger at the line of planes rumbling through the night sky towards them.

George stifled a groan. It had all been for nothing. The Nazis were coming and there was nothing he or a bunch of old runes on a crown could do to stop them now.

Adler's finger twitched against the trigger. 'Well?'

George threw a quick glance at Kitty. 'Only . . . only if you let my friend go.'

Kitty shook her head. 'No, George. I am staying with you.'

'Such loyalty!' Adler's lips quivered into a mocking sneer. 'Very well. It is no matter anyway. We will be rounding her up with the rest of her kind soon enough.' He jabbed the gun at Kitty. 'Go!'

She folded her arms across her chest and glared back at him.

George swallowed against the fear clogging the back of his throat. 'Please, Kitty. Your granddad. He needs you.'

'But—'

'Go on!'

Heaving a sigh, she turned and limped past him. But as

she reached the side of the hut, she spun round and called back to him. 'Help will come, George. I know it will.' She shot Adler a fresh look of defiance, then disappeared into the darkness.

George's heart fluttered. He wanted to believe it too, but how could he when an army of Nazi soldiers were about to parachute down on top of them?

Adler stepped smartly behind him and jabbed the gun against his back. 'Stop wasting time!'

George puffed out a breath. Better get it over with. At least if he showed the Nazi where the crown was, it might stop them from killing all those innocent people.

A loud roaring sound filled his ears. He jerked his head up. The planes were almost directly overhead now, circling like a flock of great black vultures, the small fighter planes buzzing around them like flies.

His heart clenched. He'd been stupid. Stupid for thinking he could get the better of a bunch of Nazis. Even more stupid for believing in a daft fairy story that said a crown with a dragon on it could save the day. He'd let Charlie down, and now the whole country too . . .

'Come on. Move!' Adler gave him another sharp shove with the gun.

As George stumbled forwards, the scar on his hand began to throb again. He frowned and pressed his fingers against it, but the throbbing grew stronger. A chill breeze skimmed his face and a peal of thunder echoed through the air. He started and looked up. A thick black cloud had bubbled up and was snaking its way across the sky.

The planes dropped down to avoid it, but the cloud followed, swirling in amongst them, forcing them to drop lower still.

And then he saw them.

Two Spitfires, flying high above the Jerry planes. Adler had spotted them too. Yanking a torch from his coat pocket, he flicked the beam on and arced it above his head.

But the enemy planes were too busy trying to steer away from the cloud. George held his breath and watched as the Spitfires tilted their wings and swung down through it, diving on a pair of Messerschmitts beneath, peppering them with bursts of orange gunfire.

As the bullets struck their targets, the two enemy fighters spun out of control and hurtled towards the horizon, engines screaming, tails smoking.

George gave a whoop and shot a fist above his head. He glanced at Adler. The Nazi's face wore a look of cold fury. George shivered and turned his gaze back to the sky. The Spitfires were circling back in readiness for another attack. As they dipped down towards the main group of planes, the beam from a searchlight shot up and raked the air, doing its best to light their way. Two more Messerschmitts broke away from the pack. They lifted up sharply and angled round. The Spitfires gave chase, but as they did, a second pair of Messerschmitts joined the fight. Now it was four against two. Except the Spitfire pilots hadn't realized it yet . . .

George screamed a warning and leapt up, waving his arms wildly above his head. But even as he did it, he knew it would be no use. And now, as the newcomers bore down on them, guns blazing, it was the Spitfires who were the prey. They ducked and dived, doing their best to dodge the bullets. But the Messerschmitts had smelt blood. As they homed in for the kill, George flinched and turned away.

Beside him, Adler gave a sharp barking laugh. 'Fools! Did they really think they could take on the might of the German Luftwaffe single-handed and win?'

His words were drowned out by a sudden ear-splitting crack. George's heart lurched. He took a quick breath and flicked his eyes back at the sky, expecting to see one, if not both Spitfires, hit and spiralling out of control. What he saw instead made his eyeballs almost pop from his head.

The cloud had reared up into a smoking black pillar. Now, as he watched open-mouthed, it lunged at the enemy fighters, spitting out forks of flame as it went. They swerved to avoid it, but whichever way they went, it was on them, blocking their escape.

It wasn't happening. It *couldn't* be. George blinked and shot another look at Adler, but the Nazi's slack jaw and wide-eyed stare told him it was.

He looked up again. The cloud had got the enemy fighters surrounded and was coiling itself among them, forcing them into the Spitfires' path. The two RAF pilots held their course until they were almost upon them. Then, as they opened fire, there was another mighty crack of thunder. The cloud sprang back up, lighting the sky with fresh forks of flame. One by one, the enemy fighters spun away and roared off down the river in the direction from which they had come. The rest of the Jerry planes looped round in confusion and disappeared after them, back into the night.

'*NEIN!*' Adler jumped up and waved his arms in the air, but it was too late: they had gone. As the Spitfires flew victory loops above their heads, he wheeled round, face white with rage. 'Take me to the crown. Now!'

George thrust his hands on his hips and stood his ground. 'No! You ain't getting it. And neither's old Hitler either.'

'In that case . . .' Adler took a step forwards and raised the gun. As he took aim, a dark shape barrelled towards him, head down, teeth bared.

George's blood turned to ice. Spud! He must have broken free. 'No, boy! Don't!' He jumped out in front of him, legs spread, hands raised, but Spud swerved past him and carried on. George turned and watched heart in mouth as the dog smacked into Adler, knocking the gun from his hand.

The Nazi staggered for a moment, then righted himself and delivered a sharp kick to the side of Spud's head. The dog gave a loud yelp, crumpled to the ground and lay still.

George's stomach twisted up inside him. He dashed over and flung himself down beside him. 'Spud?' He shook him, gently at first, then more forcefully, but the dog didn't move. Hot tears sprang to his eyes. 'You've killed him, you monster!' He jumped to his feet, fists raised.

Adler had picked up the gun, but now his attention shifted back up to the sky. A bolt of panic shot through

George. Were they coming again? He threw back his head, following the Nazi's gaze. But it wasn't the planes; it was the cloud.

It hovered above them, coiling and uncoiling like a great black snake. Adler gave a strangled cry and backed away. The cloud followed, bearing down on him. He jerked up his gun and fired, but still the cloud kept on coming. As he squeezed the trigger again, it reared up and spat out a fork of orange flame. Flinging the gun to the ground, he turned tail and ran. But the flame was quicker. Darting in front of him, it shot up, snapped open like a pair of huge, fiery jaws and *struck*. There was a hiss, a crackle, a single gut-wrenching scream, and then . . .

Silence.

George sank to the ground in a daze. He lay there for a moment, eyes closed, head spinning, trying to make sense of what he'd just seen. And then he remembered . . .

'Spud?' He crawled over to where his friend lay and put an ear to his chest listening for a heartbeat, but there was nothing.

'You were so brave, boy.' Slumping down beside him, he pressed his face in the dog's fur and wept until the tears ran dry and sleep stole in to take away the pain.

CHAPTER 29

Early morning – Monday 9 September

George woke with a start to see the ground spinning beneath him. Someone was lifting him; swinging him through the air.

He blinked and looked up. A man in a dark coat loomed above him, his head silhouetted against the pink-tinged sky.

'Put me down!' He tried to break free, but the man gripped him tighter.

'Steady on, lad. I'm not going to hurt you.'

'Who are you? Where're you taking me?'

'Just trying to make you more comfortable. Isn't that right, son?'

A white-faced figure appeared at the man's right elbow. 'Yes, Father.'

Raymond Scroggins! George heaved a sigh. He never thought he'd be so glad to hear the sound of the other boy's voice again. He slumped back against the rough wool of the inspector's coat.

'Here we go.' The inspector lowered him gently to the ground in the shelter of the hut and wrapped a thick, scratchy blanket around him.

George lifted up on his elbows, blinking against the gathering light. 'Kitty? Where is she?'

Inspector Scroggins squatted down beside him. 'It's all right. Your friend's safe. She's down at the police station having her ankle strapped. You can see her later.' He turned and nodded at Scroggins. 'Fetch him something to drink, would you, Raymond?'

Scroggins frowned. 'But where—'

'Initiative, son. You've shown you've got some. Now don't forget to use it.'

Scroggins flushed. 'Yes, Father.' He shot George an embarrassed-looking smile and darted away up the slope.

'So, George.' The inspector leant forwards. 'Tell me, what happened?'

He closed his eyes, doing his best to collect his thoughts. But all he could see was a great black cloud rearing up and then plunging down on Adler's head. He blinked and shook his head. 'I ain't sure I can remember. Leastways, not yet . . .'

The inspector put a hand on his shoulder and gave it a

squeeze. 'I know it's not easy, but if you could try? It would help us to clear up a few things we're not sure about.'

George frowned. Best keep it simple. The inspector didn't look like the sort to believe in legends and the like. 'There was a German spy, a man called Hans Ritter. Kitty and me came across his camp in the woods. We didn't know he was a Jerry at first, then we saw him down on the bridge signalling to the others.'

The inspector grunted. 'It must have been him and his friends that put those two Home Guardsmen out of action.'

'Did they . . . did they kill them?'

'No. They were lucky. Just tied them up and took their guns and uniforms off them. Go on, lad. You were saying?'

George swallowed and set off again. 'Ritter jumped out on us and locked us up in there.' He nodded back at the hut. 'Then more Nazis arrived, and their leader – Adler – he said they'd put the radar out of action so our boys wouldn't see the Jerry planes coming. Then he pulled a gun on us. I tried to stop him and—' He shuddered. Something bad had happened after that. Something to do with Spud . . . A dull ache started up in his chest: the same ache he got when he thought about Charlie. He pulled the blanket tight about him. He didn't want to think about it. Not yet . . .

The inspector scowled. 'You can rest assured that Nazi won't be causing any more trouble; not to you or anyone.' He nodded to where a bunch of soldiers and coppers stood huddled round a black shape on the ground.

George's heart jolted. He threw back the blanket and hauled himself to his feet.

'Wait a minute. I'm not sure—' The inspector made to block his way, but George was too quick for him. Sliding past him, he darted over to where the other men stood. He shouldered between them and jerked to a stop.

It was Adler. Or what was left of him anyway. His clothes and hair were scorched, his skin black and blistered. But worst of all was the look he wore on his face – mouth gaping, eyes fixed in a terrified stare, as if the last thing he'd clapped eyes on had been the Devil himself.

George gagged and bent double. A spurt of hot sick shot from his mouth, splatting across the shiny black boots of the policeman standing next to him.

'Hey, you! What do you think you're—' It was the pinch-faced copper, the one who'd arrested Kitty's grand-dad.

'Leave him be, Constable. It was an accident. Come on, lad. This isn't a sight for young eyes.' Inspector Scroggins steered George back to the hut. He sat him down again and grimaced. 'You were lucky the lightning didn't get you too. The storm put on quite a show. It's why we made such slow progress getting up here after you and Raymond raised the alarm.' He flashed George an apologetic smile. 'Still, it gave those two brave Spitfire pilots we managed to get scrambled a fighting chance. It's thanks to you children and the pair of them the place isn't swarming with Nazi paratroopers. It doesn't bear thinking about what would have happened next.'

George shivered as fresh pictures of the battle filled his head. It hadn't been any old storm. He knew that now. But if he told the inspector what he'd seen, he'd think he was barmy. They all would. Except for Kitty . . .

'George. Are you all right?' The inspector looked at him, eyes full of concern.

'Yes, sorry, I . . .' He shook his head. 'What about Ritter and the others?'

The inspector gave a grim-faced smile. 'They're down at the station under lock and key, awaiting questioning. They'll be off to a prisoner-of-war camp before you can say Winston Churchill. Which reminds me.' He dug in the pocket of his uniform. 'Here, I think this belongs to your friend.'

George's heart lifted at the sight of the star-shaped pendant glinting back at him from the inspector's outstretched palm. He reached out and took it from him. 'Thanks. She'll be pleased.'

The inspector nodded. 'Ritter gave it to me along with some garbled tale about having disobeyed orders to do away with you both.'

'He's telling the truth. He did.'

'Well, I suppose that might go in his favour when the army speaks to him.' The inspector's eyes clouded over. 'Now, I'm afraid I've got a bit of bad news for you, lad. It's about your dog . . .'

The ache started up in George's chest again. He looked away, eyes smarting. 'Where . . . where is he?'

'We put him in the hut.'

George made to stand but his legs buckled beneath him.

'Steady on, lad.' The inspector helped him to his feet again and walked him towards the entrance. 'I'll come in with you if you like?'

George shook his head. 'No. It's all right, thanks. I'd rather see him on my own.' He took a deep breath and stepped through the door.

It was dark inside. He blinked, waiting for his eyes to get used to the light.

And then he saw him. They'd laid him out on a piece of tarpaulin against the back wall. Stumbling over, he dropped to his knees and combed his fingers through Spud's dusty fur. A tear rolled down his cheek and dripped on to the dog's snout, leaving a dark patch where it fell.

A pair of footsteps sounded behind him. Scroggins knelt down alongside him, a thermos flask clutched in his hand. 'What happened?'

George clenched his jaw. 'He tried to save me, but the one in charge, he—' He broke off, shoulders heaving.

Scroggins patted him on the back and gave a sympathetic sigh. 'You were lucky; to have a friend like that.' He offered him the flask, but George pushed it away.

He stroked his hand slowly across Spud's muzzle, then sat back and drew in a breath. 'I've got to bury him.' He wiped his face and glanced about him.

'What? Now?'

'Yes.' George jumped to his feet and darted over to the pile of gardening equipment in the corner. Pulling the old wheelbarrow free, he pushed it over to where Spud lay and set it down on the ground. 'Help me, will you?'

Between them, they lifted up the tarpaulin and set it down inside the barrow. George tucked the corners over to hide Spud from view, then slipped back to the pile of gardening stuff and fetched the shovel.

Scroggins frowned. 'Where are you taking him?'

'A special place; where he'll be safe.'

'Do you want me to come with you?'

He shook his head. 'No. Thanks. I've got to do this on my own.' He slid the shovel in alongside the tarpaulin. 'Now do me a favour. Go and keep your dad busy for a bit while I get away.'

'How?'

'I dunno. You've got initiative, ain't you?'

Scroggins flashed George a quick smile and headed back outside.

George lifted up the handles of the barrow, wheeled it over to the door and peered out. Scroggins was busy pointing at something away down the slope, tugging at the inspector's sleeve. He waited for them to disappear round the side of the hut, then set off up the hill in the direction of the mounds.

When he reached the edge of the field, he paused and gazed about him. Curls of steam rose from the top of each mound. For a moment he thought it was smoke. Then, as the early morning sun warmed his back, he realized it must be the dew. Tightening his grip on the wheelbarrow, he lifted it up again and set off towards the tree.

As he approached it, his heart fluttered. It looked different from how he remembered. Leafier. Taller too; the tips of its branches seemed almost to be touching the scattering of gold-pink clouds overhead.

He drew round behind it, scanning the ground until he spotted the square of earth between the two tree roots Kitty had pointed out to him – the place where the crown had lain undisturbed for hundreds of years until Ritter dug it up and stole it away.

A warm glow spread across his chest. It was a good place to bury Spud. And he'd always know where to find him too. He put the wheelbarrow down, picked up the shovel and began to dig.

When he'd finished making the hole bigger, he set the shovel aside. Gripping the four corners of the tarpaulin, he heaved Spud out of the barrow and laid him down into it as gently as he could.

His eyes blurred with fresh tears. Blinking them away, he bent down and stroked the dog's soft black fur. 'Goodbye, boy. I'll come and visit you soon, I promise.'

He covered him with the tarpaulin and picked up the shovel again. As he dug it into the pile of soil, a sudden breeze lifted. It rustled through the tree's branches, parting them so that a shaft of sunlight slanted into the hole. George shivered and took a step backwards.

And then he heard it. A whimper. Coming from inside the hole.

He frowned and shook his head. His ears were playing

tricks with him. They must be.

The whimper came again. Louder this time, and more insistent.

Sucking in a breath, George crept back to the edge of the hole. As he peered into it, the tarpaulin twitched. A brown snout poked out from beneath it and sniffed at the air.

Flinging down the shovel, he dropped to his knees and yanked back the cover. A pair of dazed brown eyes blinked up at him.

'Spud!' Reaching in, George lifted him out and held him close, feeling the small *thud-thud* of the dog's heart beating against his chest. He shook his head again in disbelief. How was it possible? Spud had been a goner, and now . . . He looked up, eyes sieving the shadows beneath the tree.

A rustle of feathers made him start. The raven swooped down in front of him and landed on the pile of soil next to the hole.

As it swivelled its head to face him, George's skin prickled. It was carrying something shiny in its beak. Taking a deep breath, he edged closer and held out his hand.

The bird fixed him with a bright black eye. Then, with a loud *craak*, it dropped the object into his outstretched palm.

George's throat caught as he stared down at the small circle of gold nestled against his skin. Heart racing, he held it up to the light. Two words shone back at him. Mum and Dad's words. His and Charlie's too.

Together Always.

He clutched the ring to him, eyes filling with fresh tears. He'd got Spud back, but what about Charlie? As he opened his fingers to stare at it again, a memory flickered up inside him. Something Kitty had said about ravens being messengers. Was this a message? And if it was, what did it mean? His stomach knotted. He glanced up again quickly, but the raven had gone.

Spud nudged the back of his hand.

George blinked. 'You're right, boy. Kitty will be wondering where we've got to.' Giving him another hug, he slid the ring on to his right thumb. Then, grabbing the handles of the wheelbarrow, he drew in a breath and stepped out into the morning light.

CHAPTER 30

When they reached the Regenbogens', the front door was ajar. George pushed it open and stepped inside, Spud padding close behind. As they headed along the hall-way towards the stairs, voices echoed down to them. Kitty's first and then a man's. Her granddad. George's heart leapt, then shrank back down. They'd not want them here now, not when the old man had only just been let go.

'Come on, Spud. They're busy.' He made a grab for him, but the dog was quicker. He ducked, and with an excited yip, streaked off up the stairs.

George rolled his eyes and set off after him. He reached the top just in time to see the white tip of Spud's tail disap-pearing through the study door, followed a few moments later by cries of delighted-sounding surprise.

'George?' Ernst Regenbogen appeared at the door. He beamed at him over the top of his glasses and held out his arms. 'Come in, dear boy, come in!'

George shook his head. 'I'm sorry. We didn't mean to disturb you. Spud got a bit carried away. I'll fetch him. We'll go...'

'Nonsense!' The old man limped towards him and took him by the shoulders. 'You are most welcome. Kitty is bursting to see you again. Inspector Scroggins assured her you were safe, but she won't believe it until she has seen you with her own eyes.'

George flushed. 'All right then, if you're sure, but we won't stay long.'

The old man frowned. 'Are you going somewhere?'

'No. I don't know. I—'

'Then come inside and join us. Please. We have so much to thank you for, not least my granddaughter's life.' His eyes filled with grateful tears.

George looked away, embarrassed.

The old man lifted his glasses and dabbed at his cheeks with a handkerchief. 'Take no notice of me. I shall go and make us all a cup of tea and give you and Kitty the chance to catch up on last night's adventures.' Throwing George a quick wink, he limped past him, along the hall, and disappeared into the kitchen.

Taking a deep breath, George stepped inside. Kitty lay on the sofa, her left foot bandaged and propped on a cushion, Spud at her side. The dog jerked up when George came in and bounded over to him, tongue lolling, tail wagging.

'George!' Kitty made to sit up.

'No. It's all right. Stay there.' He walked over and perched on the chair opposite.

Her cheeks flushed pink. 'I am so glad to see you! I thought . . .' Her lip trembled. 'I thought that man might have killed you.'

'He would have done if old Spud hadn't come to the rescue.' George leant forwards and tickled Spud's ears.

'You were so brave, the pair of you. But tell me. I want to know everything.'

'Everything?'

She nodded.

He drew in another breath and began. He started with what had happened back at the pit with Ritter and Scroggins. Then he told her about the break-in up at the big house and how he'd got Scroggins to raise the alarm. When he got to the bit about burying the crown, her eyes lit up with excitement.

'Did you see him – King Redwald?'

His chest tightened. He thought for a moment about sharing his fears – that it was Charlie's ghost he'd seen beneath the tree – then decided against it. He might tell her, but not now. 'No. It – he – wasn't there.'

A look of disappointment slid across her face, but she perked up at the mention of the bird.

He faltered again when he got to the bit about the storm.

Kitty frowned. 'Why have you stopped?'

'I don't know. It's just that, well, it's all a bit confusing.

There was this cloud and . . .' His shoulders slumped. He shook his head and stared down at the floor. How could he explain it when he wasn't sure what had happened himself?

She drew a sharp breath and sat up. 'So you saw it too?'

He blinked and looked up at her. 'Saw what?'

'Will you pass me the box of photographs please?' She jerked her head in the direction of the desk. 'There, it's by the inkwell.' George got up and fetched the box over. Taking it from him, Kitty opened it and rifled through the pictures until she found the one she was looking for. She held it out to him. As he took it from her, he saw it was the photograph of the dragon; the one on the king's shield.

He glanced up again, frowning. 'What about it?'

She leant forwards. 'Remember about the dragon's blood. How the legend says Wayland bound the charm with it.'

'Yes, but what's that got to do with what happened up there last night?'

'It is obvious. When you kept your promise to make the crown safe, the dragon's spirit came to your aid.'

George remembered again what had happened after he'd buried the crown: the rumbling noise and the feeling of the earth shifting beneath his feet. Then the great black cloud snaking up and joining with the two Spitfires to send the enemy planes packing and blasting Adler with a single fiery breath. And he thought about the scar on his hand too; how it had pulsed and twisted beneath his skin.

Had that been the dragon's spirit stirring inside him as well? He stared down at it wonderingly, then back at the photograph.

'You see, Saint George. Sometimes stories can be true.' Kitty flashed him a grin, then her mouth turned down and she let out a sigh. 'But I suppose I should not call you that any more. Because Saint George killed the dragon, whereas you have tamed yours.'

'Ha ha!' He frowned. 'You said before you thought the ghost had picked me. You still haven't told me why.'

'I was not sure then, but now I think I know. The clue is in the charm.'

'The charm?'

'Yes.' Her face took on a teacher-ish look. 'I think it might have two meanings. Like a riddle. The Anglo–Saxons were very fond of them, you know.'

George shook his head. 'I don't follow.'

'Remember what it says: "He who has me has the kingdom."'

He rolled his eyes. 'I know that.'

'So, the first meaning, the most obvious one, is that whoever owns the crown will be the ruler of the kingdom. But what if it is also about the importance of being brave? Of standing up for what you believe in?'

'Go on.'

'So then, another meaning might be: "He who has *courage* has the kingdom."'

George pulled a face. 'I don't know about that. I—'

'What was that about courage?' Ernst Regenbogen appeared at the door, a tea tray in his hands.

'Oh, nothing, *Opa*.' Kitty took the photograph and slipped it quickly back inside the box.

George jumped to his feet. 'Can I help you with that, mister?'

'I have told you before, you must call me Ernst, please.' The old man stepped into the room and set the tray down on the desk. 'Kitty told me about the crown and how you stopped those Nazis from getting their hands on it. But tell me, where is it now?'

George's face grew hot under his gaze. 'I, er—'

Kitty gave a loud cough. 'What George is trying to say is that he buried it. After he raised the alarm. He wanted to make sure that, if the Nazis did invade, they would never find it, didn't you George?'

George shot her a grateful look and nodded.

The old man glanced down at the pile of mud scrapings still sitting on the desk and sighed. 'It is a shame not to have the chance to see it again.'

'I could tell you where it is if you like, Mister Re— I mean, Ernst?'

The old man shook his head. 'Thank you, but no. I think it is probably better that we keep it a secret rather than risk tempting fate a second time, don't you?' He patted George's shoulder and handed him a cup of steaming brown tea. 'And of course, I have you and Kitty to thank for my release too. When Inspector Scroggins discovered how brave the pair of you were, standing up to the enemy, he let me go at once.'

George frowned. 'It wasn't right, them taking you away and locking you up like that.'

Ernst Regenbogen gave another sigh. 'It is true. But

when people are frightened they do not always do what is right. And at least the British Government treats its so-called "enemy aliens" better than—' He broke off suddenly and turned away.

Kitty stood up and hobbled over to him. 'We must do what you told me when I first came here, *Opa*. Think about the happy times.' Her hand fluttered to her throat, searching for the pendant. She bit her lip and dropped it quickly back down to her side.

'Wait!' George scrabbled in his pocket. 'Look, it's all right. I've got it here.' He pulled out the necklace and handed it to her.

Kitty's eyes lit up. 'Thank you! But how—'

'Ritter gave it to the inspector before they took him away.'

'Oh!' Her cheeks flushed.

Ernst Regenbogen clicked his tongue against his teeth and shook his head. 'What a waste of that young man's talent. Though we must be grateful he found the courage within him to do the right thing at the end.' He blinked and gazed down at Kitty. 'You are right, *Liebling*. There were happy times. And, now we are back together, there will be more to come, I am sure of it.' He stroked her cheek with a wrinkled finger. Then, taking the necklace from her, he fastened it back round her neck.

George's heart clenched. He was glad Kitty had got her granddad back, but, though he was ashamed to admit it, he couldn't help hurting too. Curling his fingers over the ring, he pressed it to his chest and whispered Charlie's name.

A hand squeezed his shoulder. 'George. I am sorry. How selfish of us to be speaking like this in front of you when your brother is still missing. Please forgive us.' The old man peered at him over the top of his glasses, his eyes full of concern.

George swallowed hard against the lump rising in his throat. 'Is . . . is there any news?'

He drew in a breath. 'I am afraid not, no.'

A loud *rat-tat* sounded from down below. Spud scrambled up barking.

Ernst Regenbogen frowned. 'I wonder who that could be?' He adjusted his glasses on his nose and limped towards the door, Spud padding along behind.

A sick feeling rose up inside George's chest. He made to go after them, but Kitty held him back. 'I think there is something you have not told me yet. Where did you find it?'

He frowned. 'Find what?'

'Your ring.' She nodded at his hand.

George uncurled his fingers. He stared at the ring again, then took a deep breath and told her what had happened that morning under the tree. When he got to the bit about burying Spud, then hearing his whimper, Kitty gasped and clutched at his arm. 'The ghost! It must have been.'

He shook his head. 'I ain't sure.'

'I am!' She pressed her lips into a stubborn pout.

George sighed. He didn't have the energy to argue with her. And anyway, after everything else that had happened, he didn't rightly know what to think.

'And the ring?'

As he told her about the raven, her eyes grew wide with amazement.

'It must have found it on the street after your fight with Raymond Scroggins and taken it up to the tree.'

'Maybe.' He wanted to believe it too, but now a fresh memory of the ring on the ghost's pointing finger was filling him with a renewed sense of dread. He shivered.

She reached out and slid her fingers into his. 'It will be all right, George, I know it will.'

He shook his head. He wanted her to be right, but she didn't know. None of them did.

A voice called up the stairs. 'George! Kitty! There is someone to see you.'

George blinked. It couldn't be about Charlie then.

He felt a sharp tug on his sleeve. 'Come on. We should not keep them waiting, whoever they are. Besides, I need your help.' Kitty pointed at her bandaged ankle.

When they reached the bottom of the stairs, Ernst Regenbogen was waiting for them outside the museum door, Spud by his side.

'Who is it, *Opa*?'

'You will find out soon enough.' He gave them a mysterious look and gestured for them to enter.

'Ain't you coming in with us?'

The old man shook his head. 'No, George. Our visitor would like to see you both alone.'

They exchanged puzzled glances then, taking a deep breath, George pushed the door open and stepped inside.

CHAPTER
31

The room was in shadow, the blackout curtains half-pulled across the window.

As the door clicked shut behind them, a cloud of spicy-smelling smoke wafted through the air, making Kitty sneeze.

'Mmm? Ah, there you are!' The short, stout figure of a man dressed in a dark hat and coat stepped out from behind the suit of armour. He strode towards them, his walking cane clicking against the floorboards, another smoke-cloud puffing from the cigar clamped between his lips.

Spud curled himself round George's ankles and gave an uncertain growl.

'And I see you have brought your faithful hound too.

Splendid!' The man bent and rubbed Spud between the ears with his pudgy fingers. As he rose and the smoke cleared, Kitty gave a loud gasp.

The man gave a throaty-sounding cough. 'What am I thinking? We have not been properly introduced.' Removing the cigar from his mouth, he bent and ground it against the sole of his shoe, then lifted up again and held out his hand. 'Churchill. Winston Churchill.'

George's jaw dropped. He blinked and sucked in a tangy-tasting breath. 'You mean, *the Prime Minister?*'

The man's eyes sparkled with amusement. 'The very same one. A pleasure to meet you, Mister Penny.' He seized George's hand and pumped it up and down, then turned to Kitty. 'And you too, Miss Regenbogen.' He doffed his hat to her and gave a small bow. 'I have been looking forward to meeting you both since I got the news first thing this morning. The country and I have a lot to thank you two for.'

George's cheeks grew hot. 'We didn't do much really; it was—'

The Prime Minister held up his hand. 'I admire your modesty, but fighting off a bunch of Nazi commandos is no small matter; especially for a pair of young whipper-snappers – if you'll pardon the expression.' He shot them a mischievous wink, then his face grew suddenly serious again. 'These are dark days. Not content with trying to gain supremacy over our skies, Mister Hitler is now pounding our cities with his bombs. He seeks to strike fear into our hearts so that we will give in to him. However,' – he pressed his lips into a determined-looking smile – 'as you, and our valiant troops and airmen have shown, we are not so easily defeated. Courage, grit and common decency. It is with these that the battle against tyranny will be won.'

As the last of the words rang in their ears, the blackout curtains billowed into the room and a shaft of yellow light spilt across the floor. Kitty gave a small cry and clutched George's sleeve.

'What?'

She pointed to a spot in front of the window. George's mouth dropped open again at the sight of a large circle of gold metal gleaming back at them in the morning sunshine.

He licked his lips. 'It . . . it can't be!'

'But it is!' Kitty whirled round on him, eyes flashing. 'Did you dig it up again?'

George's skin prickled. 'No, I swear!'

She folded her arms across her chest and frowned.

'It's the truth. Please, you've got to believe me.'

She wavered for a moment as if considering, then puffed out a breath and nodded.

'Come now. What is all the fuss about?' The Prime Minister stepped alongside them. His eyes widened as they fell on the crown. Thrusting his stick at George, he bent down and picked it up. He drew in a breath as the dragon's red garnet eyes glittered in the light. 'Fascinating!' He turned to George and Kitty. 'Would you care to tell me about it?'

George nudged Kitty forwards. 'You say.'

She tucked her hair behind her ears and cleared her throat. 'It came from the site of the ship burial, sir; the one that was discovered last year. *Opa* – that is my granddad – he thinks it might have belonged to the king they believe was buried there.'

'Ah yes, I remember! Redwald, isn't it? But tell me, what are these markings here?' The Prime Minister tilted the crown and pointed a stubby finger at the runes.

'George can tell you about them.' Kitty flashed him a quick smile.

George's cheeks flushed. 'It's a charm, sir. From an old Anglo–Saxon legend. It says that whoever has the crown will have the kingdom too.'

The Prime Minister peered down at the runes again, then back up at George. 'I see. In that case, you must be sure to keep it safe, young man.' He held the crown out to him, fixing him with a firm, level gaze.

George felt a shiver of pride, but he knew – even as he took it – that it wasn't his to keep.

'I think King George should have it, sir. He can look after it a lot better than we can.'

Kitty clutched George's sleeve again, an anxious look on her face.

'It's all right, honest.'

She hesitated, then let her hand fall.

As George passed the crown back to the Prime Minister, he felt a small tingle in his fingers, then ... nothing.

The Prime Minister tipped his hat. 'Thank you, both of you. I am sure His Majesty will take excellent care of it.'

Kitty gave a small cough. 'It has a name, sir. It is called the Kingdom-Keeper.'

'Kingdom-Keeper, eh?' The Prime Minister's eyes took on a fierce gleam. 'How appropriate! Well, given the circumstances, I think perhaps for the time being its whereabouts are best kept secret. Do you agree?'

George and Kitty nodded.

He opened the top button of his overcoat and slid the crown down inside it. 'Excellent. Now, what time is it?'

George frowned. 'Hang on a minute . . .' Fumbling in his trouser pocket, he pulled out Bill Jarvis's watch. 'Eleven o'clock.'

The Prime Minister raised his eyebrows. 'Already? I must go. I am due at the police station to thank our local constabulary for their actions last night – I believe it was the inspector's son who helped you raise the alarm?'

George nodded. 'That's right, sir.'

'Very good. I shall ask to see him too. And then I must make my way to the airbase to congratulate our brave lads there for all they have been doing to keep the Luftwaffe at bay.'

George's heart lurched. 'Er . . . excuse me, sir. I've got a favour to ask.'

The Prime Minister frowned. 'Yes, of course. What is it?'

'My brother, Charlie Penny. He's a Spitfire pilot at the airbase. He went up on a mission a couple of nights ago and he's . . . well he's been missing ever since. I was wondering if maybe you could try and find out what's happened to him?'

The Prime Minister reached out and squeezed his shoulder. 'Of course. Leave it with me.' He took back his stick and shook them both by the hand. Then, after bending to give Spud another quick pat, he spun round and headed for the door.

As it closed behind him, Kitty stepped back over to the window and stared down at the spot where the crown had been.

'I do not understand. How did it get back here? Unless—' Her eyes flickered with a sudden gold fire.

George shivered and glanced around the room. As he turned back, something brushed against his leg. He wheeled round. 'Spud! You gave me a fright, boy.' He bent and stroked his head.

'Are you coming?'

'Not just yet.' George pushed Spud gently away. 'Will you take him? I'd like to be on my own for a bit.'

She nodded. 'Come on, boy.' She patted her leg. 'Let us go and find you a drink.' Turning, she limped towards the door.

As it closed behind them, George sank down against the wall with a sigh. They'd had a lucky escape last night, but the war wasn't over yet. The Prime Minister was right though. They had to keep on fighting; fighting for what was good and fair. For the truth ...

He slid off the ring and stared down at the inscription again. If it was bad news about Charlie, he'd do his best to bear it. Because that's what his brother would want. And like Kitty and her granddad, he'd try and remember the happy times too.

He rested his head on his knees and closed his eyes. A few moments later, he was sound asleep.

A loud *rat-tat* sounded at the front door again. George blinked and sat up. Someone had draped a blanket over his shoulders. Kitty. She must have come back to check on him. He frowned. How long had he been asleep? He pulled out the pocket watch. Nearly one o'clock. The door-knocker sounded again. He leapt up and darted out into the hallway. There was no sound of movement from the floor above. Maybe Kitty and her granddad were taking a nap too.

As he glanced at the front door his stomach knotted. What if this time it was a message from the airbase? He steeled himself. There was only one way to find out. Taking a deep breath, he walked up to it and pulled it open.

A figure stood in front of him, silhouetted against the sunlight. George shielded his eyes against the glare. 'Can I help you?'

'Hello, Georgie.'

His breath caught in his throat. He opened his mouth, then snapped it shut again, afraid that if he spoke his name – said anything at all – the figure might snuff out.

A pair of strong hands gripped his shoulders. 'I'm real. Honest I am.'

'Charlie!' George threw his arms around him and they hugged and hugged until he was sure his heart would burst.

CHAPTER
32

Later, after George had introduced Charlie to the Regenbogens and they'd plied him with tea and lebkuchen in the study, he told them about what had happened to him. How he'd flown off with the others to defend London from the Luftwaffe bombers, but then, on the way back to base, he'd been chased down by a Messerschmitt and forced to bail out.

Ernst Regenbogen shook his head. 'You were lucky to survive.'

'I know.' Charlie heaved out a breath and took another gulp of tea.

George frowned. 'What happened after you jumped?'

'I don't know exactly. I must've got a knock on the head. When I came to, I was dangling from the end of my parachute halfway up the side of a bloomin' great tree.' Charlie gave a sheepish smile.

Kitty helped him to another cup of tea. 'How did you get down?'

'I shouted for help and in the end a farmer heard me. At first he thought I was some kind of Nazi spy, but when I managed to convince him I was RAF, he went and fetched a ladder and cut me down. What with all that and then having to find myself some transport, I didn't make it back to the base until yesterday evening. By which time they were at sixes and sevens because the Luftwaffe were busy attacking London again.'

George's eyes widened. 'You didn't go up again, did you?'

'Not to London, no. The squadron leader told me and another pilot who'd gone through the same thing to rest up. Except . . . well, it didn't quite work out that way.'

'What d'you mean?'

'We were in our quarters doing our best to get a bit of kip when a call came through that a whole bunch of enemy planes were heading this way.' He shot George a knowing look. 'Though from what Mister Churchill told me earlier, you and Kitty know as much about that as I do.'

George's jaw dropped. 'You mean it was *you* up there, fighting off those Messerschmitts?'

'Me and Flight Sergeant Walters, yes. Looking back on it, we must've been mad. Spits aren't much good for night flying, and the Jerry fighters outnumbered us at least five to one. There was a moment, just before the storm blew up, when I thought we were both goners. But then this dirty great cloud came rolling in and the thunder and lightning got going, and after that the Jerries couldn't get away fast enough. It sounds daft, but we both felt at the time like the cloud was fighting on our side.' Charlie fell silent and gazed off into space.

Kitty made a small choking noise.

'Careful, *Liebling*.' Ernst Regenbogen patted her on the back. 'I have told you before, it is dangerous to eat and drink at the same time.' He frowned. 'Are you all right, Mister Penny?'

Charlie blinked. 'What? Yes. Fine, thanks.' He cleared his throat. Mister Churchill wants to give me and Walters a medal each, but I think these two deserve it more than us, don't you agree, Mister Regenbogen?' He flashed a smile at George and Kitty.

'I do. But you must call me Ernst, please.'

'Don't forget Spud.' George pulled the dog against him. 'You saved my life, didn't you, boy?' Spud wagged his tail and gave a pleased-sounding yip, then rested his head on George's knee.

Ernst Regenbogen got up off the sofa and walked across to the desk. 'Well, I cannot help with awarding medals, but I can offer you all another lebkuchen.'

As the old man handed round the plate of biscuits, Charlie gave George's shoulder a quick squeeze. 'I'm sorry for not listening to you when you came to see me at the base, Georgie. I'll find you somewhere else to stay, I promise.'

Ernst Regenbogen set the plate down again. 'But there is no need. George must stay with us, mustn't he, Kitty?'

Kitty clapped her hands together. 'Oh yes, *Opa*! That is a wonderful idea!'

Charlie shook his head. 'I don't know, Ernst. We've put you to quite enough trouble as it is.'

'It is no trouble. No trouble at all. We would love to have him here, though only of course if you, George, would like it too?' The old man looked at George, his tufty white eyebrows raised in question.

A warm glow spread across George's chest. 'Yes, Mister Regenbogen . . . I mean, Ernst. I'd like it very much.'

'Well, it looks as if that's settled then.' Charlie reached over and shook Kitty's granddad by the hand. 'Thank you. I'll let you have the money for George's keep as soon as I get my next pay.'

George gave a quick cough. 'It's all right, Charlie. I'll be getting some money off Raymond Scroggins the next time I see him. He owes me . . .'

Charlie shot him a puzzled look. 'Scroggins? Who's he?'

George was about to explain when the sound of raised voices echoed up from the street outside. He leapt up and darted to the window. 'Hey, come and look at this!'

As the others stepped alongside him, a pair of policemen came marching down the street, a man in handcuffs sandwiched tightly between them.

George frowned. 'Looks like they've gone and arrested someone.'

As the small group drew level with the house, Spud jumped up at the window and gave a growling bark. The man in handcuffs jerked up his head. His mean, ferrety eyes scanned the glass blindly before dropping back to the ground.

George took a step back, heart bouncing against his ribs.

Charlie turned to him, eyebrows raised. 'What's wrong?'

George licked his lips. 'It's Bill Jarvis.'

'Don't you worry, Georgie.' Charlie slipped an arm round his shoulders and pulled him close. 'That great bully ain't going to hurt you and Spud again – ever.'

At the mention of his name, Spud gave another bark. George reached down and ruffled his head. He sucked in a breath and peered out into the street again. But Jarvis and the policemen had gone.

'Do you think he'll go to prison?'

Ernst Regenbogen sighed. 'At the very least. Kitty has already told the inspector how he tried to break into the museum last night to steal – how did you put it, *Liebling*? Some of our exhibits. But if his dealings with Ritter ever come to light, he risks being treated as a collaborator and a traitor and that might mean the sentence will be more severe.'

George gasped. 'You mean he might hang?'

'Possibly, yes.'

'But he's a thief, not a spy.'

'And not a very good one at that.' The old man laid a

hand on George's shoulder. 'Look, I doubt Ritter will want to confess to the police about his business with Mister Jarvis, but if they do find out, you can always speak up for him.'

George nodded. Jarvis had been nothing but mean to him and Spud, but he didn't deserve to hang.

Charlie blew out his cheeks. 'He's a nasty piece of work whatever way you look at it. Did he get away with anything when he broke in?'

Kitty shook her head. 'Spud chased him off, but he left this behind.' She pulled a grimy patch of material from her dress pocket and gave a quick grimace.

'And this too.' George fished the pocket watch out of his trousers.

The old man took the watch and the material from them. 'We will hand them in to the inspector as evidence. But tell me, why did the pair of you really go across the river last night? Kitty told the inspector you were taking Spud for a walk, but then he does not know how fond my granddaughter is of fairy tales.'

Kitty's cheeks flushed pink. She shot George a desperate look.

He sucked in a breath. 'She's right. We did take Spud for a walk. But we took something back where it belongs too.'

The old man's eyes flickered with a look of sudden understanding. 'Ah yes! The little digging expedition you spoke about earlier.' He gave George a knowing wink.

Charlie frowned. 'This all sounds very mysterious. You'll have to tell me all about it when I get my next leave,

Georgie.' He glanced at his wristwatch. 'Lummy! I'd better get going. The Squadron Leader said I'd to be back at the base at four sharpish.'

George's throat knotted. 'Will the Luftwaffe be coming back to bomb London again tonight?'

Charlie sighed. 'We've been told to expect them. And if it's not tonight, it'll be tomorrow or the day after.'

'Are we going to beat them?'

Charlie's frown deepened. 'I don't know, George. But we're doing our very best.' He ruffled a hand through George's hair. 'Do you want to come downstairs and see me off?'

The lump in George's throat grew bigger. He'd been dreading this moment. But he had to be strong, for Charlie's sake.

After Charlie had said his farewells to the Regenbogens and buttoned up his jacket, the pair of them headed downstairs. As they stepped out into the light, Charlie took George's hand and gave it a quick squeeze. 'You've still got the ring then?' He glanced down at the band of gold on George's thumb.

George nodded.

'Good lad.' Charlie slid off his own ring and touched it to George's. '*Together Always.*' Remember?'

George's eyes stung with sudden, hot tears. He bit his lip and brushed them away, but fresh ones sprang quickly in their place.

'Come on now. Chin up.' Charlie drew him into a hug. They stayed there like that for a while, arms wrapped tightly about each other, until at last Charlie pulled free. He gripped George by the shoulders and looked him squarely in the eye. 'I'll come back to you, Georgie, I promise I will.'

George drew in a deep breath and nodded.

'That's the spirit!' Charlie gave him another quick hug. As he turned to go, a sudden thought flashed into George's head.

'Wait! I've got something for you.' He dashed back into the house. He reappeared a few moments later, carrying the knapsack. Chest heaving, he opened the flap and dug around inside until he found what he was looking for. 'Here.'

Charlie raised an eyebrow. 'What is it?'

'A raven's feather. A lucky one.' George thrust it into his hands. As Charlie turned it over, it shimmered in the sunlight with a blue-black sheen.

'Thanks, Georgie.' He stroked his finger along it. 'I'll make sure I have it with me every time I go up.' He smiled at him one last time, then, throwing him a quick salute, he hurried down the steps and strode away down the street.

As George watched him go, a fresh ache started up in his chest. But this time the pain was mixed with something else too. A sort of warm shivery feeling. He didn't know what was going to happen next. But the crown was safe. And he was going to do his level best to keep the ring safe too. As he stared down at it again, his eyes blurred with more tears. He scrubbed at them with the back of his sleeve and took another breath.

He was about to head upstairs when a small yip sounded next to him. He glanced down. Spud sat at his feet, the lead between his jaws.

'Good idea, boy.' He stepped back inside and called up to Kitty. The sound of footsteps echoed above and a few moments later her head appeared over the banisters.

'I'm taking Spud for a walk.'

'All right, Saint George. But do not be long. *Opa* has found another jar of honey at the back of the cupboard. He says we can bake some more lebkuchen. If you are going to be living with us, you will need to learn how.' She flashed him a grin. Then before he had the chance to reply, she pulled back her head and disappeared.

George set off down the street, Spud trotting ahead of him, tail raised. When they reached the river, he bent and let him off the lead. As the dog scooted away up the path, George stared out across the sparkling green water at the ridge opposite. It looked peaceful in the afternoon sunshine. So peaceful it was hard now to believe that what had happened up there last night was true. But it was, and it was something neither he nor Kitty would ever forget.

A sudden breeze rippled towards him. He shivered and whistled to Spud. The dog pulled out from the rabbit hole he'd been burrowing into. He shook himself and came bounding towards George, tongue lolling. As he reached his side, a harsh call echoed across the water. George's heart jolted. He stumbled down on to the shoreline, shading his eyes.

A great black bird was circling in the sky above the

ridge. Beneath it, silhouetted against the sun, stood the lone figure of a man, head held high, shoulders thrown back, the folds of a dark cloak billowing out around him.

A shiver ran up and down George's spine. He scrunched up his eyes, trying to get a better look at him. But it was no use; the man was too far away.

He stood there for a moment, as if watching George. Then, turning, he reached beneath his cloak and drew out a long thin blade. He thrust it up high above his head and swung it round. As the sunlight hit the blade, there was a blinding flash of red and gold light. George gasped and looked away. When he looked back, both man and bird had gone.

A whiskery nose tickled his shins. He shivered again and ruffled Spud's head.

'Come on, boy. Let's go home.'

About the book

The inspiration for my story is a real event – the discovery of the great Anglo–Saxon Sutton Hoo ship burial during the summer of 1939, just before the outbreak of the Second World War.

Described at the time as the British equivalent of the famous Tutankhamun tomb discovery of Ancient Egypt, the burial is one of the richest ever found in northern Europe. It was discovered beneath the largest mound on the site by a small team of archaeologists who had been invited to come and excavate it by the landowner, Mrs Edith Pretty.

Inside the ghostly imprint of a great wooden longship, 27 metres in length, the archaeologists found a unique collection of priceless treasures. Because of the richness of the finds, it is believed the ship burial was the memorial for a person of high standing, possibly the Anglo–Saxon king, Redwald of the East Angles (died around 624) – though no trace of a body was actually found. According to Anglo–Saxon records, Redwald was referred to as 'Bretwalda' or 'Britain-ruler' which suggests he may have been a sort of early high king of Britain. It is his ghost which Kitty believes is haunting the burial site in the story.

The ship burial dates from a time once popularly known as 'The Dark Ages'; a term which reflects how little we know of that period due to the relative scarcity of surviving documents and archaeological finds. The Sutton Hoo treasures are famous not just for their beauty and craftsmanship, but also because they have helped historians shine a light on the culture and beliefs of the earliest Anglo–Saxon settlers in England.

Today, thanks to Mrs Pretty's generosity in gifting the find to the nation, the major artefacts from the burial are on public display in the British Museum in London and are regarded as one of the highlights of its collection.

I first learnt about the Sutton Hoo ship burial when I studied early medieval history at university. But it was when I visited the site – now in the care of the National Trust – over twenty years later that my imagination really caught fire.

The field of around eighteen grassy mounds, set on top of a ridge overlooking the estuary of the River Deben in Suffolk, is both beautiful and mysterious. What intrigued me most though was the timing and significance of unearthing the long-lost treasure of an ancient English king on the eve of an event as cataclysmic and world-changing as the Second World War. This set me thinking about what might happen if a young boy, exiled from his home during the very darkest days of the conflict with Nazi Germany, makes a discovery, linked to the ship burial site, which has the potential to influence the future course of the war.

Though my story is set in a real time and place, it is a piece of fiction. So I hope readers will forgive me for taking a few liberties with local scenery and real personalities, together with the creation of imagined characters and events, in the interests of telling as exciting a story as possible.

Treasure, dragons, runes and ravens

The treasures discovered in the Sutton Hoo ship burial date from a time when, although people were beginning to convert to Christianity, many still held to traditional pagan beliefs. It is from elements of these beliefs that I have woven my own myth linking the fate of wartime Britain to a piece of undiscovered **treasure** – the so-called Kingdom-Keeper or dragon-headed crown.

There is no actual evidence that early Anglo–Saxon kings such as Redwald wore a crown; the helmet in the ship burial is considered the closest thing to it. But though no trace of one has been found at Sutton Hoo, I have enjoyed imagining what it might have looked like if it had existed.

The giving of treasure was an important part of early Anglo–Saxon warrior society. Ring-giving in particular signified the bond of loyalty between a king and those who fought for him. This theme is echoed in my own story when my hero, George Penny, promises to keep safe the ring his brother, Charlie, gives him as he goes off to join the RAF and fight.

Courage, loyalty and the importance of staying true to your word, or oath, were all central to the relationship between a king like Redwald and his warriors. They are also qualities displayed by both the fictional Pennys and Regenbogens in the story, and the real servicemen and women and ordinary people who lived through the dark days of the Second World War.

Dragons were believed by the Anglo–Saxons to love treasure, keeping jealous guard over hoards of gold buried beneath the ground. This may be why they have been used to decorate many of the objects found at Sutton Hoo – including the helmet, the shield and the sword belt.

At the end of the Anglo–Saxon epic poem, *Beowulf,* we learn of how a great dragon takes terrible revenge on King Beowulf's kingdom after the theft of a golden cup from its treasure hoard. This was the inspiration for *The Legend of the Dragon-Headed Crown* which Ernst Regenbogen recounts to George and Kitty. And, of course, dragons appear elsewhere in the story too. Real or imagined? I'll let you decide.

The runic inscription in the story is based on real **runes**, or letters of the ancient Germanic alphabet used by both the Anglo–Saxons and the Vikings. It is thought that such inscriptions on Anglo–Saxon weapons, rings and other precious objects were used as charms to give them magical and often protective properties.

The runic charm on the Kingdom-Keeper links it back to another mythic character familiar to both Anglo–Saxons and Vikings: **Wayland the Smith**. In my story, Wayland uses the charm, written in dragon's blood, to invest the crown with the magic which will make the person who seeks to possess it the all-powerful ruler of the country; though as Kitty suggests after George cuts his hand on the crown, perhaps the dragon's blood itself is capable of other magic too.

Kitty also thinks the charm might be a **riddle**. Anglo–

Saxons certainly enjoyed inventing and trying to solve these cleverly worded puzzles. And perhaps she is right . . .

As for **ravens**, the Anglo–Saxons believed they were birds of ill omen that, together with their fellow 'Beasts of Battle', the eagle and the wolf, foreshadowed great slaughter. In Norse mythology, which is strongly linked to the early Anglo–Saxon pagan belief system, a pair of ravens, Huginn and Muninn, acted as messengers for the god Odin. There's a sense of both these characteristics in the raven in my story, though it brings good luck too.

Finally, a quick word about **ghosts**. Anglo–Saxons believed that spirits from the Lowerworld were able to travel into the Middleworld, or world of men. Is the ghost in *The Buried Crown* real or imagined? Again, I'll leave you to decide . . .

Miracles, Spitfires and invasion plans

The Buried Crown opens not long after what is considered one of the lowest points in the war for Britain when the Allies lost the battle for France and nearly 340,000 British and Allied troops had to be rescued by the Royal Navy and hundreds of private boats – the so-called 'little ships'– in what became known as the **'Miracle of Dunkirk'**.

Although the retreat of the Allied Army was a significant defeat, the successful evacuation of so many troops from the beach at Dunkirk paved the way for a new determination to stand up to Adolf Hitler and to do everything to stop him from conquering Britain and winning the war.

The south and east coasts of England, including Suffolk, were heavily fortified at this time due to heightened invasion fears. Beaches were mined and covered with barbed wire; a chain of radar stations had been constructed along the coast to detect enemy aircraft; and civilian volunteers working in the Royal Observer Corps helped keep a track on planes once they were over land.

In reality, the area around Sutton Hoo became a restricted zone because of the fear of a German glider-led invasion and there were anti-glider ditches built across the mound field.

In addition to the fortifications and the creation of the **Home Guard** to act as a secondary defence force in case of invasion, the Government used posters and information leaflets to warn ordinary people to be on the lookout for German spies and 'enemies within'.

As everyone in Britain held their breath during the summer of 1940, waiting to see if Hitler would invade, the Royal Air Force (RAF) was engaged in a desperate battle to keep the German air force, or Luftwaffe, at bay in what the Nazis called **Operation Eagle Attack,** but which became known as **The Battle of Britain.**

At the start of the story, George's brother, Charlie, is about to complete his pilot training and earn his 'wings'. In reality he would have trained at a specialist training centre before joining a squadron to go up and fight, but in the interests of keeping the story tight, I have him finishing his training at an active combat airbase.

Charlie is a **Spitfire** pilot. In reality, Spitfires weren't very well suited for night flying and in spite of special adaptations the RAF stopped using them for this purpose in June 1940. But I have used a little dramatic licence to suggest that perhaps one or two might still be in service when my story opens in September that year. Coincidentally, I discovered as I was writing the story, that the word 'spitfire' comes from the Anglo–Saxon word meaning a fiery person.

It is due in large part to the bravery of the RAF aircrew who fought in the Battle of Britain – nearly 600 of whom were killed and many more injured – that Hitler eventually decided to cancel his seaborne invasion plan – codenamed **Operation Sea Lion** – and the country lived on to fight another day.

Although the attempted landing of Nazis troops in *The Buried Crown* didn't happen in real life, there were rumours that a failed German invasion attempt had actually occurred at around the same time as my story takes place at Shingle Street, a few miles from Woodbridge, on the Suffolk coast. However this was never proved and it's now regarded as a piece of wartime **propaganda**.

What is true is that Hitler tried to destroy British morale by ordering a campaign of intensive bombing of London and many other cities and industrial targets by the Luftwaffe. This *blitzkrieg* or 'lightning war' began on 7 September 1940 and continued for eight months until May 1941. **The Blitz** was responsible for the deaths of over 43,000 civilians, the serious injuring of tens of thousands more and the destruction of huge numbers of homes, factories and other buildings up and down the country.

Evacuees and refugees

Wars and conflicts force countless numbers of ordinary people to flee their homes and to travel many miles, often at great risk, in desperate search of a safe refuge. The Second World War was no different, and the idea of exile and being parted from your loved ones is an important theme in *The Buried Crown*.

Both George and Kitty experience this first-hand, George as an **evacuee** from London and Kitty as a German Jew, who has to leave her homeland to escape persecution and, ultimately, almost certain death at the hands of Adolf Hitler and his Nazis during what became known as the **Holocaust** – the mass murder of millions of Jews and other groups of people the Nazis deemed 'undesirable'.

Kitty is one of the 'lucky ones', given safe passage thanks to the **Kindertransport** (German for 'children's transport'). This was a series of organized rescue efforts, developed in response to widespread violence against Jews in Germany by Nazi paramilitaries and German civilians on 9–10 November 1938 during what became known as **Kristallnacht** (German for 'Crystal Night' after the mass of broken glass from damaged properties on the streets afterwards). The transports brought approximately 10,000 mainly Jewish children and young people from Occupied Europe (mainly Germany, Austria, Poland and

Czechoslovakia) to safety in the UK principally between December 1938 and the outbreak of the war in September 1939.

Meanwhile, in 1940, when invasion fever was at its height, Germans, Austrians and Italians living in Britain were labelled 'enemy aliens' and many were sent to **internment camps** or deported to penal colonies in countries like Canada and Australia. Incredibly, this included Jewish refugees, amongst them some of those who had arrived via the Kindertransport. Due to protests in the British Parliament, the first internees began to be released from August 1940 until eventually only those believed by the authorities to present a serious risk continued to be detained.

I hope in some modest way, besides being an entertaining story, *The Buried Crown* helps to shine a light on the bravery and resilience of the real Georges, Kittys, Charlies and Ernsts of this world, who, in the face of great and seemingly overpowering odds, have the courage to accept and stand up for what they know to be right and true.

A note about the real people who feature in *The Buried Crown*

In real life, **Adolf Hitler** and some of the other leading Nazis were indeed treasure-thieves: they even created a special Nazi theft unit to steal artworks from the countries they invaded to build their own collections. The Nazis were also interested in runes and ancient myths for their propaganda value. If the crown had really existed, and if Hitler had managed to have it stolen, I think there is a strong chance he would have made use of it in the Nazi propaganda war against Britain.

(Note: there is some debate about Hitler's eye-colour – blue or brown? Based on my own research, I have plumped for blue, but it is worth noting that this is the subject of some controversy.)

Prime Minister **Winston Churchill** is credited with leading the country to eventual victory against Hitler and his Nazis, with the help of its allies. But this victory was not a foregone conclusion. At the time when *The Buried Crown* is set, Britain stood alone against what seemed impossible odds. Churchill recognized the significant challenge the country faced, as did the reigning king, **King George VI**. Between them they gave ordinary people the courage to stand firm in the face of great hardship and loss. I like to think that if the crown had existed, and had come into their hands, it would have helped further strengthen their resolve to win the war.

More information

Read:
About the Sutton Hoo Ship Burial:
Sutton Hoo by Steven J. Plunkett – National Trust Guidebooks
The Sutton Hoo Helmet by Sonja Marzinzik – British Museum Objects in Focus Series – British Museum Press
British Museum web pages on Sutton Hoo
http://www.britishmuseum.org/visiting/galleries/europe/room_41_europe_ad_300-1100.aspx

About the Second World War:

BBC websites:
The Battle of Britain – http://www.bbc.co.uk/history/
histories/battle_of_britain
The Blitz – http://www.bbc.co.uk/schools/
primaryhistory/world_war2/air_raids/
Dunkirk – http://www.bbc.co.uk/archive/dunkirk/
Evacuees – http://www.bbc.co.uk/schools/
primaryhistory/world_war2/evacuation/

Other websites and publications:
The Association of Jewish Refugees – www.ajr.org.uk
(for information on the Kindertransport initiative)
Imperial War Museums pages on the Second World War –
http://www.iwm.org.uk/history/second-world-war
The National Archives –
http://www.nationalarchives.gov.uk/education/
sessions-and-resources/?time-period=second-world-war
Evacuees of the Second World War by Mike Brown – Shire
Publications Ltd
The Home Front by Guy de la Bédoyère – Shire
Publications Ltd

Visit:
'Kindertransport – the arrival' memorial sculpture by
Frank Meisler – Liverpool Street Station, London
RAF Museums (Cosford and London) –
https://www.rafmuseum.org.uk/

Second World War exhibits at The Imperial War Museums – http://www.iwm.org.uk/
The Sutton Hoo Ship Burial Site – https://www.nationaltrust.org.uk/sutton-hoo
The Sutton Hoo Treasures at the British Museum – http://www.britishmuseum.org/

Acknowledgements

Researching and writing a story is a bit like going on an archaeological dig – you might have some idea of what you are looking for, but you are never quite sure what you will find. That has definitely been my experience with *The Buried Crown*. And of course, like the business of uncovering buried artefacts and treasures, writing a book is a highly collaborative process too. So I have many people to thank for helping me excavate this story from the shadowy cave of my imagination and bring it out into the light.

First and foremost my parents: my dad, George Burt, whose memories of his time spent as an evacuee during the Second World War are one of the archaeological layers in our own family history, packed full of shiny nuggets of inspiration. And my late mum, Beryl, also an evacuee, who, through her own love of books, encouraged me into reading, so giving me the tools to begin uncovering my own stories.

As ever, I am also indebted to my writing friends – especially the members of the two critiquing groups I belong to – who encouraged me in the early days to think that this particular patch of ground was worth further exploration.

I also owe a very big thank you to the people who have freely and very generously given of their time to share their expert advice and insights into the key historical elements of the story: my former university professor, Professor Richard N. Bailey for checking the details relating to the Sutton Hoo ship burial and providing me with the runic and Anglo–Saxon versions of the Kingdom-Keeper's inscription; Kindertransport refugee, Bernd Koschland, who left his home and family in Bavaria to seek shelter in the UK from Nazi persecution all those years ago and who has kindly reviewed and commented on my representation of the Kinder experience in the story, and also to Chairman, Sir Erich Reich and all the other members of the Kindertransport special interest group of the Association of Jewish Refugees who I had the privilege of meeting with and talking to about their experiences, and to Susan Harrod, Lead Outreach and Events Co-ordinator, for the invitation; Bryan Legate, Assistant Curator (Archive and Library) at the Royal Air Force Museum Hendon and Bill Reid, former wartime pilot in the Fleet Air Arm for their insights into the recruitment and training of pilots during World War Two and the design and handling of Spitfires; Bob Merrett at Woodbridge Museum, for information about the town during the war; Sally Metcalf, Volunteer Programme Manager at the National Trust, Sutton Hoo, for information relating to the ship burial site and Tranmer House (the 'big house' in the story) and the staff at Woodbridge Library for making available archive material relating to the original Sutton Hoo discovery. And finally to our good friend, Till Ruessmann for his advice on my use of German phrases and terms.

While I have tried to stay true to the historical background and geography of the area where possible, the book is, of course, a work of fiction and so I hope I will be forgiven for taking certain liberties in the interests of telling a good story. All errors and inaccuracies are my own!

My sincere thanks too to the brilliant and passionate story excavators extraordinaire, Chicken House Books and in particular: Treasure-Seeker-in-Chief, Barry Cunningham for encouraging me to dig deep and bring *The Buried Crown* to the surface; my wise and eagle-eyed editor, Kesia Lupo for helping me cut through the layers of grime to discover the treasure beneath and to Rachel Leyshon, Esther Waller and Sue Cook for helping to make it shine. Also to Rachel Hickman, Jazz Bartlett, Laura Smythe and Elinor Bagenal for showing it to its best advantage and to the talented trio of Rachel H., artist Alexis Snell and designer Steve Wells for the glittering and gorgeous cover.

And above all, my deep and heartfelt thanks to my husband, fellow adventurer and best friend, Steve, whose support, encouragement and love are, for me, the most precious treasures of all.

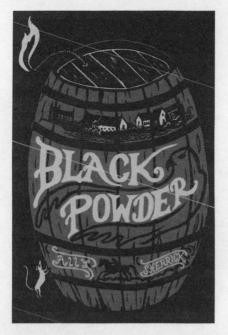

BLACK POWDER by ALLY SHERRICK

England, 1605

Twelve-year-old Tom is in a terrifying race against time to save his father from the hangman's noose. In desperation, he makes a deal with a fearsome scarred stranger, known only as the Falcon. But what's really at stake in this murky world of plotting and gunpowder? Tom must rely on his wits and courage, as his loyalty is put to the ultimate test . . .

This historical tale is steeped in intrigue, mystery and danger.
BOOKTRUST

. . . a wonderfully explosive adventure . . . I loved reading about (and rooting for) Tom, though I have to admit developing a rival soft spot for his mouse.
JULIA GOLDING

Paperback, ISBN 978-1-910655-26-9, £6.99 • ebook, ISBN 978-1-910655-65-8, £6.99

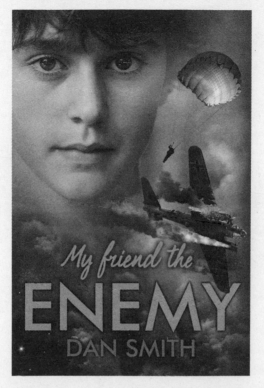

MY FRIEND THE ENEMY by DAN SMITH

1941. It's wartime and when a German plane crashes in flames near Peter's home, he rushes over hoping to find something exciting to keep.

But what he finds instead is an injured young airman. He needs help, but can either of them trust the enemy?

. . . an exciting, thought-provoking book.
THE BOOKSELLER

Paperback, ISBN 978-1-908435-81-1, £6.99 • ebook, ISBN 978-1-909489-06-6, £6.99